# TUSK

A NOVEL BY
## J.T. BORGMAN

Cover and Interior Design by KUHN Design Group | kuhndesigngroup.com

Amazon, the Amazon logo, and Thomas & Mercer are trademarks of Amazon.com, Inc., or its affiliates.

Published by Thomas & Mercer, Seattle | www.apub.com

ISBN: 979-8-9926026-2-3 (paperback)
ISBN: 979-8-9926026-4-7 (eBook)

*This book is dedicated to
my old friend Adam; to my grandma,
who encouraged me to become a writer; and to all
the elephants of Africa that have lost their lives in
this vicious struggle.*

# ACKNOWLEDGEMENTS

I would like to sincerely thank my copy editor, Robin Fuller, for the professional touch she provided for this book. Her nuanced skills were invaluable in bringing this novel to fruition.

I would also like to thank photographer Will Burrard-Lucas for allowing me to use his captivating photo taken in the African bush for the cover, and designer Steve Kuhn for his outstanding work in bringing this cover to life. The elephant was photographed in the Maasai Mara National Reserve region in Kenya—coincidentally, or perhaps synchronistically, quite close to where much of the story takes place.

I also must thank my parents, Mike and Christina, for their unending love, and for always believing in me, encouraging me in anything I set out to do in life, including writing this book.

And finally, I'd like to thank Misha, my love, for giving me the support and inspiration I needed to complete this meaningful project. Without you, this book would not exist.

# ONE

It felt like an eternity since I had last ventured to Shady Cove, but on this crisp morning, I couldn't resist. It felt right—necessary, even. The trailhead, marked by a weathered post at the top of a precipitous rocky headland, zigzagged a couple miles down to a secluded crescent-shaped beach with fine pearly-white sand, the kind that caressed one's toes. However, I had no intention of strolling the beach barefoot as I often did, nor had I set out for a casual dip.

The rays that penetrated the patches of dense morning fog, typically a welcome sensation, only irritated my bloodshot eyes. I'd been awake for almost three days, delirious and sobbing for most of them. As I trudged along the sandy path accented by vibrant lavender and yellow wildflowers interspersed with poison oak, I felt more tears forming in the corners of my eyes. *Thirty-eight-year-old men aren't supposed to cry*, I thought to myself, but once again, I disregarded that taboo.

About halfway down, the trail vanished for about thirty feet, where jagged pieces of slippery loose rock had to be carefully negotiated. A faulty step could prove fatal, with nothing to catch my fall into the unforgiving tide pools below. Ever since childhood, I'd been apprehensive of heights, but this bitter day was different. She was gone. I no longer cared if I fell.

IT HAD BEEN HER FAVORITE PLACE ON EARTH. Granted, she hadn't been many places in her all-too-brief existence, but whenever I took her to Shady Cove, her face would light up. Her smile stretched from ear to ear as I sang her classic eighties tunes while she rode on my shoulders across the dangerous stretch until we reached the sand. But there was no one to sing to anymore, except for a few gulls perched on a conical rock being battered by the angry sea.

I caught myself reaching for her tiny hand at the bottom of the trail, where about twenty worn wooden steps completed the trek. I always used to grab her hand, knowing her youthful instincts would kick in and send her sprinting towards the crashing waves. She had adored playing in the water, jumping and splashing around, only distracted by the occasional sight of a washed-up sand dollar, a gift from the retreating tide. Hours could pass, and she would barely notice, so engrossed by the changing patterns in the shallow water, which I found equally mesmerizing. But the current at Shady Cove was not to be taken lightly, so I made her wade close to me, and never past her knees. She was not yet old enough to hear about the people who had tragically drowned at her cherished spot, and I did not want to break the news that I feared might break her heart.

I sauntered over to the reddish-brown triangular rock forma-
tion that jutted out of the shallow surf just to the right of where
she used to play. It was littered with large black mussels and flu-
orescent-green anemones, and when the tide was right, bright
orange bat stars could be seen clamped to the base. I tiptoed into
the water, shoes and all. Salt water soaked the lower portion of
my jeans. I tried to explore the rock as she once did, hoping to
catch a glimpse of her favorite creatures, but the tide was too
high; only the mussels were on display.

I gazed out into the choppy grey Pacific. The horizon—or
"the edge of the earth," as Lily preferred to call it—sparkled with
the faintest hint of blue from the sunlight that escaped the elongated purplish fog bank. I imagined myself in a vessel, heading straight for the edge and beyond, not stopping until I either
found a whole new life, or ran out of food and starved to death—
whichever came first.

*Maybe I'll voyage all the way to China*, I irrationally pondered.

*"Daddy, help!"*

My daydream was interrupted by a familiar flashback that
felt like a sledgehammer to my chest. Those two words that had
come screaming from my daughter's mouth pounded in my head
and tore at my heart. Selfishly, I couldn't help but wonder how
long this recurring nightmare would endure.

# TWO

A brisk wind whipped through the dark, cavernous cut-out at the base of the seaside cliff, pelting me in the lower back, where my bare skin was exposed. I must have fallen asleep listening to the rhythm of the crashing waves. For how long was anyone's guess. As the fog began to lift, the bashful sun peeked into the chilly cave, providing some much-needed warmth as I noticed the remnants of an old bonfire a few feet away.

As I arose, countless grains of damp sand were stuck to the side of my face, but that was the least of my concerns. I squinted in pain as I clutched my forehead with both hands. My head was splitting, a common occurrence just about every time I had awoken since the incident. My daughter's petrified, helpless face was seared into my mind.

LILY HAD LOVED THE ZOO, as most five-year-olds did. If she didn't want to go to the beach, she wanted to engage with the animals, not yet recognizing the misery of their captivity. I too shared a fondness for creatures, but preferred them in their natural state, without the blank stares of hopelessness. But what daughters want, daughters get, and I took her there whenever her little heart desired.

But ever since her mother and I had divorced, she had become more reclusive and lost interest in some of her favorite things. How could I blame her? A divorce was challenging for any young child, and Lily was no exception. She loved her mother immeasurably, even though I had stopped years ago.

Lily was a natural introvert, just like her dad. So, when she turned even more inward following the split, I was concerned, but not alarmed. As an only child, Lily could entertain herself with the best of them, but also recognized the peace and tranquility that came from constant solitude. Making friends did not come easily for her, but it was not for lack of effort. She was liked, but misunderstood, as introverts could often be.

"Am I weird for just listening and not speaking much in school?" she would ask.

"We are not weird, sweetheart. We're just different and special," I would tell her.

I wanted so badly to explain to her all that I'd learned about growing up in the world as an introvert, but I knew she would not yet be able to process such complexities—such as the unfortunate, detrimental stigma placed on introverts in Western cultures. "Shy," "quiet," and "awkward" were words commonly associated with what society seemed to think was closer to a crippling disease than a personality type. I was waiting a few more years to convey to her that introversion was simply an innately different and often beneficial way of processing stimuli, and certainly not something to be ashamed of.

I relished any opportunity for us to spend time exploring the world together. So, when Lily had begged me to go to the zoo last Saturday, although we had just gone two weeks prior, I was happy to grant her wish.

It was a strangely warm, almost summerlike day in early November. Other than a light breeze and a few high clouds, I could've mistaken it for early September. As I retrieved the morning paper from our U-shaped driveway, I was greeted by a pungent aroma that reminded me of beached seaweed, a smell I had learned to enjoy since moving near the coast. During the Great Recession, I had gotten a steal on a single-story house with light brown shingles and white trim, one that reminded me of Cape Cod, where I'd spent a few summers as a teenager. Lush green grass with a mature, prolific blood orange tree accentuated the front yard. I picked up the newspaper from the flower bed of pink and red azaleas, and although it was rolled up and rubber-banded, my peripheral vision could not avoid the front-page headline. *GHOST TOWN* caught my eye in its oversized bold lettering. I accidentally snapped the rubber band, which left a red welt on the side of my hand just above the base of my thumb. I immediately regretted my eagerness to read it, as it turned out to be just another story about an abandoned neighborhood in Detroit, a remnant of the housing crisis a few years back.

"Daddy, let's go see the giraffes!" Lily exclaimed.

"Be right there, pumpkin."

As cute as a button, she stood in the doorway in her little pink dress and matching shoes, with a petulant lip that I was worried she might trip on if I didn't move with more urgency. I hustled back to the porch, when a familiar annoying, high-pitched voice pierced my eardrums.

"Joe! Is that you out there?"

"Yeah, morning, Gary," I said unenthusiastically, trying to hustle back into the house. I was almost to the door when loafers clicked behind me across my driveway, the pace increasing with every step.

"Say, Joseph, what are you doing next Sunday?" he asked, grabbing me by the shoulder. Gary was very touchy-feely and paid no mind to personal space. He reeked of cheap cologne—the kind they handed out as samples at department stores. Because he was dressed in his typical navy-blue Saturday suit, I knew where he was headed.

"Another open house today, huh, Gary?" I said, attempting to dodge his question.

"Yeah, you know, business is booming! And when you're the top producer in the company, expectations run high. Gotta keep the wife satisfied, so I stay satisfied ... if you catch my drift." He winked, apparently oblivious to the fact that I had recently separated from my own spouse.

Gary was one of those folks who would not stop spouting off at the mouth, no matter what hints were given to him. Self-awareness was not his forte. And he never asked anyone anything meaningful about their life. His only concern was boasting about how much money he made and how great his life had become. But I knew it was mostly a façade.

His irritating rant continued for what felt like an hour. I glanced through the front window and saw Lily on the couch, playing with Ellie, her stuffed African elephant she'd gotten at the zoo gift store about a year prior. Lily adored elephants.

I returned my attention to Gary, wondering how I was going to cut the maniac off, when *bang*! A car backfired three houses down—just the opportunity I needed. As Gary spun around to look, I made a break for the door.

"Gotta go! We'll catch up later, Gary!" I called, praying it would not be for weeks, at least. The door slammed as I kicked it shut with fervor.

"I'm ready, sweetheart," I said, feeling guilty, but relieved when I saw Lily smile as she leapt off the couch and into my arms.

"Daddy, can I bring Ellie?"

"Of course, darlin'!"

I threw on a baseball cap, grabbed my keys, and headed out the door with her, but not before peeking out the window to make sure Gary was safely back inside.

The zoo was about a twenty-minute drive, but I didn't mind; it was more one-on-one time with Lily. Furthermore, I had recently purchased a newer black Range Rover Sport and loved driving it, especially with the sunroof open.

I asked Lily how she liked her kindergarten teacher, Mrs. Gallaway. I was not trying to turn her giddy smile into a frown, but I inevitably did so.

"She's okay," she said without conviction as she attempted to reach her hands up through the sunroof to feel the wind rush through her fingers. Disappointment flashed across her face when she quickly realized she was not yet tall enough.

I frequently made sure I asked her about school, constantly stressing the importance of education. I knew Lily wasn't fond of her teacher, and unfortunately, it was reciprocal. Only a month into the school year, Mrs. Gallaway had pulled me aside one afternoon while I was picking up my daughter from school.

"There's something I think you need to know," she began, scrunching up her stern, unappealing face. "Lily is a dreamer. She stares off into space when I'm teaching, and when we do group activities, she basically sits outside the circle and says nothing. Frankly, I don't think she takes anything pertaining to education seriously!"

I tilted my head and looked at her in utter bewilderment as I pictured what I had been doing when I was five.

Mrs. Gallaway was the type of woman whose deadly serious expression rarely changed. Laughing—or even smiling, for that matter—was a foreign concept. With greyish hair pulled back impossibly tight in a poor attempt at a ponytail, she often lowered her bushy, unkempt eyebrows in a V that suggested something was drastically wrong when she addressed anyone. And with a raspy but strict tone, she spoke as though the world were on fire. I had a hard time taking her as seriously as she wanted to be taken, but she seemed like a lonely older woman who'd had a bumpy road, so I tried my best to act concerned when she spoke of Lily.

I gazed out the window at the countless varieties of massive trees that lined the streets of our suburban neighborhood. I admired the foliage that had morphed into stunning autumn hues. Vivid reds, oranges, and yellows danced in my eyes as I forgot all about Mrs. Gallaway.

I also forgot I was driving.

"Daddy, stop!" Lily yelled.

I swung my head around just in time to spot a fluorescently attired jogger obliviously crossing the street, not wanting to break stride, as if he owned the road. I slammed on the brakes, narrowly missing the jogger by a few feet as he shot a fierce glare my way. Ellie, whom Lily had placed in the back seat, catapulted forward and smacked into the dashboard, ending up in Lily's lap. Ashamed, I turned to her, thankful that she was buckled in tight, especially since I knew she was not supposed to ride up front. With worry draped over my face, I couldn't believe the carefree expression on hers as she giggled in amusement.

"Brakes work, Daddy," she said, smiling, as I burst into laughter.

We pulled into the gravel parking lot of the Pacific Coast Animal Park, which was oddly devoid of vehicles for a sun-drenched Saturday. I was about to ask Lily if she was ready, but there was no need. As I looked over, she was beaming with anticipation, clutching Ellie in her left arm and thrusting the door open with the other.

I went to cut the engine when out of the corner of my eye, I noticed the title of the song scrolling across the oversized screen on the dashboard. In big, bold capital letters, the old eighties track "GHOST TOWN" by The Specials rolled across the display, a song I hadn't heard in literally decades, on the radio or anywhere else, for that matter. Alarmed, I stared at the script as my curious mind quickly correlated it with the morning newspaper headline. I had always believed in signs from some unearthly realm—especially after my mom, Christina, who was also in tune with the universe, saw the hands on a clock in my grandfather's greenhouse operate in a counterclockwise fashion the day Pa passed.

My mind raced as I stared even more intently, whispering softly to myself, "Some things are almost *too* coincidental to be just a coincidence." I tried to decipher the possible meaning, but my thoughts were interrupted.

"Daddy, let's *gooooooo*," Lily whimpered from outside the car.

I locked the car as Lily and I walked to the gift shop to purchase zoo passes. To my surprise, there was only one other family in the parking lot, about twenty paces behind us: a rail-thin, blonde soccer mom type, carrying a colossal Louis Vuitton handbag that could have nearly held her two wild little sons.

Lily, as the polite young lady I was grooming her to be, noticed them and held the door to the shop open for an extended duration as the family approached. I immediately filled with pride. She tried to make eye contact as each one strolled through, but they were oblivious to the courtesy being extended to them. Smiling, she waited patiently for a thank you, which I had repeatedly taught her was the proper response, but it never came. The mother, squawking on her sparkly gold cell phone, didn't even look at Lily, as if she had just walked through an automatic door.

Lily shrugged it off. Nothing was going to ruin her jovial mood. I, on the other hand, was steaming inside.

We entered the park, and Jimmy, an aspiring young environmentalist, was there to greet us. He attended the local junior college and had a passion for wildlife. He was tall and lean with short dark brown hair, not unlike my own, and he was one of those pleasant, genuine people who spoke with an enthusiastic smile.

"Hi, Mr. Lockett! Hey, Lily!" he greeted us, remembering our names from several previous encounters. "Would you guys like today's brochure?"

"Jimmy! Sure, thanks, bud. What's the good word?" I asked, impressed that he remembered our names.

"Well, so far, it's strangely quiet today, but at least you'll have the place more or less to yourselves. And make sure you stop by our newest exhibit; I think Lily will love it! Details are in the brochure," he said, winking, not wanting to spoil the surprise.

"What is it, Daddy?"

I glanced at the brochure, realizing why Jimmy didn't want to ruin the surprise.

"We'll just have to find out, love," I said, maintaining the suspense.

I looked to the left and noticed that the woman and her two boys had stopped to check out Bali and Gigi, the two female chimpanzees stationed near the entrance. One was half lying on a thick tree limb, looking hopelessly bored, playing with her rear end to pass the time. The other was nervously shaking the chain-link fence with her strong humanlike hands, clearly in some sort of distress. The obnoxious boys began to mimic and mock her, pretending to be a caged animal while curling their hands under their armpits, grunting and shouting, the way apes were portrayed in cartoons. I turned to their mother, wondering if any discipline was forthcoming. Her hand waved wildly as she paced back and forth, prioritizing her phone conversation, ignoring the boys. The mocking escalated when the agitated female chimp let out a ferocious scream that seemed to frighten the boys, and they backed off.

"Why do people do that, Daddy?" Lily asked in a distraught tone. "Aren't we supposed to be nice to the animals?"

Before I could answer, I looked over at the expressionless, carefree chimp lounging in the tree. There was a calmness to her, as opposed to her cellmate, as she dangled her leg over the branch, leisurely swinging it in an elliptical pattern. Then something changed. All movement halted. Appearing pensive, she sat up straight, yawned, and stared keenly at the boys standing by their mother, with deep, dark, mysterious eyes. Suddenly, she began picking at her rear with much more haste and intent. The fierce staring intensified. The shorter boy became increasingly anxious and grabbed his mother's leg. Then in what seemed like slow motion, the chimp cocked her arm behind her head like a major league pitcher, holding something in her palm. Just as quickly as I realized what was happening, I saw a sizeable dark brown clump shoot through the chain-link fence, straight towards the two lads and their mother. The feces missile was a direct hit, smacking the taller of the two boys right in the shoulder and neck as a large remnant broke off in midair, landing in the woman's perfectly flat-ironed, bleached-blonde hair.

"What the hell?!" she yelled, unsure of what exactly had hit her. She pulled the phone away from her ear and looked at her son, who was covered in malodorous brown filth, when it finally dawned on her. Redness engulfed her cheeks, and a blood-curdling sound shot from her mouth. My jaw nearly hit the ground. Two female primates were screaming at the top of their lungs— the chimp and the woman—and I couldn't tell which was louder. Mortified, the woman snatched up the boys and headed straight for the exit, but not before demanding an explanation, unfortunately for Jimmy.

"I am absolutely irate!" she shouted. "How could you allow this to happen, dammit?! I've never been so appalled in all my life! My husband's a lawyer! I'm gonna slap a big, fat injunction on this place if it's the last thing I do! I want those monkeys *out* of here!"

"Actually, they're chimpanzees, ma'am," Jimmy said. "But I am very sorry. We have a sign; did you not see it?"

"I don't give a rat's ass what they are!" she said as she peeked at the bright orange sign on the side of the cage.

CAUTION: CHIMPANZEES WILL THROW FECES.
PLEASE DO NOT AGGRAVATE.

Her face turned red as a tomato as she stormed out of the exit, children in tow, phone finally put away.

Unable to contain ourselves, Lily and I watched in utter delight. We hadn't laughed like that in quite a while.

We were walking through the courtyard over to the koala, our first attraction—when suddenly, an indescribable, eerie feeling swept over my body. Something in the air gave me chills. Goose bumps draped the back of my neck as I looked around at the desolate park. Something was amiss. The gorgeous North American mountain lion was frantically pacing back and forth in his cage. The macaques, which were normally content to swing in the trees and eat the provided fruit, were howling uncontrollably. Even the antelope, which were usually calm while grazing, were cowering in the corner of their pen.

I began to sweat as a wave of heat came over me. A gut feeling raced through my body, churning my stomach, alerting me that perhaps we should not have been there that day. Mouth dry and hands clammy, I looked at Lily. I wanted to ask if we could come back another day. But all her bright blue almond-shaped eyes could see were the animals, and she seemed totally unaware of anything amiss.

"This is her day," I told myself under my breath, not wanting my strange, unexplainable perceptions to spoil it for her.

We stood in front of the glass of the koala's enclosure. Kiki was a fluffy male koala from southwestern Australia who was content to spend most of the day munching on his favorite meal, eucalyptus. But even Kiki was behaving peculiarly. With his back turned to the glass, he sat motionless on a crate, staring at a wall six inches in front of his face. He appeared statuesque and devoid of life.

"Daddy, is Kiki sleeping?" Lily asked.

I wanted to tell her yes, but I saw that his visible eye was wide open.

"I think Kiki wants some alone time, sweetheart. Would you like to go feed the giraffes?"

She looked puzzled, but nodded with excitement as we walked away, looking over her shoulder to see if Kiki would acknowledge her just once. He did not.

*Click.* I heard the front gate latch as I noticed a few more families entering the park.

As we stood on the elevated feeding deck, a familiar friend gracefully strolled over with inquisitive interest. Emma, the remarkably tall West African female giraffe, was a staple of the animal park. With her beautiful patterns, unending legs, and large brown eyes protected by lashes that any woman would envy, she was truly magnificent. She had just recently given birth to a calf, but due to minor complications, he was being tended to and was not out for our viewing pleasure.

I propped up Lily as Emma's caretaker gave her a handful of carrots, a favorite alternative snack of the gentle giant, since acacia trees didn't grow in our region. With an agile, dark purplish-black tongue well over a foot long, Emma examined Lily's offerings. Lily giggled as the giraffe's tongue began inspecting her left ear. She held out a carrot, which Emma tenderly took with grace. The zookeeper explained that giraffes had nimble, extra-long tongues so they could get to the acacia leaves while avoiding the pesky thorns. Lily, utterly happy and satisfied, gifted me her last carrot to give to the long-necked marvel. Her selflessness came so naturally, and for the second time that day, I beamed with pride and adoration.

Lily was in her element. Something about animals fulfilled her spirit; she felt at peace in their presence. Completely blissful after her visit with Emma, she could never have imagined that she would receive an even greater thrill that day.

As we made our way to the back corner of the property, we passed by Captain, the orphaned young male grizzly bear, who was resting in the shade on his large hindquarters. He looked tired. He had been a fixture of the park going on three years. Every time I saw him, I couldn't help but envision him back in the wild where he belonged, roaming countless miles of mountainous Alaskan terrain. Judging by his expression, he longed for that day as well.

Suddenly, I became consumed with guilt over the thought that my dollars were going toward an operation that kept such special creatures in captivity. Only the notion that many of them had been injured and rescued allowed me to breathe a sigh of relief. Well, that, and Lily's unbridled enthusiasm.

We walked hand in hand as we admired the various wonders of nature. I felt her tiny palm in mine as I became overwhelmed with emotion, pondering the random nature of her own being. She was a perfect creation. It seemed statistically impossible that I could have been so fortunate. I thought of my ex-wife, Victoria, and instead of animosity, my heart overflowed with warmth and gratitude.

Abruptly, Lily slid her hand out of mine and skipped over

to the enclosure occupied by Amadeus the armadillo, one of the more unique species at the park. I sat down on a bench and watched Lily as she knelt by the fence and coaxed him over to her. She had a way with all creatures, almost as if she could speak to them. She looked them deep in the eyes with a genuine tranquility that sparked connection. They did not fear her, and perhaps they could sense that she did not fear them.

"Lil, are you ready for your big surprise?" I asked.

She was so engrossed by her encounter that I had to call to her twice.

"Lily, love, let's go see something new!"

She ran over, her glowing blonde ponytail thrashing around with every step. "What are we going to see, Daddy?"

I grabbed her by the hand again and smiled. "C'mon, it's right over here," I said, trying to my best to mask my own excitement.

She yanked my arm as she surged ahead, searching for something foreign, something unfamiliar. Her head swiveled continuously, her eyes stuck wide open, like the lemurs we had passed earlier. We skipped over the zebra pen, only shooting the striped wonders a quick glance, her little pink Chucks picking up speed with each eager step. We made a right turn around a corner, and there he was. Lily's feet ceased moving, and her body froze so suddenly that I nearly slammed into the back of her. If not for my nimble feet, I would have. Her saucer-like baby blues locked onto the behemoth in disbelief. Her mouth was ajar, yet no words could form. She had never seen anything like it.

A grey male African elephant towered before her, waving his

massive ears back and forth, fanning the air. A young boy stood a couple feet to the left of us in front of his parents, arm raised, carrot in hand. When Lily's muscles finally loosened, she looked down at the stuffed animal in her right hand, still gripping mine with her left. She swung her head skyward and stared at the real pachyderm, and then back at Ellie. She repeated this four times, increasingly stunned at the striking resemblance.

"Is that a real Ellie?" she asked when her mouth worked again.

"I believe it is, sweetheart! Would you like to feed him?"

She paused and looked at me for a moment, perplexed, as if she couldn't believe she was about to interact with an actual elephant in the flesh. They had previously only existed in her fantasies, spurred on by various children's books I had given her.

"Hi, folks! Would you like to meet Kemba?" the zookeeper said as the boy and his family departed.

Lily stepped up to the feeding area, just in front of a tall iron gate that had a hole large enough for an elephant trunk. She was handed three carrots and an orange.

"Just give him one at a time," said Joanna, Kemba's trainer. "He loves the orange for dessert."

Lily held a carrot high in the air as Kemba's agile trunk snaked out of the hole and latched onto the treat. He curled it into his mouth, seemingly smiling as he chewed. Before he finished swallowing the first morsel, he was already searching for more. His trunk scoped out Lily's arm and lightly grasped onto her shirt near her armpit, tickling her as she giggled, leaving a trail of slime on her shoulder. She gave him the carrots, and lastly the orange, as instructed. The two fingerlike appendages at the end of his multipurpose trunk suctioned onto Lily's hand when grabbing for the orange. She didn't pull away. He let go, raising his trunk up to the sky, and softly trumpeted in appreciation—or perhaps dissatisfaction, I couldn't tell which.

"Oh, don't mind Kemba, he can be a little too curious," Joanna said. "Sometimes he mistakes a hand for a snack. Not to worry though, he has no teeth in his trunk, but it is a multifaceted tool. It can act as a snorkel in water, and with its millions of receptor cells, an elephant's extraordinary olfactory senses are substantially keener than even a bloodhound's. And with its eight different muscle groups, it can even topple full-grown trees."

I stared at the enormity of the majestic creature. His amber eyes were warm, yet secretive. There was a depth to them. I had heard elephants could sense things humans could not, and as I stared him deep in the eye, I could almost feel his concealed wisdom. His weathered skin was cracked like the Sahara Desert, and his ears were roughly the shape of his native continent. Five gargantuan humanlike toenails surrounded the front of his extrapadded squishy feet. As I scanned his massive frame, I noticed that one of his tusks was severed in half.

"So, Kemba is our twelve-year-old bush elephant who comes from Kenya," Joanna explained. "Do you know where Kenya is?" She directed her question to Lily, who looked at her with a blank stare before shaking her head.

"Kenya is in Africa," said Joanna. "Kemba is an adolescent who's nearly full grown, almost ten feet tall at the shoulder, and he weighs close to six tons. Elephants are the largest living land-roaming animals on the planet."

"Why is his tusk broken?" Lily asked astutely.

"We aren't sure, but he possibly lost part of it in a fight when he was younger. However, the break is pretty clean, so it's also possible that it was the work of a poacher—although that would be unusual for a poacher to just take a portion of the tusk. We got him from a wildlife reserve in Kenya. His mother was shot and killed when he was young, and sadly, he was separated from his herd, and he most likely would not have survived had it not been for the reserve taking him in. Elephants are in dire need of their mothers when they're calves, largely for protection. Fortunately, he survived."

"Protection from what?" Lily asked.

"Well, when they're still calves, they're susceptible to lion attacks if there are no adults around to protect them," Joanna replied. "But a full-grown adult rarely has to worry about an attack. Due to elephants' sheer size, lions don't bother them unless they sense substantial weakness. But adult African elephants have a much graver concern." Her voice became noticeably higher-pitched and more emotional. "The fate of Kemba's mother is a common one for many elephants in Africa. Poachers are decimating the population much faster than it can be countered with reproduction," she said, clearly passionate about the issue.

"How bad is it getting?" I asked, taking over the question duties, recognizing that the vocabulary being used by Joanna was a little too advanced for Lily.

"Poachers have killed more than one hundred thousand elephants for their ivory in just the past few years. Over fifty percent of the wild population has been destroyed in the last decade. If extreme measures are not taken, and soon, elephants will become extinct in the wild in the not-so-distant future," Joanna explained as I shook my head in disbelief. "There will be no more—"

"What's ivory?" Lily inquired, unintentionally interrupting.

"I'm sorry, I get a little worked up when I think about the atrocities being committed against these amazing animals," Joanna said, turning from me to Lily, softening her tone back to that of an educator instead of an advocate. "Their tusks, which are basically big incisor teeth needed for protection, foraging, and digging, are made of ivory," Joanna replied, displaying her wealth of knowledge on the topic. "Poachers kill the elephants for the ivory, which can be sold for huge profits around the world."

"How can people help?" I asked, feeling hopeless. "What can be done?"

"Well, obviously the battle is waged on the front lines in African regions, where poachers are prevalent. There are wildlife groups who have teamed up with tribes from African villages to combat the situation head-on using military tactics, albeit somewhat primitive ones. It is getting better, however, with some ex-military people joining the fight and leading some of the teams. But their courageous efforts aren't enough; the scope of the killing is too great. Away from the front lines, donations to the various organizations involved can be beneficial for necessary supplies and training. But the fact of the matter is, none of it will end the catastrophe until demand for ivory wanes around the world. This can be accomplished partially through legislation, but more effectively through social movements, as was the case in the United States when fur garments became taboo a few decades ago. Did you know that the United States is one of the largest markets for ivory next to China?"

"I had no idea," I said, again shaking my head as I looked at the ground. Joanna nodded, her eyes noticeably glossy. "Thank you so much for all the information. You're obviously very passionate about your work. And we really enjoyed meeting Kemba."

"It's my pleasure. Thanks for stopping by."

I looked down at my daughter, but before I could even tell her to say her goodbyes, she was already fully engaged with her new friend. Kemba once again snaked his trunk through the hole, but this time, a treat was not his focus. He placed the tip of his trunk on Lily's head and gently caressed her scalp, moving from side to side. Without an ounce of trepidation, she stood motionless, her eyes shut, and a grin swept over her face. She looked completely at peace, perhaps embracing the tranquil oneness of it all. She slowly reached her hand towards her head and softly rubbed the end of Kemba's trunk as her way of saying thank you.

As we walked away, I couldn't help but feel bittersweet about our encounter with Kemba. I was so grateful for the experience Lily got to enjoy, but I also felt melancholy and was overcome with a strange sense of duty. However, I wasn't exactly sure what my feelings were telling me.

I was pondering what Joanna had said as I stared off into

space, when Lily suddenly stopped walking. She looked at me and tugged at the side of my shirt, the way she did when she has something important to say, and she spoke with a conviction I had never really heard from her before. "Daddy, when I grow up, I want to go help save the elephants," she professed.

I didn't know how seriously to take her, but moreover, I couldn't believe how many times a daughter could make a father proud in one day. I swooped her up in my arms as she clung to the front of me like a baby bonobo. I planted a big kiss on her rosy cheek and received one in return.

"I love you, baby. You're such a sweet and thoughtful little girl, and I'm so very proud of you."

"I love you too, Daddy," she said, wrapping her arms around my neck as her head rested on my shoulder. I wondered why time couldn't stop in that moment.

It was getting late, and the warm bright blue sky was fading to its typical late fall afternoon haze. A coolness chilled the air. I put Lily down and grabbed her hand as we headed towards the exit.

"It's getting late, Lil. Should we head home?"

"Okay, but can we get ice cream first, Daddy?" she asked, spotting the ice cream stand strategically positioned near the exit, just to the right of where Leo the lion was kept.

"Of course we can, love. What flavor would you fancy?"

"Ummmm … vanilla," she said after a long pause.

"Vanilla? I thought you were a chocolate kind of girl. But okay then, vanilla it is! In a cone, right?"

She quickly nodded.

I stood in front of the ice cream stand, tempted to join her in the delights of an afternoon sugar rush. I surveyed the flavors in an attempt to convince myself that I might actually branch out and select a different flavor than my go-to: vanilla with chocolate syrup. I stared at the pistachio flavor for a while, not even noticing that Lily had wandered off.

"I'll have a vanilla scoop in a cone, and one in a cup with chocolate syrup, please," I said, feeling unadventurous.

"Here you go, sir," the attendant said as I handed her some cash.

I turned around to hand Lily her cone—and realized I was alone. Lily was not usually much of a wanderer, so I was briefly concerned, until I spotted her across the walkway, peering down into Leo's pit. The lion had a flowing mane and devilish golden-amber eyes. His head was frighteningly large, with powerful jaws to match. He looked at the patrons as if he'd been starving for weeks, and he was a truly regal but chilling sight—when he was actually awake. But as most male lions did, he spent most of his time sleeping, so Lily and I usually didn't give him much more than a passing glance.

As I thanked the girl for the ice cream, the eerie feeling that had hit me earlier but subsided during our encounter with Kemba resurfaced, this time with heightened intensity. I looked up to the sky, trying to put my finger on it.

Suddenly, from the far corner of the property, Kemba began to trumpet incessantly. It had a much different tone than before, this time one of panic and rage. The chimps, also near the entrance, began to shout and swing around their cage uncontrollably. The jet-black puma stationed next to the lion, who was also normally content to snooze the day away, used his powerful hind legs to thrust himself halfway up onto the fence, gripping it with his massive claws. He began to growl with fervor, whipping his head from side to side as fear spread to his iridescent yellow eyes. In seconds, the entire park sounded like a chilling mammalian concerto.

At that moment, I felt something profound deep within me. It was as if there was a flavor in the air that my human senses couldn't pick up. I knew—perhaps instinctually—that an animal's instincts and senses derived from a realm that we humans could not perceive. They could sense something coming, like an earthquake about to shake the ground. The screams, trumpets, and howls grew louder and louder and more violent. The few people left in the park began heading for the exits. I took that as my cue; I did not want to find out the reason behind the uproar.

I took a few brisk strides toward Lily, who was still looking down into Leo's open-air enclosure, focused and apparently oblivious to the commotion. I anxiously called out to her, and she spun her head around as she looked at me in a state of confusion. She was about to take a step towards me, when over her shoulder, I saw a face more terrifying than Satan's. I completely froze; my muscles ceased to move. The ice cream fell from my hands, my eyes locked in horrified disbelief. My mouth tried to communicate sounds, but none would form. Leo's deadly paws were gripping the top of the enclosure wall, just a foot away from my daughter, whose back was turned, and she didn't hear his stealthy maneuver. Realizing I couldn't cover the twenty yards between us in time, I finally regained the use of my voice and screamed in desperation at the top of my lungs.

"Baby, *ruuuuun!*"

She instead turned her head toward the enclosure. "Daddy, help!" she screamed.

Leo's massive claws grabbed her by the shoulder, ripping into her flesh, smashing her into the wall. Somehow still gripping the slick interior of the high wall with his hind legs, he used his raw power to hold himself up with his left foreleg, grasping her with his free paw, placing much of Lily in his crushing jaws.

Instinct took over, and adrenaline raced through my body, prompting my legs into action. Fully sprinting, I knew I had mere seconds to save my little girl's life, although I did not know how I would pry her from the lion's clutches. She was like a rag doll, incapable of putting up a fight. I was closing in when Leo looked right at me, snarling, and began lifting her off the ground. With no regard for my body, I threw myself at her in a desperate full dive, extending my arm as far as it could reach, hoping to grab a piece of her clothes. When my face hit the ground, I realized I had come up short. His razor-sharp canines clamped down, puncturing her skin as he flung her back over the wall. They both dropped twenty feet down into the pit. Leo landed like a cat, securely on all fours. Lily lay motionless, face down in the dirt, her body limp, bloody, and mangled.

I sprang to my feet as blood poured from my brow. Looking over the fence, I saw my daughter, lifeless, being straddled by the ferocious beast. I had never felt so helpless as hope began to vanish from my mind. Every ounce of me wanted to leap down and save her, but something in me kept my feet planted on the cement. Perhaps I knew we would both be doomed. My survival instinct must have overpowered my willingness to die for her. Ironically, because of my cowardice, I began to wish I was dead.

"Lily! Get up! *Please* get up!" I screamed down at her, trying to will her off the ground.

I yelled for help at the top of my lungs as I searched for something large I could throw at the lion, but found nothing. People scrambled toward the exit as every worker on site came running, walkie-talkies pressed to their mouths as they shouted for assistance.

The big cat crept around her body as if it were an antelope carcass. Blood discolored his muzzle. He hovered over her, bending down to pick up the smell of her blood, which covered half of her upper body, staining her hair a deep maroon. He sniffed around her head and deliberately swiped his tongue across her cheek. His mouth opened as he stood panting for what felt like forever. Still yelling and now crying, I could not bear to watch my daughter get devoured.

But then, to my astonishment, Leo backed away from Lily's body. He paused for a moment before he looked up and again stared right at me with his penetrating eyes as if to say, *"This is what happens when you cage us up."* Slowly strutting away from his conquest, he lay down next to a boulder, exhausted, breathing heavily. He was licking his lips and yawning in apparent disinterest when two tranquilizer darts whizzed through the air and struck him in the neck. He growled and hissed in anger, until his head finally fell to the earth. Immediately, my eyes darted to Lily. I prayed that she had not just taken her final breath.

# THREE

The room was as dark as a dungeon. The blackout curtains kept any light from peeking through. Musty clothes were scattered throughout my bedroom, and unwashed plates littered the floor. An odor worthy of a landfill permeated the room, but I hardly noticed. I only rose to eat and relieve myself. When I wasn't asleep, which was rare, I stared at the wall in a trance-like malaise until I fell asleep again. I didn't even mind that recurring nightmares filled my subconscious as I drifted away; I was just grateful to see my daughter one more time.

I wasn't exactly sure what day of the week it was, but it had been approximately three weeks since I'd left my life for the sanctuary of my bedroom. Following the funeral, guilt had become anger, which turned into misery, and eventually, a dense fog bank of depression hovered over my being. Suicidal thoughts became the norm as I wasted away under my comforter, and I genuinely wondered how much longer I could endure the pain. I had lost everything that mattered in my world. Hell, even my meaningless desk job as a research analyst for an investment company had been stripped away. It was my fault, however. I had just stopped showing up. No email, no call; I just vanished. I didn't want any-one to know what had happened, and I hated the job anyway. I was a washed-up former minor league baseball player, and there was no way I was going to spend the rest of my life in a cube in the corporate rat race, working for the man.

I poked my head out from under the smelly, unwashed sheets, opened one eye, and stared at the soft red glow from the digi-tal clock, which was mostly covered by previously worn black underwear. I reached over and uncovered the clock, turning it towards me. It blasted me as I opened the other eye: 8:28. Feel-ing like a vampire who'd been struck by the sun, I jerked the cov-ers back over my face, wondering if the time was a.m. or p.m. I truly didn't know, but it didn't matter; 8/28 was Lily's birthday. Another sign? Perhaps. But I was sick and tired of thinking about signs, and the reminder boiled my blood. I threw off the com-forter, jumped out of bed, grabbed the clock, and fired it at the wall. I couldn't see the effect, but I heard several plastic pieces hit the hardwood floor and was satisfied.

It was good to stretch my legs. It felt like at least a full day had passed since I had last risen. I yanked the chain of the light that sat on the nightstand. Squinting until my eyes adjusted, I scanned the room and noticed the cyclone that had spun its way through while I was sleeping for the better part of the month. The room was a disaster. But I certainly wasn't going to clean it.

I put on some navy-blue plaid pajamas and navigated my way through the room, trying not to step on any dishes, broken or otherwise. I made my way over to the bathroom sink and turned on the faucet. The warm water soothed my hands. I splashed water on my grimy face and ran it through my unwashed, messy brown hair that was quickly fading to grey. As a former athlete, I had always been religious about fitness, but the reflection in the mirror revealed the effects of being sedentary. An unusual soft, pudgy spare tire was growing on my stomach. I stared deep into my hazel eyes for several minutes, contemplating life, contemplating death. I couldn't get her out of my mind. All the moments we had shared raced through my head like a slideshow on repeat, only stopping at the sight of her face down in the dirt, lifeless. The doctor's words, *"shattered neck vertebrae,"* kept ringing in my head.

No matter how hard I tried, I couldn't withstand the overwhelming feeling of guilt. In my mind, I was culpable. Nearly everyone at the funeral, including the parents of my ex-wife, Victoria, tried to reassure me that what had taken place was just an accident. However, Victoria didn't see it that way. I'm not sure I did either. I never should have let her wander off. If she hadn't previously, Victoria certainly despised me now, as evidenced by the civil suit she was preparing to file.

Snapping out of my daze, I made my way back to the bed and sat down. I reached for my phone, which had been shut off all through my hiatus from the world. I clicked it on and saw the countless missed messages, and I felt like hurling it at the wall to accompany the clock. But I refrained. I scrolled through my contacts until I found Adam Rorbach. He had been a former teammate of mine in college, and was the one person in the world I truly trusted, family aside.

The call went to voicemail. I dialed again. On the third ring, a concerned voice answered.

*"Joe! Where are you, man? Are you alright?"*

"Yeah, thanks, brother. I'm alive ... barely," I said in a soft, raspy tone, clearing my throat. It had been a while since a word spilled from my mouth.

*"Where have you been? I thought you were dead! It's all over the news. I know I told you at the funeral, but words can't describe how sorry I am. I want you to know that it wasn't your fault. I wish I could do something to help you see that."*

"Thanks, Adam, I appreciate it. You're a good man. But there is actually something you can do for me."

*"Name it."*

"You know that .357 Magnum you have? I need you to let me borrow it."

*"Very funny."*

"Not joking."

*"You want me to bring you a gun? Have you gone crazy?! We're great friends and all, but I can't do that for you in your state."*

"Adam, I'm okay. Really. It's not what you think. I just need to get away for a while. I'm going to the mountains to clear my head. It's just for protection," I said, blatantly lying.

I HAD MET ADAM RORBACH on the first day of baseball tryouts. It was the spring of our freshman year in college. He came across as a joyous fellow who loved life and loved to be around people. Most of the players gravitated towards his outgoing nature, and even as a freshman, he became a leader on the field. Being reserved, I kept more to myself and went about my business of playing the game.

I was on a scholarship, but Adam was a walk-on trying to make the squad. He was a uniquely gifted athlete who stood six feet tall, with a tan, chiseled frame and a friendly smile that was often on display. He walked tall with an enthusiastic swagger, and he had a mop of sandy-brown hair. He didn't grow much facial hair, just a little dark stubble on his chin, which I imagined irked him slightly, considering that beards and goatees were such a rite of passage in the game of baseball. He was a right fielder and could swing the bat equally well from both sides, which wasn't terribly unusual, but Adam was different than the rest. He was ambidextrous and could throw with both arms as well. In high school, he had been a three-sport athlete, playing football and basketball before baseball season started in the spring. The basketball coach would yell at Adam because he couldn't decide which hand to shoot with, so instinctively, he would fire up jump shots with both. Although that was not the best idea in basketball, it was quite the asset to him playing baseball, especially as a switch-hitter.

But as effective as Adam was on the field, and especially at the plate, the inevitable slumps that happened to every player throughout the course of the year were particularly hard on him. A short memory and an even-keeled disposition were vital to regaining form in baseball. Not getting too up or too down helped keep a player focused, and the better coping mechanisms a person had for the lows, the easier it was to get back to hitting at a high clip. Hell, even an outstanding player failed seven out of ten times at the plate. A player had to be able to accept that reality.

But Adam had been diagnosed as bipolar as a teen, which was why, when he was exuberant and high on life, people loved his company. But the lows were extraordinarily hard and led to a complete shift in his demeanor and behavior. After a critical Friday night road game that we lost in extra innings—a game in which he had extended his hitless streak to fourteen—he went out drinking while the rest of us went to get pizza. I wasn't there, but I was sure he'd hit the bottle with intent. Adam also had a rare and detrimental ability to drink in massive quantities. Not surprisingly, he didn't make it to practice the next morning and showed up late to the game. Coach sat him on the bench, which didn't sit well with him and only sent his depression spiraling further.

By the latter half of the season, Adam and I had become quite close and shared a great deal of personal stories. I wasn't sure why, exactly, but he liked me more than he did the rest of the guys. Perhaps it was my complementary quiet, consistent nature that leveled him out. Perhaps it was my sincere and genuine personality. Maybe it was my similar athletic giftedness. Once, he told me that he greatly respected my athleticism, as I was also a multisport athlete, competing at a high level in basketball, golf, and tennis in addition to baseball. Occasionally, we would sneak off after practice, find a basketball court, and play one-on-one for hours, against the advice of our coaches. I won most of those hard-fought battles, and Adam seemed to respect me for that.

But by our junior campaign, the toils of the game had begun to take their toll on him. As a perfectionist, in combination with his difficulty with remaining even keel, Adam lost the ability to cope with failures at the plate. And since baseball was a game of failures, he began to hit rock bottom.

As a team, it was our worst season in three years; we missed the postseason by a wide margin. For Adam, as the drinking increased with every strikeout, his play suffered and he hit just .212, barely above the Mendoza Line, and he was dropped to eighth in the batting order for the last month of the season. Once the season finished, I turned the page and wiped the slate clean. Unlike Adam, I was looking ahead to the final year, hoping to impress the scouts enough to be drafted.

As spring led to the alluring days of summer, I did not see or speak to Adam for several weeks, as we had a break in our mandatory training schedule. I figured he had gone home to see his folks for a while, but it was odd not to hear from him. I stayed on campus that summer and kept on training on my own time, six hours per day, six days a week. I was determined to finish my college career strong.

One evening in late June, I was out with some classmates at a local pub near campus called the Bird's Nest. I was enjoying a cold one at the bar, when Josh Honnold, our starting shortstop, greeted me with an alarmed expression.

"Joe!" he said, slapping me on the back. "You hear about Bach?"

Intuitively, I knew the news was not going to be good as I calmly shook my head, staring Josh in the eyes with concern.

"He beat the hell out of some old guy last night!" he said. "I think it happened down by the river."

"Wait… I thought he went back home," I said.

"So did I, until this girl from my math class told me she saw him at a bar last night, pounding shots with a three-inch gash on his forehead."

"Dammit, that guy is a wild man. He's gonna get kicked off the team if Coach finds out," I said. "Where is he now?"

"Not sure. He's probably still at the bar," he said, only half kidding.

I knew Adam, and my instincts told me this was more serious than just a fight, so I decided to go over to his apartment the following morning. "I'm going to go find him tomorrow. I'll let you know if hear anything," I said as I shook Josh's hand and walked out.

The following day, a heavy downpour canceled our optional afternoon workout. The tops of the trees were shooting leaves from their branches in every direction as the car's windshield wipers struggled to keep up with the steady rain. I pulled up to the large new apartment complex, jumped out of my car, and found cover under the nearest eave. I did not see Adam's old light blue Ford Bronco out in the lot, but that did not mean he wasn't there. Adam frequently left his truck at the bars—not because he cared about getting a DUI, but because he enjoyed the few-mile stroll home. As I approached apartment 4, I noticed a broken handle of Popov vodka lying in the grass next to Adam's door. If I hadn't had a queasy feeling before I got to the complex, I certainly did as I began to knock.

Old-school rap was blasting inside, so I began to pound harder. Four more knocks on the door, but still no answer. Perhaps he had a girl in there, I reckoned, but I was not going to give up. An intense anxiety made me persistent. For whatever reason, my hand made its way to the doorknob, and I gave it a turn, just in case. To my surprise, the door opened, allowing me to peek through the crack with one eye. Before I could holler out his name, my eye froze wide open in disbelief.

Stuck to his couch and facing a muted TV, there was Adam, wearing only red boxers, as dried blood streaked down the side of his face from the gash on his forehead. He was staring at the wall in a catatonic state, eyelids open so wide that they seemed glued to his brow. A chilling expression was draped over his face, as if he'd seen a ghost. Perhaps he had.

As I nudged the door open a little further, several seconds passed without any movement from him, and I thought maybe he was dead. That was when I scanned down to the coffee table and saw the culprit. Plastic baggies, a razor blade, and off-white powder littered the glass.

His jaw was repeatedly clenching, his pupils the size of saucers as sweat dripped from his face. It was chilly and raining, so I ruled out the weather as the reason for the intense perspiration. I had dabbled with drugs in high school, so I knew the signs to look for.

"Adam, what in God's name are you doing?!" I asked forcefully, but received no acknowledgement.

"Rorbach!" I yelled.

Finally, he snapped out of his catatonic state, and his eyes darted to me, unblinking. A maniacal grin crept over his face as he opened his mouth, relieving his clenched jaw. "Lockett! My brotha! What brings you this way?" he asked in an upbeat and hurried tone. He was suddenly and oddly chipper, considering the blood all over his face.

I was astonished. I didn't know what to say.

"I thought you went to your folks'!" I shouted. "Are you actively trying to get kicked off the team?"

He didn't reply.

"Do you even know that you have blood all over your face?"

Still no response, just a blank stare.

Finally, he let out a cryptic laugh. "I love this stuff!" he exclaimed as he reached for a baggie on the table. "You want some?"

I was stunned that he had the audacity to ask me if I wanted drugs, but I decided to let it go, since I understood the state he was in. "No, I gave up cocaine years ago," I said.

"It's not coke. It's meth. Even better!" he said with a half smile. "Man, I love this stuff," he repeated.

Adam had been introduced to meth just a month prior, and it hadn't taken long for his addictive nature to relish the opportunity of a new vice. He was hooked.

As he reenacted the story of his gash, it began like any other drug deal gone wrong. He had met the dealer down by the river. But a new guy showed up, not the one he had previously dealt with. The new guy was older and even rougher around the edges. Adam said he looked like he was homeless, with rips all over his filthy clothes. He had dirt on his face, as if bathing was not part of his daily routine. Adam was not hesitant, however. He was not the fearful type, and he needed his fix. But as he went to make the exchange, the dealer pulled out a six-inch kitchen knife, activating Adam's fight-or-flight mechanism. But Adam was an accomplished fighter, and in typical Rorbach fashion, he chose to fight.

Adam had grabbed the man's arm just before the blade entered his midsection, and with his free hand, he landed a right uppercut square on the man's chin, snapping his head back. The dealer was shaken, but maintained a firm grip on the knife. They wrestled for control of the weapon as they hit the ground, with Adam landing on top of him. In the process, the knife had swiped across Adam's forehead, leaving an open wound that gushed blood onto the man's face, getting in his eyes. Adam sensed an opening and pounded him five times in the nose with his strong left hand. The dealer released the knife as blood overwhelmed his face. He stopped moving. Adam grabbed the weapon, and with terror in his eyes, thought about ending the man's existence. But something powerful came over him in that moment, and he refrained. He tossed the weapon into the bushes, grabbed the drugs, and fled the scene—but not before he dished out one last swift kick to the perpetrator's head.

I stood there listening, stunned, trying to absorb the gravity of the situation as he acted out the drama while feeding his addiction. I had heard awful stories about meth and how rapidly it could rip a person's life apart, and I was thankful I had never ventured down that dark road. I watched as he inhaled line after line, speaking a million miles a minute. I knew at that moment that I would never play baseball with Adam again. I tried to tell him that his actions were setting in motion a future he would come to regret, but he wanted no part of it. All he could see was his reflection in the table as the dirty white powder inched closer to his face. Then I remembered that an addict can only stop himself. So, I hugged him, told him I loved him like a brother, and walked out.

It would be several years before I saw Adam Rorbach again.

THE DOORBELL RANG SEVERAL TIMES, followed by a fierce pounding on the door. It sounded like the police. Whoever it was didn't seem too pleased. I must have dozed off again.

"I'm coming, dammit!" I said angrily as I threw on a T-shirt and stomped down the hardwood-floored hallway. One more knock reverberated through the room before I reached the door.

"Adam!" I said with great surprise. When we had hung up the phone, it did not seem like he was on board with my request. But here he was, carrying a blue duffel bag, which piqued my interest. It was nice to see him, for it had been a while, and he was looking better since the last time I had seen him. True, he'd gained some weight, his hair was still shaggy and unkempt, and his teeth were decayed in places—remnants from years of drug abuse. But every time I saw his face, I was just happy he was alive. And although he lived just over an hour away, we unfortunately didn't hang out all that often.

"Hey, man. It's good to see you," he said after I gave him a lengthy bro-hug. "Against my better judgment, I decided to bring you this." He held out the blue duffel bag. As I received it, the weight gave away its contents.

"I didn't want to," he continued, "but you helped me kick my vices, which saved my life, so I owe you. I always told you, if you ever needed anything, I'd be there. So, here I am," he said with calm sincerity.

I looked down at the blue bag as guilt swept over my entire body. I think he instinctively knew why I had really asked for the gun, but as a man who'd been to hell and back, he understood my bleak situation and didn't further question my intentions. A part of me wished he had.

"So, you're going to the mountains?" he asked. "Where, exactly?"

"Honestly, I'm not sure," I said, somberness returning to my voice. But I was sure; I knew exactly where I was going. It was a beautiful stretch of cascading river where my parents and I used to fish every summer in the western part of the Sierra Nevadas.

"I could go with you. I'm pretty handy in the wilderness," he said.

"Thank you, brotha. And thank you for bringing me this. But I need to be alone up there."

We chatted a bit more, but when I invited him in, he said he had to run. I supposed it was because he wanted to avoid the urge to sit and have a drink with me, like in the old days. Adam had been clean and sober for over two years now and didn't want to compromise his success with temptation.

I thanked him again, and instinctively, our hands interlocked in an old baseball victory handshake we used to do whenever the final out was recorded in our favor.

"You take care of yourself up there," he said. "The safety's on, but the gun is loaded."

As I watched him drive away and the nostalgia simmered, I lamented him granting my request. I wished he had never come.

MY EYELIDS FELT LIKE BRICKS as the white divider lines and endless dark green pines raced by with mesmerizing effect. However, my mind's eye was fixated on the blue bag on the floor of the passenger side. It haunted my thoughts the entire drive up to the river. A light mist began to coat the windshield, hindering visibility, as dusk was fast approaching.

It was late in the year, and Gold Creek Campground was already closed. But the snowfall had been very light, and the roads were still clear. I knew exactly where I was heading: campsite 17. The site rested on top of a granite hillside, right along a flowing stream surrounded by numerous varieties of towering pines that lined both banks.

I had fond memories of campsite 17, not only as a young lad learning to be an outdoorsman with my parents, but also with Lily. I had taken her twice, and luckily, both times, the site was available for me to pass on the family tradition. My dad, Ken Lockett, a bona fide outdoorsman, had taught me several valuable lessons at Gold Creek, from how to make a fire and pitch a tent to catching trout and shooting cans with a handgun. Little did I know as a child that one of those lessons I would someday regret ever learning.

After several hours of driving, the light rain subsided, for which I was thankful, since I had not remembered to bring the waterproof rain fly. Finally, I arrived at the campground, and as I expected, it was devoid of humans. It was very quiet until what sounded like a large crow in the trees let me know that I was not totally alone. I wondered what else was watching me.

I parked as inconspicuously as I could, behind two large tree trunks, each at least five feet in diameter. The entrance gate was locked, so I grabbed my axe, tent, bottle of whiskey, and the blue duffel bag out of the car and walked a few hundred yards down a slight grade to campsite 17.

It was just as it always was: the perfect campsite, spacious and flat, with just the right amount of mature trees and a centered firepit. But what set the site apart was its setting along the cliff's edge, with a view of the stream from the entire plot, accompanied by the tranquil and continuous sound of rippling water.

I set the items on the picnic table and walked a few feet to the edge, where the sloped granite hill made its way down to the stream that cut through the canyon about thirty feet below. As I gazed upstream at one of the most scenic and productive fishing holes along the stretch, a wave of nostalgia rushed through my mind, interrupting the serenity of the moment. Fishing with my mom and dad. Fishing with my daughter. Images of learning, and then teaching. Teaching—and then nothing. I had to turn away; the emotions were too raw. All I could think about were the words *gone too soon*. The three most important people to me—gone too soon. I truly was alone, and not just literally. But then I remembered, that was why I had come to the camp in the first place. And if it had to be done, I figured it might as well be in a place that had brought me great peace in the past.

Darkness was creeping in, so I quickly set up the tent and gathered enough scattered wood and pinecones to make a fire. I knew the temperature was supposed to drop to near freezing. The cold air began to overtake my extremities, as well as my senses. Making a fist became a chore. I no longer noticed the sweet odor emanating from the evergreens as I managed to gather the materials needed for the fire, but the kindling was damper than I expected. I used my left hand as a shield and lit the only two napkins I found in the glove compartment, but the wood resisted the innocuous flames. I struck six more matches, but each time, the napkins I had twisted flamed out before any wood could ignite. I was now down to my last match. I did not wish to face the prospect of a fireless night in bitter cold; that was not the way I wished to go out.

Feeling stupid and angry for not bringing enough supplies, I took a long pull from the bottle of whiskey and sat on the picnic table. The whiskey burned my throat, making me cough. I put the bottle down and looked around, but it was getting too dark to see much more than ten feet in front of me. Snot began to drip from my nose as the wind picked up, smacking my exposed face.

I walked around the campsite, desperately feeling the ground for something dry to work with. After minutes of searching, I came across a small patch of pine needles—exactly what I had hoped to find. Because of their thinness, they were drier than the twigs. I scurried over to the firepit and scattered the needles all over what was left of the two napkins as I knelt down and shielded the pile from the wind as best I could. I pulled out my last match, praying for ignition. My hands, shaking and fumbling, struck the match, and I watched the flame move its way from the napkin towards the needles as if in slow motion. Finally, a flame began to take shape.

"Fire!" I blurted out, knowing the potential ramifications had I failed. I started blowing and waving my hands frantically in an effort to spread the flame, and as I fed the fire, it began to grow, and I began to thaw out.

My stomach was churning with hunger, but I was almost too sick to eat. I hadn't brought much, but I had an old Snickers bar in the car. It pleased my taste buds as I ate it, as close to the fire as possible without melting the chocolate. It was satisfying, but not as a potential last meal. I grabbed the bottle of whiskey to wash it down. My senses dulled more and more with each gulp until my body could feel very little, not even the cold. The fire was helping, the heat finally overwhelming the damp wood.

I sat there motionless on the edge of the table, staring at the flames as they danced around the ring, changing colors with each unscripted move. My physical senses were numb, my eyes at half mast, but my emotions were growing with every memory that raced through my mind, like a slideshow I couldn't pause. All the love. All the laughter. All the pain. I peered deep into the fire and marveled at the vivid orange glow that only the sun could replicate. The flames above the glow were flickering and dancing around with two outstretched arms, and for a brief moment, I saw Lily frolicking in the grass near the oak tree in our backyard. I wouldn't allow myself to blink in fear of losing the image, but eventually my eyes gave in, and the flame took on a different form. Finally warmer, I noticed tears running down my cheek.

I loaded up the fire with all the somewhat dry sticks and pine cones that I could gather, then finished the entire bottle of whiskey. I stumbled past the fire, trying not to fall in as I hurled myself into the tent and zipped it shut. The tent was relatively warm from the nearby flames. I threw a sleeping bag over my entire body and attempted to pass out immediately. I did not wish to struggle to sleep on my final night on Earth, and I desperately hoped to dream of my daughter.

THE BITTER MORNING CAME QUICKLY, greeting my body with uncontrollable shaking and quivering. Was I cold, or fearful, or both? A jackhammer was implanted above my left eye, and the construction that was being conducted on my skull would not stop. The fire was gone, but so was my numb state, and I did not want to exit the comfort of the sleeping bag. The sun was nearly an hour from its daily welcoming as pins and needles shot through my body from the unbearably cold air. I had no more matches to make a fire, and the pounding in my skull kept me from dozing off again.

"I could just get this over with right now," I muttered to myself.

I may have dreamed of my daughter, but if I had, I did not remember. However, I did remember dreaming that I'd heard something sniffing around the tent. Or perhaps I wasn't dreaming; I couldn't be sure.

After several minutes of resisting, I muscled up all the will I had to leave the shelter of the tent, but not before grabbing the blue duffel bag next to the sleeping bag. I unzipped the tent, and a penetrating chill slammed my face, my eyes still squinting from the hammering in my frontal lobe. I poked my head outside the tent and immediately wished I were back home in my warm bed. But I had a job to do. "Nobody said it was going to be easy," I murmured in a daze.

I figured it couldn't have been much past 7:00 a.m., as the glow from the sun was just starting to reach the tips of the tallest pines across the stream. The morning dew had again saturated the ground, as well as the tent. I struggled to locate my shoes, and putting them on with frozen fingers was no less challenging. My body was quaking, but I still couldn't tell if it was from the cold, the hangover, or the fear of what was about to happen. Perhaps it was a combination of all three.

I put on every article of clothing I'd brought, grabbed the blue bag, and walked down to the water, where a path hugged the bank. I followed the trail upstream around several bends in the river for about a half mile, dead leaves crunching beneath my feet. I kicked a few pine cones off the granite boulders, sending them toppling down into the stream that was still flowing somewhat swiftly in places, considering the time of year. Some of the holes were deep enough to fish, and even though trout season had ended, I lamented not bringing my gear for one last go at the wily rainbow.

I stopped and admired the picturesque beauty around me. The sloping granite banks had been carved out by the untamed waters below, forming a V-shaped canyon that made me think of the angling classic, *A River Runs Through It*. I inhaled the fresh mountain air as deeply as I could, held it, and slowly exhaled, trying to savor every last moment of what it felt like to be human. I looked down upon my favorite spot along the river, and a sensation rushed over me, sending chills up my spine.

It was time.

With the blue bag in one hand, I headed down toward the water's edge. I had to move cautiously, as the boulders were slick from the morning dew. But I knew where to place my feet, as I had descended the hillside countless times before. The sound of the rushing stream intensified as I neared the spot I had dubbed "the famous hole" years ago as a teen. It was famous for its fruitful fishing—but soon to be infamous, I thought.

A ground squirrel poked his head out of his hole just as I arrived at the rock where I'd first taught Lily how to fish. As he looked at me, I smiled, thankful for one last moment with another living creature. The large granite slab underneath my feet had a flat area on its crown, then dropped off like a ramp down to a deep pool ten feet below. I put the bag down and sat with my legs crossed as the moisture seeped through my pants. I closed my eyes for just a few moments and entered into a meditative trance, and a calmness crept over my body. I imagined myself as a Native American, connected to the earth and the singular oneness that was shared between every living thing. I grinned as a peace that I hadn't felt since my daughter was alive briefly took over. A loud silence enveloped my blank mind. It was filled with nothingness. Free, finally—if only for a moment.

The squawk of a crow interrupted my trance and forced my eyes ajar. They ignored the large bird, immediately darting to the blue bag next to me as crippling anxiety filled my body. I started to sweat. The sun illuminated a portion of the water twenty yards downstream, but I was still cast in shade. I tried to calm myself by looking for shadows of any fish swimming about as I began to shake even more uncontrollably, attempting to maintain focus. Nothing was going to bring Lily back, and I knew what I had come for.

I took off the glove covering my right hand and reached for the bag, unzipping the pouch, my hand trembling with every movement. I extended my hand into the bag like I was trying to disarm a bomb and clutched the butt of the gun. The steel felt like ice, sending pins and needles through my near-frozen extremity. I slowly turned the .357 Magnum to the side, made sure it was properly loaded, and then just stared at it, shocked by the sheer size of the weapon. Guns had always made me uneasy. The tremor in my core shot vibrations through my entire body. I was scared ... but I was ready.

I took one last long look at the shimmering stream and the towering trees, the jagged rocks and the crystal-blue sky as a ray of light hit my lower leg. It felt warm, but not comforting. I stood and marveled at the beauty of the earth, pondering how something so magnificent could be counterbalanced by such cruelty. But then I remembered the natural yin and yang of life, the revolving ebb and flow.

"Nothing lasts forever," I whispered, my cracked lips barely opening wide enough to make a sound.

I set the hefty pistol on the ground and took my other glove off as I reached into the front left pocket of my cold, stiff jeans. I pulled out two creased pictures: one of my parents, and one of Lily and me. With my head drooped, I focused intently on the photos of three of the only people that had truly meant anything to me in my life. Vivid images from my childhood and then Lily's raced through my mind, one after another. As my life flashed before my eyes, I felt a tear roll off my nose, landing on the picture of Lily and me, with her riding on my shoulders at the zoo. I wiped the tears from my face, looked up at the sky, and felt unrelenting regret that my parents had never gotten to meet their granddaughter before they passed.

I put the photos in my coat pocket, slowly bent over, and nearly vomited as I picked up the gun, which was warmer now after resting in the direct sun creeping further up the hillside. I gripped it tightly with my dominant hand and braced my feet on the wet boulder. I inched it from my side up to the underside of my chin. With the butt facing the stream, I felt the cold steel of the tip press against my skin, which tightened as my head stretched skyward. My finger entered the hole and made contact with the trigger as tears streamed down my face.

The rapid slideshow in my mind intensified, almost as if someone or something were trying to get me to see all the past joy in my life, but I was resisting. I began to pull ever so gently on the trigger, not remembering how much pressure was needed to actually fire a bullet. But my survival instincts were attempting to overtake my will. My hand was shaking, but I gently kept squeezing, knowing that time was running out. I clenched my jaw and braced myself.

All of a sudden, the mental slideshow stopped, and with it my finger. My daughter's face lit up my mind as a ray of sun caressed my eyelids, the background of my mind's eye changing from black to a warm reddish hue. I could see her golden hair as I stared into her mesmerizing blue eyes. We were at the animal park on that fateful final day. My finger was still frozen as her eyes peered directly into mine. I felt her essence almost like she had taken over my spirit. Even as I tried to pull the trigger with finishing force, she wouldn't let me. She kept gazing up at me, tugging on my hand, acting as if she had something to say, but as was customary in dreams, words struggled to find form. Finally, her lips opened...

"Daddy! Daddy!" she cried with vigor. "I want to help the elephants! Help me save the elephants!"

The tears streamed down in greater volume as I felt my finger begin to release the trigger. I wasn't sure what was happening. I was supposed to be dead. Was I dead? Was it a dream, or an out-of-body experience? I wasn't totally sure. I opened my eyes, and the vision of Lily subsided—yet I felt so alive.

I tossed the gun aside and let it all out. All the emotions one could possess, from the moment of near death to the feeling of rebirth, released as I keeled over with my hands gripping my knees, bellowing and dry heaving simultaneously. I crouched down and cradled my head in my hands. I didn't know what was happening to me, but whatever it was, it felt like nothing I had ever felt before.

"You saved me!" I shouted—followed by a blood-curdling scream. My voice echoed through the canyon as I attempted to conjure more images, but my mind was now blank. I was just happy to be alive. Not just alive, but alive with purpose—a new purpose. I was to live out my daughter's dreams of which she had been stripped. I felt reborn.

After several minutes of staring at the ripples in the water, a smile crept across my face as the tears ceased. My eyes opened, and suddenly the world seemed more beautiful, all the colors enhanced, and I could feel every breath seep into the deepest caverns of my lungs. I leaped to my feet, anxious to get back to the car and get on the road to salvation. In my haste, I pivoted quickly to trek up the hill, when my feet lost contact with the slick, icy rock. I was momentarily airborne. My rear end slammed down on the hard surface as I tried to dig my nails into anything that might slow my slide, but the rock was too slippery, like a slide on a playground. The bottom edge of the slab was just a foot above the rushing water, and I had built up ten feet of momentum as I slid backwards down the granite slab, giving in to the inevitable and bracing for the ice-cold tributary. Time seemed to slow as I prepared for impact.

The freezing water jolted my core and numbed my extremities, but adrenaline kicked in shortly after the initial shock wore off. The surface current, which had appeared somewhat negotiable from the hillside, was just an illusion. Upon entry, an underwater force beyond my control catapulted me downstream. It threw me left, then hard to the right, then back to the left. The deep pool was narrowing, and I could see large boulders up ahead in the middle of the stream, marking an eight-foot drop-off that formed a waterfall into another deep pool below. I didn't know if I could slow my momentum before the drop, but I was going to give it everything I had. I tried not to panic, using all the strength I could muster, and pulled myself closer to another group of large boulders lining the bank, all saturated and sloping towards me. I inched closer to them and searched for something to grab hold of, but there were no tips to the boulders and no tree limbs or bushes in sight. I placed my hands on the slimy surface and tried to hoist my body out of the water, but all I could feel were my fingertips scraping the rock, unable to secure a grip. My hands slid right off, and I was forced to submit to the power tugging at my legs. I was at the mercy of nature, headed for the drop-off whether I liked it or not.

Once more, time began to slow. Accepting the reality of my situation, I began to think of the irony of the morning. After

I had barely escaped a self-inflicted death, the forces of nature weren't going to let me off so easily. The life that had been in my hands just seconds earlier was now in the hands of Mother Nature. As my will to fight waned, my body relaxed as the boulders marking the edge of the drop-off approached. They were even slicker than the shore stones, and I was unable to grab onto any of them as they rushed on by. I held my breath, faced downstream, and braced for whatever was to greet me in the harmless-looking pool below.

But as I reached the drop-off, underneath the darkness, I could see a massive immoveable object with a pointed tip that rested just below the surface—the kind of large boulder that trout used for shelter. But there was no time to admire it, and even less time to avoid it. I was catapulted over the waterfall, landing with my feet hitting the backside of the sharp conical boulder. For a moment, I thought I had escaped harm once again. But the momentum of my fall swept my legs out from under me and threw my upper body in reverse, whiplashing my neck until the back of my skull slammed into the granite slab. I thought I heard a crack. But before I could understand what was happening, all thoughts ceased, and only blackness remained.

# FOUR

The sounds were increasing in decibels. A wavy, oscillating murmur gave way to recognizable words that altered in tone and pitch. The words faded in and out, striking my ears simultaneously, but I could not put them together. Where I was, I had no clue. But who I was was gradually becoming clearer, as the name "Joe" was being repeated by the various voices.

I began to expand the range of my alertness as I picked up shuffling footsteps, some moving around to the right of me, some to the left, and intermittent door-latching sounds. My awareness heightened as my senses gradually became more acute.

I could tell I was supine, but darkness still consumed my view as a familiar odor swept across my face that I could not quite make out. I tried to move my index finger and realized it was being clamped by something small but hard. The odor wafted through again, this time with more aromatic intensity. Suddenly, a childhood image of me with a broken leg flashed in my mind, but it was interrupted.

*Beep . . . beep . . . beep . . .* An electronic pulse, smooth and rhythmic, rang out over and over as my mind tried to place it. Four more latches, accompanied by footsteps intermixed with beeps. I tried to force my eyelids ajar, but they felt glued shut. I attempted to piece together all the information my senses could gather, but all that resulted was confusion. I went to lift my arm, but it remained motionless. Panic was setting in once again.

*Beep … beep … beep…* The beeps became more frequent, and the footsteps moved around with more haste, some coming from behind my head, when all of a sudden it hit me. I remembered the unmistakable smell. I was in a hospital.

I gasped for air. My eyes jolted open as the rapid beeps morphed into one flat, continuous tone.

"We're losing him!" a voice shouted, and I felt something hard placed over my mouth.

The noises that surrounded me and the words I could previously make out began to fade, and any thoughts lost their form. The vivid darkness returned until there was sheer nothingness.

And then, something happened. Something unfamiliar. Something unearthly. Somehow, I was outside of my body, suspended in the air near the foot of a hospital bed, and I could see my physical self lying there some five feet below. There were machines and tubes and people in green scrubs working frantically over my lifeless body. A sheet covered my head and face. There was tranquility to the moment, despite the frenetic action being observed. It was as if the outcome were irrelevant, the procedures futile. Whatever would be would be.

The room was square and fairly small, with off-white walls, a grey paneled ceiling, and a floor painted deep blue. Multiple screens of all different sizes lined the walls, and robotic-like arms hung down from the ceiling with a bevy of equipment attached. I looked over to the right—my physical form's left—and as I had envisioned, there was the latching door I'd been hearing.

As I swung my head back to the proceedings taking place on the bed, I noticed something in my peripheral vision. A figure was standing in the corner, no more than three-and-a-half feet tall. It was not moving or making any sound, but it seemed to be holding something. The figure's form appeared humanlike, as I could make out four limbs and a bipedal stance. It was blurry and partially translucent; I could see the off-white wall right through it. But something about it seemed oddly familiar. I peered more closely, as if my vision could zoom in like a camera. The clearer the image became, the more detail I could determine. I began to pick up hints of blonde hair, pale skin, and bright eyes, but could not ascertain their exact color. Then I looked down and saw small white tusks protruding near the end of the figure's left arm. A fuzzy stuffed animal came into focus, and I finally realized who the figure was, an image eternally seared into my brain. It was my daughter, holding her favorite elephant, once again standing before me.

"MR. LOCKETT! MR. LOCKETT! JOE! Can you hear us?"

I woke to a room full of faces, some of them familiar, some not. I did not know what day it was, or what I was doing in this bed, but I knew I was still in a hospital, and my body ached like never before.

I tried to survey the room, but my neck struggled to make a full pivot; a shooting pain knifed through the back of my head with the slightest of motions. The bed was partially raised, so I could see straight ahead. A television affixed to the wall was on mute, a baseball game showing, but I couldn't see who was playing; my vision was too hazy.

"Joe, do you know where you are?" asked a woman in a white coat that hung to her knees. "I'm Doctor Weatherly. You're in a hospital. Are you able to speak?"

I stared at her intently, trying to answer, but my mouth remained shut.

"Take your time, Joe," she said as she touched my shoulder, then she turned to leave the room.

"Monitor him," she said to what appeared to be a nurse. "Come get me immediately if he relapses."

Before she placed her hand on the handle of the door, control of my facial muscles returned.

"So, I'm still in a hospital, huh? Terrific."

The doctor turned back around and looked at me with a pause that made me feel stupid for asking, since I knew the answer.

"Yes, Joe. Do you remember anything that happened?"

I didn't remember much, but I nodded anyway. "I was in an accident, wasn't I?"

"Yes," she replied cautiously.

"Car?" I asked.

She looked at me for about ten seconds, seemingly trying to determine if I was stable enough to hear the news. She appeared unsure of my state as she rolled a chair over from the corner of the room and sat down.

"Joe, you had a bad accident, but it wasn't a car accident," she began. "A ranger from the Fish and Wildlife Department brought you here. You were in critical condition when you arrived. I don't want to overwhelm you with the details, because I'm worried about your vitals, but we had to perform major surgery to save your life."

My eyes froze, locked on her mouth. All of my limbs seemed intact as I began a mental checklist. I could not see under the hospital gown to take inventory of my midsection. I began to wonder which organ had been treated.

"What kind of surgery?" I asked, not really wanting to hear the answer.

She paused for a moment before speaking. "Brain surgery, Joe."

A rush of adrenaline raced through my body as dread set in. I stared at her before hesitantly raising my hand to my head to inspect the damage, only to encounter a thick bandage. Was I deformed? Was part of my skull missing? I was trying to prepare for the worst-case scenario.

"Try not to touch your head, Joe," the doctor said. "The surgery went well, but it will take some time to heal. You had a significant gash in the back of your skull that required one hundred and twenty stitches. Your skull was cracked, and you had significant cranial bleeding. When you slipped into a coma, we were concerned that you might have permanently damaged brain tissue, but we're hopeful that now that you've come to, you'll make a full recovery, with all your faculties intact."

"I was in a coma?" I asked with trepidation.

"Yes, for twelve days. You gave us quite a scare," she said with a warm smile that eased my anxiety momentarily. "Again, I don't want to overwhelm you right now, Joe. You need to rest. We're going to have to keep you here for a couple more weeks to make sure you're stable. I have to step away, but the nurses will be here for anything that you need."

She gently touched my shoulder again before she stood up and walked out of the room. I meant to thank her for saving my life, but too many swirling thoughts left me speechless. I still didn't know what had occurred; the last thing I remembered was holding a large gun near the river. As the minutes passed and I scoured my mind for clues, I began to recall images of the suicide attempt, followed by the subsequent feeling of sheer ecstasy over its failure.

A cheery brunette with a warm demeanor and vibrant hazel eyes came over and introduced herself as Samantha, asking if I was comfortable. I nodded, but really, my whole body felt like it had gone through a meat grinder. She said she would keep checking on me, and that in a few hours, they would be moving me to a different room with a more comfortable bed. For that, I was grateful. As she turned and headed for the door, I felt a mammalian instinct kick in, my eyes fixed on her curvaceous proportions, shifting ever so naturally with each step. I felt a rush of blood to my pelvic region as I wondered why I would ever want to die when there was still that kind of beauty in the world.

"Thank you, Sam," I said with a flirty grin as she turned, smiled, and walked out the door.

THE NEXT COUPLE WEEKS trudged along at a tortoise's pace. My body's atrophic state was accelerating, but my mind was defogging more and more each day. The clarity was a nice change. I was weak, however, and had lost too much weight since the accident. The doctors and nurses wanted to make sure I hadn't lost any motor function as a result of the trauma to my head before allowing my release.

When the day finally arrived, I was brimming with anticipation, so much so that I had barely slept the night before. All I wanted to see was a sunny blue sky, or anything other than white walls, but I would miss seeing Samantha. Every morning at 10:00 a.m., she came in and brightened my otherwise dreary day.

Samantha walked into my room, right on time as always. I barely knew what day it was, but I always knew the time the minute she came through the door. There had been a four-nurse rotation taking care of me, but Samantha was the only one that activated my primal clock. She was soft and kind, with a smile that gave me hope. She sat down in the chair next to my bed for what I knew would be the last time.

"So, you're leaving us today, huh, Joe?" she said with irresistible charm. "I got kinda used to you being around. Sure you don't want to stay?"

"I'd love to, but I don't want to get you in trouble with your superiors," I said playfully. "I know my handsomeness has been distracting for you."

She tilted her head and half smiled as if to say, *"Do you not realize you have a bandage covering most of your head?"*

A part of me did want to stay, and she knew that. We had talked about many things over the last couple weeks, but I had never addressed the elephant in the room. I wanted desperately to see her again someday, and I sensed that she would not be opposed, but I never let myself go down that road. I had a new mission— a mission that would take me to a faraway land and in an opposite direction in life, one that she would not fully understand. So, I kept my feelings bottled up, minus some harmless flirtation.

I told her all about my plans to go to Africa, and why I was going. I told her about Lily and the vision I'd had, and to her credit, she was enlightened enough not to dismiss it as ridiculous. In fact, she seemed to embrace the notion, being spiritual herself. When I told her the story of Lily's death, she broke down and cried, revealing her innate compassion, which did not surprise me, considering her profession. What I didn't disclose was how every day, Samantha made me want to change my plans. But despite my desire to say it, I simply couldn't. Destiny was calling, and I intended to answer.

"Well, Joe," she said, "I just wanted to tell you, it's been wonderful getting to know you, even for such a short time. I feel like I've known you for years. And I'm glad you shared your story with me. I find it inspiring."

"Thank you, Sam. I can't tell you how much it's meant to have someone to talk to through all this. I feel like I haven't really talked to anyone in a long time."

"It's my pleasure, Joe. Just doing my job," she said with a sudden indifference that made me feel like I was talking to one of the other three nurses. "I'm glad that you're healing well, and I think you'll make a full recovery. If there's nothing else you need…"

I just looked at her, puzzled. Where had the warm, playful girl gone? What did she do with Samantha?

We stared at each other for several seconds, then she got up and started for the door. I put out my arm, ignoring the pain, and gently reached for her hand, barely latching onto her pinky. By the look on her face as her eyes met mine, I could tell she was caught off guard, but not offended. A warmth returned to her face, a sudden glow as I felt her fingers clutching mine ever so slightly.

"I will miss seeing your lovely face, Samantha," I said with complete candor. "Maybe in another life, huh?"

She paused as her eyes left mine and stared at the wall, not knowing what to say. A flush swept across her cheeks as her hand began to pull away from mine. She looked at me for what I knew would be the final time.

"You take care of yourself, Joe," she said with a smile, and walked out the door.

I turned my head, closed my eyes, and tried to forget the radiance of hers, but my reconstructed brain had other ideas.

A lonely couple of hours had passed when two of the other three older nurses who had the pleasure of looking after my immobilized body came into the room, much to my chagrin.

They cleaned me up, clothed me, and went over all the necessary instructions on how to care for my wounds. The whole time, I was wishing Samantha would come and save me.

I was feeling as if I could walk out of the hospital, but not without great pain, and they insisted on a wheelchair anyway. Standard protocol, I assumed. I just didn't want Sam to see me being wheeled out of the joint.

"Joe?" The largest of the nurses got my attention. "We noticed on your file that you don't have any relatives in the area listed as an emergency contact," she said, which was a nice way of not mentioning that my parents were deceased. "Is there someone else you'd like us to contact?"

I paused and acted like I was thinking, but in reality, I knew exactly who I was going to have her call.

"Yes, please call my friend, Adam Rorbach. He owes me a ride," I said, telling her the number.

She nodded and gave me all my paperwork and charts, then left the waiting area. I didn't know how long I was going to have to use the wheelchair, but I tried to relax and settle in. Nothing was ever quick in a hospital. I tried to doze off, but my back ached like never before, and the wheelchair was too short for me to rest my head. I began to wish I was back in the hospital bed. I passed the time by flipping through all the charts and paperwork I was given, trying to get a good sense of the procedures that were done to save my life, and how to properly rehabilitate. I wanted to recover as swiftly and effectively as possible, so I could get on a plane to Africa.

As I went through all the documentation, one piece in particular caught my attention. It was the report from the ranger, detailing what he'd encountered the day he stumbled upon my body at the river. I still didn't know how I'd ended up in the operating room, and I was scared to find out, but too curious not to.

It began like any other report.

*It was approximately 8:15 a.m. when I unlocked the gate and pulled into the campground, and I did so because I saw a black SUV outside the fence. I smelled smoke and headed down toward the river to investigate. As suspected, I saw a tent and a fire that was somewhat fresh, but with no flames, just a smolder, releasing smoke into the air. There were a few miscellaneous items on the picnic table, but no one in the tent or on site. I thought something was amiss, but didn't suspect any foul play. I thought a person might be down at the river doing some offseason fishing, but I didn't notice any fishing gear. I decided to go down to the river to inspect. I trekked upstream for about a half mile, and that's when I saw the body of a man wedged between two boulders near the bank, his lower half submerged in the river. His head was cocked back and to the side, his eyes closed and mouth open. His shirt was torn, and blood covered one of the boulders, as well as his clothes. I could see trauma to the back of his skull and lacerations on his hands and forearms. He appeared deceased, but a faint pulse told me otherwise. I pried him from the rocks, tried to stop the bleeding as best I could, and managed to haul him back to the truck. We arrived at the ER at approximately 9:45 a.m.*

The report was a shock to the system and revived my memory of that day, but I didn't dwell on it; it was a blessing that I had survived.

I relished breathing in fresh air, even if I had to be wheeled to Adam's truck. The sun peeked out from behind a passing cloud, making my eyes squint, as the beams were more intense than I remembered. It had certainly been a while. The sky was a radiant blue, and I just stared out of the truck in silence, window down, drawing in as much air as my lungs could hold, feeling the wind graze my face. I still had a bandage on my head, albeit a tad smaller, but I didn't care how I looked; it was just refreshing to be out of the hospital. I closed my eyes, grinned, and rested my head on the window frame. I nearly fell asleep, until my moment was interrupted.

"I knew I shouldn't have let you go up there alone," Adam said, breaking the silence. "I should never have given you that damn gun."

"You don't even know what happened!" I exclaimed, irritated as I looked back out the window.

"I don't need the details. I already know."

"I didn't shoot myself in the head, if that's what you're thinking," I said.

"Obviously. It's a .357 Magnum. You wouldn't have a head anymore if you had."

"Well, don't you wanna know how I almost died?" I asked him.

"It doesn't matter," he said, to my surprise. "I feel responsible for giving you a gun, knowing the state you were in. But you're still breathing, so I guess that's all that really matters now."

"I was close to pulling the trigger," I said, ignoring his disinterest in my story. "But a moment of clarity, like nothing I've ever experienced before, came over me. The sun came out, like it is right now, and I suddenly had a deep desire to live to see another day. It was totally surreal. It was like—"

"So, how'd you get a brain injury?" he cut in, interrupting my story.

"Oh. Well, I slipped and fell into the rushing river and smashed my head on a boulder, apparently. A ranger found me. Ironic, huh? I wanted to die, then wanted to live, and then I nearly died, all within a few seconds. I swear all this shit happens for a reason."

Adam wasn't spiritual or much of a deep thinker, so it shocked me a little when he nodded in agreement. "Well, I'm just really glad you didn't blow your face off," he said. "You wouldn't make a very good wingman without a head ... not that your bandage does us much good."

I just looked at him for a few seconds, stunned by his cavalier attitude, then started cracking up. It was so like Adam to use a joke for healing.

I sat contentedly in the truck as my old friend guided us down the hill, out of the mountains, and back to the urban sprawl. There was a peacefulness to the ride, just like in the old days, when we'd cruise around town in his old blue Bronco, with the only sound coming from the stereo. An hour passed with few words, and I had time to ponder my future journey and where it would take me. I had no idea where to begin, yet I was already imagining the many different environments and people I would encounter along the way. All I knew was that my life as I knew it was finished, and my new life was to start immediately. I had just enough money saved up to buy a one-way ticket to a foreign land, with maybe a little left over for food. After that, I would have to believe in my ability to survive. I wasn't too confident, but I was willing to try it. I was excited, filled with both fear and anticipation. But mostly, I just felt alive—and not just alive, but alive with purpose.

With the city skyline in view, Adam turned down the music. The audible change woke me; I had dozed off thinking about my journey.

"You awake over there?" he asked. "You missed a car full of females driving down the hill next to us. One of them pointed at you. Must've been the bandage." He let out his maniacal chuckle.

"Too bad I missed it," I said with detectable sarcasm.

"I'm just messing with you," he said. "I didn't want to bother you with questions, but now that you're awake, what will you do going forward?"

He wasn't one to ask those types of questions, and I wasn't planning on revealing my plan until later, but since he asked, he must've been truly interested.

"I'm going to Africa," I said, without explanation.

"You're going *where?*"

"Africa. Kenya, most likely."

"What, like on a safari?"

"You might call it that," I said.

"No, really, why are you going to Africa?"

I didn't want to reveal the real reason, afraid that he wouldn't believe me and would question whether I had indeed developed permanent brain damage, so I kept it simple. "I'm going to save some elephants. Or try to, at least."

"From what?" he asked obliviously.

I shot a bewildered look his way.

"I'm kidding!" he said. "Simmer down. I've been following the news more lately. I know about all the poaching."

Adam was more of an on-the-surface person, so it didn't shock me when he didn't ask for all the details. I wanted to tell him, but I figured he wouldn't understand.

A few moments of silence passed, and I could tell his wheels were spinning. Adam's mouth opened, but often nothing would come out when he was in deep thought but didn't know what to say. Finally, he stuttered out his question.

"So, uhhh... So, when you leaving?"

"Soon," I said. "Very soon. As soon as the bandage comes off. I'm going to go home and start packing immediately."

"What about the lawsuit you filed against the zoo?" he asked. "That lion should've never been able to get anywhere near your daughter; he should've been in a steel cage, and you know it. You have a great case. You could win millions!"

"I'm not dropping the suit, but it could take years, and I don't have time to wait around," I said. "Besides, it won't bring my daughter back. So, I'm going to Africa. However, I will say, I still have no damn clue how that lion was able to grab onto a super tall and ridiculously slick surface."

Adam paused for a moment, then he looked at me and uttered the most endearing thing I had ever heard come out of his mouth. "I'll go with you."

I shot a wide-eyed look his way and nearly laughed, but I could see the seriousness in his face and knew he was not playing games. Adam was the adventurous type who instinctively knew his way around. Perhaps his skills and companionship would not only be reassuring, but useful. I gave it some thought.

"Life has run its course here for me too," he said. "I got nothing stopping me. So, let's go on an expedition. I'm game!"

I did not question his motivation; I just went with it. It was just another piece of the puzzle in a sequence of life events that was feeling more and more like destiny.

We drove the rest of the way in silence, dreaming about new beginnings, adventure, and what awaited us in the Motherland.

# FIVE

y head ricocheted off a hard surface, not too far from the scar where my skull had split, as I woke to a stiff neck, with drool forming in the corner of my mouth. A sudden jolt followed by a quick drop reminded me that I was high above the clouds, with nothing but the vast sea below. I lifted the plastic shade, but all I could see was the Earth's blue canopy for miles. How long had we been in the air? I hadn't the faintest clue.

I normally didn't sleep on planes—the discomfort of coach worked even better than caffeine—but I was so exhausted from the last few weeks post-surgery that my body had given up the fight to stay awake, despite the sardine can they called a seat.

I had made the sentimental decision to sell my house, but the choice was made for me in a way, as I knew that massive medical bills were coming that would threaten any good financial standing I had accumulated over the years. Fortunately, the market had skyrocketed significantly into green territory, and with any luck, the profits would be enough to keep me out of trouble with Uncle Sam. Not that that mattered much anymore, as I genuinely didn't know when I would set foot on US soil again, if ever.

I looked over at Adam two seats to my left, with an empty seat between us. Reclined and with a leg jetting out into the aisle, he appeared enviably comfortable. For a guy who was often hyper, he sure could snooze in many different settings.

I tried to doze off again, but the child sitting behind me had plenty of energy and kept kicking the back of my seat. He sounded about seven or so and had a strong lisp, with his R's resembling W's. He was one of those kids who would repeat fun phrases continuously for several minutes for no apparent reason, while his mom in the seat next to him was the type who didn't care about the other passengers on the plane.

"I like *whinos*. I like *whinos*. Mommy, guess what? I like *whinos*."

There was a rhythm to his tune, I had to admit, but the song was stuck on repeat, while the mom flipped through her gossip magazine like he wasn't even there. My agitation grew as my feet began shifting back and forth on the floor. I wondered how much longer we had in the air, but knew the answer was probably more hours than I could bear to find out.

Finally, my irritation reached its peak. I unbuckled my seatbelt, turned and kneeled on my seat, and uncharacteristically just stared at the young boy with spiky blondish hair and glasses.

"Hey, buddy," I said nicely. "I know you like *rrrhinos*. I like *rrrhinos* too! They're so big and massive and all dinosaur-like. And that horn! But you know what I heard? *Rrrhinos* don't like it when people kick the back of other people's seats. Okay? Thanks, pal."

His mom, a full-figured woman in her thirties with matching blonde hair, slowly lowered her magazine and revealed at least four inches of cleavage as she gave me the death stare. She opened her mouth as I braced for impact, but something got the better of her, and she looked over at her son instead. "Jackson, stop kicking the man's chair, please," she said with a Southern drawl and surprising authority. Then she looked at me and smirked. But the kicking stopped, so I was grateful and thanked her and the young lad.

I went to turn back around when she caught me off guard. "So, where in the world are you heading?"

I was taken aback by her sudden affability. I figured she must have thought I had a nice face or something. Either that, or she felt bad for me because of the scar on the occipital portion of my head, not yet completely covered by hair.

"Me and this snore machine over here are going to Kenya," I said.

"Oh, yeah? Us too! Which part?"

As lovely as she was being all of a sudden, I was hoping we were on different paths. I didn't know how much more of Jackson's *whino* infatuation I could stand. But I was pretty happy to be alive, so I made a strong attempt at tolerance.

"After we land in Nairobi, he and I are heading to a reserve in northern Tanzania, very close to Mount Kilimanjaro," I told her, but did not want to divulge why.

"Big game hunting trip, huh?" she asked.

I gave her a look of disapproval as one of my brows lowered. "A bit presumptuous, no? What makes you assume that?"

I could tell she wasn't the type to care if she offended some-one, so I assumed an apology was not in my future.

"I just figured, two guys... on a plane to Africa... heading to a big game reserve... Why else would you be going?"

She had a point, and I almost turned around, but figured the conversation was better than Jackson playing soccer with my seat.

"Quite the contrary," I said, with detectable rudeness. "Me and my longtime friend here are meeting up with a group that is dedicated to fighting the poachers that plague the elephant pop-ulation in the region." I was going to elaborate, but I assumed she didn't really care.

"Wow, that's very honorable," she said. "I apologize for the assumption."

"No, no worries. I probably would've thought the same thing."

"How long are you two going for?" she asked.

"Indefinitely, for me at least," I told her, and her eyes widened. "Yeah, these tickets are one-way. I sold my house, and I'm going on an adventure, starting down a new path. Where it will lead, I have no clue, but it's going to be exciting, I know that much. And hopefully rewarding as well."

I could see her interest growing, and I noticed others eaves-dropping with shocked expressions in the surrounding rows. One woman even whispered in her husband's ear, her eyes still focused on me. When I caught her gaze, she looked away.

The mother was about to ask another question, but Jackson interrupted her. I was glad; I didn't want to go into all the details.

"How about you?" I asked her. "What business do you and your son have in Kenya? I'm assuming he's your son."

"He is! How'd you guess?" she asked, with a plethora of sarcasm. Her feisty tone reminded me of my ex-wife.

"Hair color. Dead giveaway," I said with a little sass of my own.

"Ahhh, of course. Anyway, Jackson and I are going to meet my husband in Nairobi. He's a government official and will be there on business for a few months. And since Jackson loves safari animals, we're all going to take a few days and visit the Serengeti."

"What an incredible experience that will be," I said, turning to the boy. "Jackson, I bet I can guess what your favorite animal is."

He just looked at me, puzzled.

"Well, you two have a nice time," I said. "I hope you brought a good camera. The photo ops will be aplenty."

"Got it right here," she replied and smiled, pointing beneath my seat. "You have a good trip too. Be safe. Sounds like it could get a little dangerous."

"Thank you. I'm sure it will have its moments," I said as I turned back around.

I strapped myself back in and leaned my head against the window, wishing I had asked the flight attendant for a pillow at the beginning of the flight. I gazed out the window and listened to the drone of the engines. The low, humming rumble was soothing as I closed my eyes and thought about what we were getting ourselves into. Who would we be working with? What would the reserve be like? Would we sleep in tents, or in enclosed structures? How visible would Kilimanjaro be? I knew very little other than the name of the person we were to meet in Nairobi, a man called Kwame Ibori. Kwame worked for the organization that operated on the reserve. We had emailed back and forth several times, and he sent a few pictures and some brochures, but the details were still a bit hazy, as the marketing wasn't exactly top notch. I didn't mind. It only added to the mystery of it all.

I was very close to joining Adam in sleep when the flight attendant announced that a movie was about to begin. It was one I had seen before, *The Air Up There*, starring Kevin Bacon. *Fitting*, I thought as I chuckled under my breath. It was an oldie but a goodie about a basketball coach who reluctantly travels to a remote village in the heart of Africa on a recruiting assignment, but winds up teaching the game to a village of people who barely have shoes, let alone much awareness of the sport. In the process, he finds himself and grows to love the culture. Even though I had previously seen the film, I jumped at the chance to kill a couple hours. I scooted over to the middle seat and flagged down Katie, our long-legged flight attendant with a flowing sandy-blonde ponytail, and without waking Adam, I ordered a Jameson and ginger ale to calm my stomach and enhance the movie. It worked like a charm, and I finished the cocktail just before Adam woke, for which I was thankful. He was a still a long time sober now; I didn't want to be the catalyst for a relapse, and I sure as hell didn't want him scouting for meth in some African village.

A little turbulence jolted Adam awake. He looked around the cabin with a confused expression, like he had been sleeping for hours and didn't totally realize where he was.

"Man, that felt good. How long have I been out?" he asked.

"A little over an hour," I replied. "Movie's on. It's almost the end though."

"Is that the one where Kevin Bacon tries to pretend he's a basketball coach?" he asked, and I laughed and nodded.

"So, tell me the plan again. We're meeting a guy named Kwame in Nairobi? Then what?"

"We still have over eight hours to go in the air. I was going to brief you just before we land. But I suppose I'll tell you now," I said. "When we land in Nairobi, we need to get a shuttle or taxi or whatever is offered at the airport and get to the heart of downtown, where the African Wildlife Preservation Organization office is located. That's where we're supposed to meet with Kwame, and he'll give us directions from there. We land in the morning but aren't supposed to go to the AWPO until the afternoon. Maybe we'll try to find something to eat. I hope English is at least somewhat common there; my Swahili isn't too polished."

"Should be quite the adventure!" he said with a glimmer in his eye as I smiled in agreement. He seemed truly excited, which worried me a little. With Adam, adventure was always a stone's throw away from trouble. But I was the one who had said he could come along, so I had to deal with any potential repercussions. I knew the real reason I'd told him to come was due to my trepidation over going to a foreign land alone, and I thought Adam, who was so adept in unknown territory, would be the ideal companion—as long as he could stay out of danger. But danger was what we were in fact heading towards once we arrived on the reserve, so I figured his experience would come in handy.

We chatted for a bit longer about the prospects of tracking down elephant poachers and what that would feel like. The conversation was somewhat superficial; we didn't really delve into what it would mean to actually hunt down a man who was trying to steal the tusks from an elephant's face. But something told me it would have a different significance for me than it would for him. That didn't bother me; I understood that life's journey was distinctive for each individual on Earth. But one thing seemed inescapably congruent for both of us: we were certain to feel alive in the heat of pursuit, even if it was for different reasons.

The flight was long and arduous. I had never liked long flights, and the flight to Nairobi was nearly double my longest. After approximately twenty hours in the air, my thoracic spine felt like it was going to snap in two, and my legs began to feel like they were permanently locked at ninety degrees. In fact, if I could not see them, I wouldn't have believed they were still attached to my hip sockets. I tried to sleep but was ineffective for the majority of the flight. Adam, on the other hand, would wake up to the Nairobi skyline, refreshed and ready for whatever was to come. Conversely, I had fought tooth and nail to keep my sanity and vowed to fly first class if I ever boarded a plane again. I just kept telling myself that it was worth the pain. Lily's beautiful face kept popping into my mind, and that kept my focus on the journey.

As the aircraft finally began its descent, all I could see was my daughter holding that little elephant—but all I could feel was angst. In an attempt to calm my nerves, I opened the guide on Nairobi that I had bought weeks prior and had already read cover to cover, but I figured a second glance could only help, and it would certainly aid in passing the final hour of the flight.

I relearned that Nairobi, the capital of Kenya, was much more advanced than I had originally imagined. Whenever I had previously conjured up mental images of the country, besides the abundance of wildlife, the vast open plains brimming with acacia trees and small rural villages with homes that were more akin to huts had come to mind. But as I flipped through the pages and countless photos, I was again surprised at how large the city appeared. In fact, it could've been confused with a medium-sized American metropolitan area, particularly in the heart of the city. Dozens of tall structures, including some that might even be called small skyscrapers, dominated the landscape. Most appeared to be for residential use, but modern office and government buildings with intricate architecture were also prominently featured in the downtown sector. Museums, schools, restaurants, bustling squares, and lush parks were scattered throughout for locals and tourists alike. Even golf was available, to my surprise.

The Nairobi River, which connected to the mighty Athi, flowed through the metropolis and gave the city its name. The Maasai phrase *Enkare Nyrobi* meant "cool water," and although the waterway was the key to the city's existence, as in many large cities, it had its problems with pollution. Disease was a common and constant battle for many Africans, but large cities like Nairobi were better equipped than the villages, as there were several modern hospitals in the metro area, which had over six million inhabitants. The official languages in Nairobi were Swahili and English, I read, the latter stemming from the days of British rule, and it was still the most utilized for commerce. European colonization had left its indelible stamp on the African cultures it infiltrated, a fact I knew all too well from my studies in college.

We were about to touch down on an overcast day in the capital city. Through the tiny window, just before the buildings obstructed my limited view of the land, I spotted two giraffes with their glorious outstretched necks, roaming the golden terrain miles in the distance. I saw it as a great omen for the start of the voyage.

As we deplaned and made our way through the airport, I was surprised at how similar it felt to an American hub, minus the Swahili being spoken all around. Some parts, like the wing in which we arrived, were modern and contemporary, and others were old and run down. But in general, there was a welcoming aura about the place. I had made an effort to learn a few words and phrases in Swahili that I envisioned as being useful, but I wasn't too eager to test them out just yet. Luckily, English was commonly spoken as well, and many signs were in the world's most utilized language. We did not need to wait for our luggage; everything we'd brought fit into duffel bags small enough to take on the plane. My bag felt light, and I felt unprepared. Unlike Adam, roughing it wasn't exactly my thing.

We made our way through the airport filled with travelers coming and going. Some resembled tourists like us, but most appeared to be native, if not to Kenya, then to somewhere in Africa. It was that group that more than once shot me looks, like I wasn't following the cultural norms in Nairobi. People kept doing double takes at my feet, assessing my attire. I had on everyday black boots and could not figure out why people were acting like I had a sticker on my pants that said, PLEASE STARE; I'M AMERICAN. Anxiety began to flow through my veins, until it finally dawned on me: it was the camouflage cargo pants and white T-shirt I had chosen to accompany the black boots, mimicking the appearance of an American soldier. I had not meant to give that impression, but it was the only outfit I owned that I thought might work in the African bush—not that I anticipated actually being in the bush for at least a few days. Nevertheless, I decided I needed to change in a hurry to better blend in.

"What's the matter, bro? You look all panicky," Adam said as we made our way towards the airport exit.

"Nothing," I snapped, "I just wore the wrong stuff. I'm sticking out like a sore thumb. We need to get to a clothing store."

"Yeah, I could've told you that," he said, chuckling.

As we were about to catch our first whiffs of African air, a commotion caught our attention over by the baggage claim. Just like with a fresh car accident, most everyone stopped and turned to stare. A bone-thin, poor-looking African girl, wearing an orange tank top and torn sweatpants, was yelling while being detained by two large security officials as a third searched what appeared to be her travel bag. I picked up a few words in Swahili as she tried to break free from the officials, but the search continued, and they had no problem containing her weak, malnourished frame. Finally, the yelling stopped, and she gave up when the official pulled out something from the black luggage. I could not determine what was found, but the off-white contents contrasted with the black of the bag. I took a few steps toward the scene, but a large bald man who was observing near me grabbed my shoulder and yanked me back.

"Don't go over there," he said sternly with a Kenyan accent.

The officials began to handle the girl less like a citizen and more like a rag doll, slamming handcuffs on her meager wrists.

"Why? What did she do?" I asked, displeased about being pulled aside by the man.

"If you don't want to end up where she's heading, I would stay put or walk out the door. The police here aren't too kind to tourists who interfere with state business."

I still wanted to know why three large men were violating her rights, but before I could repeat my question, Adam interjected.

"What was she smuggling?" he asked, as if he were privy to her motives.

"It isn't coffee beans," the man said with a salty attitude.

"So, what did she get arrested for?" I asked.

He hesitated to answer, but finally said, "Blood money," and turned to walk away.

"Wait!" I said. "I'm curious. What does that mean?"

"You Americans really are naive about this region, aren't you?"

Out of the corner of my eye, I could tell Adam was heated,

and I was hoping he wasn't going to hit the man, because that would be one fight Adam wouldn't have won.

Finally, he answered the question. "Ivory," he said. "Happens all the time around here. It's a major problem for this nation, if you haven't heard. The government has been trying to pass a bill to put all poachers and their affiliates in prison for life, but there's so much corruption that it just gets stalled."

He paused for a few seconds as I started to open my mouth, about to explain to him that our motives regarding the precious material were much more involved than he assumed.

"Now you got me talking politics," he said and walked away.

Adam and I were both a little offended, but we knew we were in a foreign land and decided to let it go. We looked over at the baggage claim one final time, but they had already hauled the girl away, so we turned and headed for the exit.

A searing wave of arid heat smacked me in the face as we walked outside. Several taxis and their drivers, all male, were lined up to greet the arrivals. Some were holding signs with names in big black lettering. There were many different types of vehicles from which to choose, and it was clear that each driver's socio-economic status was reflected in the car he shuttled. There were some newish cars, but most of the vehicles were old and beat up, some even resembling a three-wheeled cart with no doors. I didn't recognize many brands, but I knew I would be getting in a car with four wheels and accompanying doors.

"Let's take that one!" Adam said, pointing at one of the three-wheelers. It was so like him to pick the most adventurous and subsequently dangerous option. But before I could even squash his idea, at least eight different taxi drivers began hollering in our direction. It was like walking through a flea market on a Saturday.

"Need taxi? Half rate for you guys. Car goes real fast," one driver said. Another boasted about his quality speakers. They were all talking at once, and it was difficult to think, let alone decide.

But one car stood out to me. The driver was just leaning against the side, smoking a cigarette, not even looking in our direction. It was an old, classic dark blue automobile, with a rounded hatchback and circular headlights, straight out of the 1940s, with a yellow stripe running down each side. I could not pinpoint the make, but the car did not look American.

"That one," I said to Adam, pointing in the car's direction.

After the driver loaded our luggage in the rear, he opened the doors, and we hopped in. The car was musty inside, but surprisingly clean, considering its age. I noticed bench-style leather seating, a plethora of legroom, and no window dividing us from the driver.

"What kind of vehicle is this?" I asked the man.

"This beauty is a 1967 Austin FX4. The Brits used to occupy this land before we won our independence in 1963," he said proudly. "They brought their cars over, and many are still running today. Look! There's another one," he said, pointing to a green one across the street. "We don't have a lot of fancy new cars to choose from here, so we take what we can get. But me? I prefer the classics."

"Couldn't agree more," Adam said.

"So, what part of Kenya are you from?" I asked him as we pulled away from the curb.

"I'm from a rural village to the southwest," he replied. He was a short, wide, jovial fellow with warm dark eyes and a shaved head. He was happy to talk to us and seemed just as interested in us as we were in him.

"So, where you boys headed? What brings you to this fine land?" he asked, sizing us up in the rearview mirror.

"Well, we're meeting someone from the African Wildlife Preservation Organization. I have the address right here," I said as I reached into my pocket.

"No need for an address, good sir, I know just the building."

"Wonderful!" I said. "But we actually have some time to kill first, and we'd like to get some proper bush attire and a bite to eat," I told the man while looking at Adam, who I could tell was in agreement. Adam could eat like a horse. "Can you recommend any places near the AWPO?"

"Absolutely I can. I'm a taxi driver. That's what I do," he replied warmly. "There's a delicious authentic Kenyan restaurant near the office, and not far from that is a shopping square where you'll find all different types of garments. I'll point you in the right direction when we arrive."

I was a little wary of eating food in unknown lands, but I had recently tried Moroccan cuisine and thoroughly loved it, so I thought we'd give it a go (not that we had many options). Adam would eat anything, so he was indifferent. We couldn't get there fast enough; even my shoe was starting to look appetizing.

"Sounds perfect," I said to the man.

"So, what brings you two guys to Kenya?" he asked again. "What business do you have at the AWPO? I know people who work there."

I was staring out the window, captivated by the bright pastel colors of the buildings we passed, and barely heard his question. Before I could reply, Adam jumped in and blurted out with a big grin, "We're gonna go kill some elephant poachers!"

Suddenly, the driver's face turned grim, his demeanor flipped, and the car began to creep as he stared at Adam, then at me, then back at him. I was horrified that Adam had put it that way. We had always referred to the mission as helping the elephants, but perhaps Adam had different internal motivations. That didn't bother me in itself; whatever it took to get the job done, I figured. But I didn't want to divulge that kind of information to a stranger in a foreign land. For all I knew, the driver could have a brother who poached for a living.

I waited nervously for a reply as his chocolate-brown eyes penetrated mine in the mirror. I could tell his wheels were turning, but it became apparent that Adam had caused him some sort of grief with his comment. I was beginning to think we might wind up in a ditch before we ever made it to the meeting.

As the taxi halted at a traffic light, Adam's stutter showed up again as he tried to backtrack and soften his words. But before anything else could spill from his mouth, the driver finally spoke.

"You boys are playing a dangerous game. Elephants are sacred to many in this land, and the cost of their protection is often someone's life." As he looked down at his lap and paused, I thought I noticed moisture in his eyes.

After nearly fifteen agonizing seconds, he continued. "One of the lives lost was my dearest cousin, Sambo. His whole life, he loved the elephants. But even more than that, he grew to hate the poachers. He fought them with bravery and saved countless animals, but eventually, his passion led to his demise. A bullet from close-range gunfire went through his neck, shattering his spinal cord." He paused again before continuing. "You boys are not the first Americans I've seen come over here to play cowboys. We are appreciative of the help, of course, but you must prepare yourself; death comes quickly in the bush. The poachers are ruthless and have nothing to lose."

I looked at Adam and he looked at me as a silence swept through the car. I didn't know if he could sense the fear in my eyes, but I could detect the excitement in his. Adam lived for thrills, which was why I was glad to have him by my side. He was my security blanket.

The taxi driver quit talking, and the tension grew with each mile as we neared our destination. I rolled down the window and drew in a deep breath, smelling the new world in which I found myself, observing the territory and its inhabitants, wondering what the war taking place outside the vibrant city walls looked like. I wasn't so sure I was ready to find out anymore, but there was no turning back now.

The taxi rolled to a stop near a crowded square with several eateries, shops, and vendors selling anything and everything one could want. We hopped out of the car after paying the man, thankful to shake off the awkward silence. Before speeding off, he rolled down the window to extend one last courtesy.

"The AWPO is right over there," he said, pointing to a run-down, two-story beige office building next to a newly built shopping center. He halfheartedly wished us luck with a thumb pointed skyward.

I could tell Adam wasn't too pleased with the driver, but there were more pressing issues. Hundreds of people flocked in the roadway, some selling, some buying, some carrying baskets on their heads, some just standing there with seemingly no purpose but to be in the way. Several cars and bright green buses were stopped in the middle of the street—not because of a traffic light, but to avoid plowing into the crowd. Horns blared, one after another, but were ignored, as the middle of the road was treated as an acceptable sidewalk.

We made our way through the mob to a slightly less crowded section of an outdoor market filled with countless varieties of fruits and vegetables. A sea of yellows, greens, oranges, and reds filled large wicker baskets, matching the bright colors worn by the countless Kenyans walking by. I paused to inspect the produce, salivating as my taste buds felt like they were going to burst. Bananas hung from the roof of the small makeshift stand, and trays upon trays of apples, mangos, pears, oranges, and many different juicy-looking fruits of unknown variety were laid out like a king's feast. I so badly wanted to sink my teeth into a mango or two, but I knew the well-armored fruit would take a sharp blade to peel, which I did not possess. I grabbed a pear and a couple bananas, and before I even turned to look for a person to take my money, a friendly-looking elderly man with a big white smile held out his hand, showing off a missing front tooth.

"Bananas and a pear? Good choice, very fresh," he said. "Twenty shillings."

"I don't have any shillings yet," I said, feeling like a stupid tourist, hoping he took dollars like the taxi driver. "Will you take two dollars?" I asked him, wishing I hadn't forgotten the currency conversion already.

His smile grew wider as he took my money and dropped it into an oval woven basket next to the apples. Then he went back to his chair, disregarding any change I should've been afforded. But it was my own fault for not having the proper currency, so I decided to be a generous tipper instead of a difficult tourist.

Adam had seen the exchange from the other side of a row of fruit. "You just gave him about two hundred shillings," he said. "He only asked for twenty! At the rate you're throwing away money, we won't even make it to the reserve!"

"I felt like giving," I said, feeling silly and lying simultaneously. "C'mon, let's go find some different attire, and some protein to go with this fruit."

"Unlike you, I don't have a clothes problem. But I could go for some meat, that's for sure," he said with a smirk.

We walked down the bustling street, taking in the city, feeling its pulse. Nairobi was a relatively diverse city, with a spectrum of economic conditions on display, all intertwined under a canopy of dry heat. As in a large American city, the business elite walked past and sometimes over those who slept in the dust with not much more than a shirt to their name. A modern pillar of commerce was often just blocks away from tin huts, where the have-nots watched and dreamed. But one thing that stood out more than what people wore or what they possessed was the upbeat spirit many of the Nairobians seemed to display on their grinning faces. Dancing was commonplace, regardless of the time of day or even if there was any music guiding the steps. The city and its sounds were the beat, and the people were the melody.

I began to feel the rhythm, until a pungent waft of street meat led our noses and our stomachs to a stand in front of a row of shops, some enclosed with glass, some not. I spotted a clothing store near the stand and wanted to skip playing Russian roulette with whatever mystery meat was being scorched by the searing flames, but my stomach was willing to take the gamble.

"Look at that chicken!" Adam hollered as he scooted in line behind five people, three of whom looked as though they hadn't eaten in days.

"I doubt it's chicken," I said. "Look at the color. Rat is more likely."

"Everything tastes like chicken if you cook it long enough. Besides, I'm so hungry, I would eat horse meat."

"That's good, because you might be in luck!" I said. Then I turned to the man taking money as another was flipping and slicing the meat with the proficiency of a five-star chef. There were no signs, no prices, just enticing aromas. "What kind of meat is that?" I asked.

"This meat on the grill? This *nyama choma* here is dog," he said with an exuberant smile and a strong accent.

I felt my stomach twist as I recalled images of Mattie, our beloved golden retriever that my family had when I was a boy. I took two steps out of line and began to turn as the man chuckled and said, "I'm just messing with you, man! I heard you stressing about what type of food we got cooking. Thought I'd have a little fun."

"Comical," I said, peeved. "So, what is it really?"

Before the man could answer, Adam interjected. "I don't care what it is; I'll take two!"

"Excellent!" he said as Adam handed him payment. "This is the finest *mbuzi* in the city—or goat, as you would call it." He handed Adam the lightly charred brownish meat, which could look a little like pork to the untrained eye, and Adam sank his teeth in. I could tell it hit the spot even before his eyes rolled back in his head.

"Never had goat," I said, "but never a better time to try, I suppose."

I popped a chunk in my mouth, and the flavor of the spices exploded like a symphony. It was slightly gamey, but utterly delicious and more than satisfying. We scarfed down the meat like we hadn't had food in a week.

With satisfied stomachs, we were ready to tackle the important business of the day: meeting Kwame at the AWPO, which we could see from the street corner. But the meeting was still over an hour away.

"Hey, Bach, I'm going to browse through that clothing store over there to see if I can blend in a little better," I said as he licked his fingers clean.

"Right on, man, I'll be here. I wonder what else I can find to grub on."

Adam was *always* hungry. I didn't think it was the best idea to split up on our first day in a foreign land, but it would just be a few minutes, and it was an adventure, after all.

"Alright, but don't go anywhere, and try not to get into any trouble," I said, noticeably concerned.

"What could possibly happen in ten minutes?"

"Well, we already saw someone get arrested today, so you never know," I said, shaking my head as I walked across the street toward the clothing shop. I was beginning to wonder if bringing Adam along had been the wisest move. Africa was no place to be cavalier.

The store was clean but hot, with a low tan ceiling, an old rusty fan, and wall art that portrayed an African safari. It was clear that I had picked the right shop for tourists who brought everything except for what they would actually need to survive in the bush. The owner of the store was a full-faced woman who looked like she'd never missed a meal in her entire life. She greeted me with perfect English, warmth, and a big smile. She glanced up and down at my attire, fixating on my camouflage pants without making me feel stupid for wearing them. She didn't have to;

I did already—especially considering that I hadn't spent a single minute of my life in the military.

I told her about our plan without revealing too many details or motivations, and she seemed more than happy to help. She had likely seen her fair share of Americans coming over unprepared for the harshness of the bush.

The clothes on the racks and along the wall were well organized and neatly presented, but something about them seemed previously worn. Some of the shoes had faint discolorations and scuffs, and the white shirts were far from sparkling in places, with pale yellow stains.

"Is this a secondhand store?" I asked the woman as politely as I could.

She stared at me as I waited for a harsh reply, but nothing came. She appeared puzzled, and I began to realize she didn't understand my question.

"Are these clothes used?" I asked. "Previously owned?"

She laughed. "Yes, of course! That's mostly what you'll find in many parts of the city. We have some new clothing stores in the prime areas, but the textile industry has mostly been destroyed here in Nairobi, due to the mass importation of used clothes, and these types of stores flourish here now. We scrub the items up, and they're just like new."

I was not a fan of previously worn clothes, but I did not have time to run around Nairobi looking for a store that sold new attire, and I assumed they would be getting thrashed anyway. So, I smiled at the woman and asked for her assistance. She fixed me up with all the necessities as she explained that the key to dressing for the bush was versatility, durability, and of course, blending in. Subsequently, I wondered why my pants weren't useful, but after she clarified that camo was often confused by poachers as a hostile military target, my curiosity quickly waned.

Not more than ten minutes passed before I was well dressed to adapt to the environment. She advised different-colored T-shirts for all conditions and landscapes: dark green, brown, tan, and clay red. She also recommended thick, canvas-like khaki button-down shirts and matching pants and shorts. Much of the thorny vegetation in the bush could scrape and slice like road spikes if the clothing was not sufficiently durable, she explained. Layering was vital, as was having many pairs of back-up socks and underwear, as monsoons could creep up faster than a horny fellow at a New York City nightclub. And as quick as they could come, they could go, leaving the unprepared saturated and desperate for dry feet. Thus, a pair of brown high-top safari boots was essential. Lastly, gloves, a multi-pocketed vest, and a full brimmed hat that made me a dead ringer for Indiana Jones rounded out the wardrobe. I thanked her for all the help and handed her the correct amount, which was far less than what it would've cost in the States. Feeling satisfied, I grabbed my luggage that I barely needed anymore and walked out.

It was less than a hundred yards back to the meat stand where I had told Adam to wait. Dozens of people came into focus as I approached the corner, but Adam was not one of them. Wide-eyed and anxious, I panned the entire area, but did not spot him.

I asked a few patrons and merchants, including the man who had sold us the goat meat, if they had noticed where he went, but shrugs were all I was afforded. I searched through various stores along the street, but there were still no signs of my adventurous friend, and the knots in my stomach began to tighten.

"I knew I shouldn't have brought him," I muttered, louder than I anticipated, and a few people turned and gave me dirty looks.

I looked across the street, where a crowd was gathered in front of what appeared to be an eatery. Some were standing around waiting, while other groups were sitting around tables as smoke filled the air. There was a rooftop area where I could see the heads and shoulders of folks laughing, drinking, and smoking. It had the feel of a place Adam would gravitate toward, so I hurried over to investigate.

I looked at the sign on the building, but couldn't make out the calligraphy. It appeared to be a Middle Eastern script, and I guessed it to be Islamic, since I'd read while prepping for the trip that Nairobi had a significant Muslim population. My suspicion was confirmed by a bright red neon light in a side window of the corner structure, illuminating the word HOOKAH in big, bold lettering. As I got closer, I saw round tables out front, with each person passing around a silver mouthpiece connected to a long tube. Thick flavored smoke filled the air as I squeezed my way through the throng of people waiting to get an outdoor table and entered the establishment through dark glass doors.

The room was large and open, with drapes covering the windows, and the only light was from dim deep red lights that hung from the high ceilings, giving the room a dark, eerie feel. It was the kind of place where one couldn't see the details of a face until the person was within arm's length. There was a mezzanine level with more tables on a beautifully crafted balcony reminiscent of a Moroccan mosque. I scanned the lower level as aromas from a vast array of cooking spices filled my nostrils. There were far more people out front and on the rooftop than there were inside, and upon entry, there was no sign of Adam. I began to wonder if my typically astute intuition was failing me. But I knew he was near; I could sense it.

As I turned towards a staircase that led to the rooftop, a striking female hostess stood before me. She was a tall and slender young woman with olive skin and flowing, wavy jet-black hair. She had deceptive almond-shaped eyes and full red lips, with a diamond stud in the left side of her nose. I had a hard time maintaining eye contact, as my instincts directed me to look at her barely covered breasts and exposed slim belly that accentuated her broad hips. Hostesses resembling belly dancers? Adam was definitely somewhere on the premises.

"Can I help you?" she asked seductively, with a slight accent.

"Actually, yes. I was just heading upstairs to look for someone. Maybe you can assist me," I said as I finally stopped gawking at her mesmerizing shape.

"And who might you be looking for?"

"I'm looking for my friend. His name is Adam. American, good-looking guy, white collared shirt, sandy-blond hair, kind of wild and crazy… Have you seen him? I really need to find him."

She barely blinked before turning and saying, "Right this way."

I couldn't help staring at the dimples in the small of her back that her top failed miserably to conceal. Her body epitomized sex appeal, alluringly illuminated by the red lighting as she climbed the first few stairs, and for a few seconds, I completely forgot why I was there. Eventually, I snapped out of it and followed her to the upper level.

We did not turn right and out the glass door that led to the rooftop that looked onto the street. Instead, she led me past the balcony into a dimly lit corridor with four private booths, hidden from those dining below. It felt like a VIP room in a nightclub, where anything could happen and no one would notice. No one occupied the first three booths, but I saw a familiar brown boot hanging out the side of the last one, and immediately, I knew I had found who I was looking for.

As I approached the table, the woman extended her arm and presented the table to me like a ringmaster would present a tiger in a circus, then strutted back downstairs, stilettos clicking with every step.

The booth was dark, with black leather seating, a white marble table, and a flickering candle in the middle that subtly lit the faces of four, Adam being one. Two seductive black-haired women, very similar to and equally as mysterious as the one who had led me to the table, flanked a man who was unlike anyone I had ever seen before. His skin was a similar deep olive, his hair, also jet black, was pulled back into a slick ponytail, and his beard was long and coarse. He had on a half-unbuttoned white shirt that revealed ink on the top of his chest behind his lengthy beard, but I could not make out the image due to the dimness. A large scar was visible, however, just above his left eye, cutting through his thick brow. His eyes were as dark as night, with a malevolence to them that gave me an uneasy feeling, which was already becoming an all-too-common theme of the excursion. The women, clinging to his sides like he was the air they needed to breathe, just stared at me intently. I was about to address Adam when the man looked up at me and spoke.

"Who are you, and what are you doing standing at my table?" he asked, flashing a shiny gold incisor, his voice twice as sinister as his eyes.

"I was looking for this guy," I said as I set my bags down and looked in Adam's direction. He was staring straight ahead at the wall, avoiding any eye contact, like he had something to hide.

"And what business do you have with this person? Better yet, what business do you have here in Nairobi?"

I could tell this man was a businessman, and a shady one at that. I paused before answering as I assessed the situation. I was about to speak when I noticed four thick lines of powder that blended perfectly into the marble table. I began to fume inside as I stared at Adam, who was still staring straight ahead. Because of the shadows covering his face, I couldn't determine whether or not he had yet partaken in the festivities.

"This guy is my friend. We're just travelers," I said, not wanting to divulge too much to this ominous character. As I looked back at Adam, one of the women leaned forward and inhaled one of the lines from the table. Her eyes rolled back in her head as she threw her neck back and wiped her nose. She returned her tempting eyes to me and smiled as if to say, *"You know you want some of this,"* which I assumed to have a double meaning.

"Adam, what the hell are you doing?" I asked with a sternness that couldn't be misinterpreted.

He kept his stone face looking straight ahead and said nothing. Before I could ask him again, the man interrupted.

"My name is Ahmed," he said with notable arrogance. "This is my establishment. These are my beautiful women. You are a guest. So, I ask you again…" He paused to flick the woman to his right in the face with the back of his hand for taking down another line of the powder. "What business do you have here? And don't lie; I can sense lies," he said, before erasing a rat-tail-sized line from the table himself. His eyes squinted and glared at me, with a devilish smirk tugging at the corner of his mouth.

I was searching for something to say, and Adam wasn't helping. He was staring at the last line on the table out of the corner of his eye. I was about to grab him and walk out, but something told me that Ahmed wouldn't approve.

"We're simply here to visit a reserve," I said.

"I heard," he replied, incriminating Adam and leaving me to wonder what else he had revealed. "Which one?"

"Not sure, exactly. Somewhere east," I said deceitfully, trying to maintain a poker face. "We haven't met our guide yet."

He stared at me for what felt like an eternity, analyzing my expression. I stared back into his evil face. I was thinking about walking out when he broke the silence.

"So, what is your business with elephants?"

I remained silent, still not knowing how much Adam had told Ahmed, but certain that he disclosed more than he should have. I was not going to answer any more questions and was willing to risk Ahmed's subsequent displeasure, so I smacked Adam on the shoulder and spoke to him with intent. "Let's go," I said, with a seriousness in my eyes that could not be misunderstood.

I grabbed my bags, and as I walked past the balcony and down the staircase, I could hear footsteps behind me, and hoped they were Adam's and not Ahmed's. As I passed a few patrons and approached the door, I turned towards the balcony and caught Adam heading down the stairs in my peripheral vision. Ahmed was standing with both hands on the sculpted railing, his gold rings shining in the red light as he glared directly at me. I locked eyes with him ever so briefly before I rushed out the door, with a sick feeling in the pit of my stomach. I couldn't exactly pinpoint why, but something told me that we would someday meet again.

# SIX

The fiery African sun peeked over the horizon as dawn inched ever closer to daylight. We had been picked up by a tan Land Rover that was rolling along a neglected stretch of highway as I sipped my black coffee, which threatened to spill on my pants with every pothole we negotiated. The coffee, which our driver had mentioned was a main export of Kenya, tasted earthy and deep, and it was beyond needed, as I had barely slept a wink in the cramped, un-air-conditioned room Adam and I had shared in Nairobi. From the back seat, I could see the back of Adam's head, propped up on the passenger's side door. I assumed he was catching up on some sleep as we made our way out of the city towards the Tanzanian border. I just stared at him, wondering what additional trouble he would bring my way with his recklessness. But ultimately, it had been my decision to bring him along, so I had to accept whatever transpired. I was just glad he hadn't participated in the drug platter being served at Ahmed's table, although I'm sure my presence had interrupted his intentions—or his desires, at a minimum.

An initial awkward silence allowed me to reflect on our meeting with Kwame at the AWPO, which had gone smoothly, despite us being fifteen minutes late. He was a gargantuan, militant native Kenyan who did not smile much, unlike others we had met in Nairobi. He took his work very seriously, but I understood why. We went over the details as he mapped out our route and told us about the reserve and what to expect. He then called our driver and contacted the head of the organization leading the fight against poaching on the reserve, telling him when we were to arrive.

While Adam slept, uninterested in the very territory we needed to study, I took mental notes of the terrain, until my focus was interrupted.

"When we arrive, you will meet with Captain Stewart," the driver said, breaking the silence. I was already privy to that information from our proceedings with Kwame, but I chose not to interrupt him. "Captain Stewart is a good man. He has been a godsend to the area, not only for the elephants, but for the villages surrounding the reserve. He's easy to work with, but whatever you do, always look him in the eye when you speak."

"Why is that?" I asked.

"Because he can sense fear, which is why he's so adept at tracking poachers. He was a former captain in the British Royal Marines and spent about a decade fighting proxy wars in East Africa. Tracking the enemy, the *hasidi*, runs in his veins. But he has a soft spot for wildlife and anyone who risks their lives trying to help the cause. So, you will be in good hands," the driver said with a smile.

"And what about you?" I asked him. "What is your connection to this operation? First of all, what's your name?"

"My name is Mohammed," he replied warmly in near-perfect English.

"I'm Joe. Nice to meet you. And that's Adam. He sleeps a lot."

"I can see that," he said, and we both chuckled.

Mohammed was a thin-faced man with a short, wispy beard and warm eyes. His smile was inviting, despite missing a couple bottom teeth.

"So, what's your story, Mohammed?"

"Well, I was born in a small village very near the southern foot of Mount Kilimanjaro, near the town of Moshi. Moshi is somewhat of a tourist town, now that it has been steadily growing because of all the interest in the great volcano, but where I come from, there used to be far more cows than villagers. My father had a fair number of cows, which translated into relative wealth. But when I got older, I did not want that life, despite my father's deepest wishes. When I was fourteen, I went to Nairobi to be educated. It really opened my eyes to what else the world has to offer, and when I finished at the university, I wanted to see more. I had a friend in school who had family in America that he decided to go visit. He liked it so much that he stayed. Eventually, he asked me to go too, but I was scared to go that far at first. But I felt like I had to see more of the world, so I saved up money working as a dishwasher in Nairobi, then boarded a plane when I was finished with school."

"Wow! Where did you live in the US?" I asked.

"Seattle."

"Ah, yes, I know it well," I said. "The Emerald City! Beautiful!"

"Yes, it is!" he said. "Very clean. And friendly people!"

"Indeed! So, what did you do for work?"

"I drove a taxi. It was a pretty good business. I had a great experience there and met a lot of nice people, and many native Africans as well. It's quite the ethnic and diverse place!"

"So, what brought you back?" I asked.

"I missed home. But perhaps the real reason was when I started seeing the horrific stories on the news about the murders of so many elephants so close to my home. I felt something deep within me pulling me back. I wanted to be a part of the fight, you could say. But since I'm not much of a militant, I chose to aid the conservation efforts through transportation services from Nairobi to the battlefront, which comes naturally, after my business in the States."

"It sounds like you're happy to be home," I said.

"I am, yes. I feel great pride in the work I do. Plus, I get to eat all the African food I was missing, and upon my return, I found a wife to cook for me!"

"Hard to beat that!" I said, and we shared a laugh. "I tried goat meat for the first time yesterday. It was quite good! I can't wait to sample what else the region has to offer."

"Just wait until you try goat stew!" he said.

"Mmmm…Love me some stew," I replied, feeling my stomach yearning for something hearty. Adam and I had woken up too late to eat much of a breakfast. "So, Mohammed, approximately how many elephants are in the reserve where we'll be working?"

"I'm not sure of the exact number, but I believe there are still around forty or so that live in the reserve, and at least that many that roam the terrain outside the reserve, which the organization tries to aid as well. But those figures could be less. I was recently told that the poachers have been more active lately, and they've been more successful with their methods. And obviously, the mothers can't have calves fast enough to keep pace with the ones that have been lost."

He cleared his throat. It was apparent from his tone that elephants meant a great deal to him.

"Elephants are sacred around here, aren't they?" I asked.

"I would not say 'sacred' in the religious sense, but revered and beloved by most in the region. As long as there have been humans on this land, there have been elephants, living together with us in relative harmony, until recently. They are a symbol of strength to the villagers, who rely on the elephants economically as well. Kenya makes over fifty million dollars per year in tourism from people coming from all over the world to see the elephants. And Tanzania, which we'll be crossing into in about ten miles, also relies heavily on the business of tourism. That's where the bulk of the Serengeti is, as you know."

We drove along in silence for a few minutes before Adam began to snore, the side of his forehead pressed up against the window, his breath fogging up the glass. I, on the other hand, was no longer tired. I was anxious and excited to reach our destination and begin working on the reserve. So many thoughts were rushing through my head, so many wonders.

I looked out the window, rolled it down a few inches, and

studied the land. I wanted to get a sense of the environment. The air was dry, but mild, and it had a fresh, unpolluted scent. There were a few cirrus clouds hovering high in the distance, but mainly, a deep blue sky spread as far as the eye could see. Level, barren land began to give way to a more rolling and rugged topography, with scattered green vegetation here and there, as trees with an artistic form that I assumed to be acacias sprouted in random order amidst the scattered brush.

Along the two-lane road (which was paved, but not terribly well), a few dilapidated wooden structures could be seen that couldn't have had more than two or three rooms at most and appeared to be missing key windows. Yet there were telephone poles lining the road, which surprised me. I couldn't help but laugh under my breath at the paradox. It reminded me of images I had seen of teenagers in third-world countries, with barely enough clothes to cover their bodies, but holding fancy new cell phones.

As we drove on a few more miles, the low, rolling hills near the eastern horizon began to morph into more defined peaks, and the road became more undulating the farther we headed south toward the border. I gazed out into the distance toward the mountains and spotted a small grove of acacias, and I imagined a small herd of elephants grazing beneath them. It was hard to believe that my dreams would soon become my reality.

Mohammed vanquished my daydream as he again broke the silence. "I think it's so admirable, what you guys are doing," he said. "I've seen many volunteers come over to help with the struggle. But I don't want to paint too rosy of a picture; this work is not for everybody. Not everyone can stomach what they end up witnessing. Not only is it dangerous, but it can be quite grotesque as well. It can change a man. I've seen it happen. In fact, it changed me."

He paused for a moment. My thoughts began to swirl as my imagination shifted to what that could mean. Then he continued his story.

"When I was a young boy, about seven years old, I was tending to my father's cattle when a stocky white man with slick black hair, spectacles, and a cream suit pulled up in a large beige truck. I had never seen a truck before—or a white man, for that matter. He got out of the truck and began to negotiate with Ruhiu, who was the head of our neighboring village. Finally, the white man handed him something that I would later learn was some form of currency. In exchange, Ruhiu pointed off in the distance, away from the mountain. The man pressed a black piece of equipment up to one eye that I would also later understand to be a scope. He seemed satisfied and took out a long, thin brown-and-silver item that looked like a partially metal pole from my vantage point, but it had a triangular wooden end. He also took out a serrated blade. He put his scope in his pack, threw on a pair of tall brown boots, and began walking in the direction he was inspecting. He didn't walk far before I could no longer see him, and soon after, he disappeared into the bush. Then the loudest noise I had ever heard rattled my eardrums, followed by violent trumpeting cries that slowly tapered off. I wanted to go see what had happened, but fear kept my feet planted right where they were.

"It wasn't long before the man began walking back to the truck as I pretended not to stare. He had the blade in one hand, the long pole over his left shoulder, and his large pack over the other. I didn't understand what had happened until I saw something I recognized. Two medium-sized white tips were jutting out the top of his pack, one coated with a blood-red streak. I wasn't familiar with most of the possessions the man had taken into the bush, but I knew what he was bringing out, and I knew tusks didn't belong to him. I'll spare you the rest of the heinous details of what I saw when I went to inspect the scene. I don't want to deter you before you even get started, and I'm sure you'll see it for yourself. I wish I could do the work you two will be doing, but as I came to find out that day, I don't have the stomach for it. So, I can only drive for those who do."

As he finished his story, my stomach began to churn with even more vigor than when I thought I had lost Adam the day before. The sight of blood and open flesh had never sat well with me, and again, I wondered what I was getting myself into. But I knew the risks and told myself to breathe deeply and stay focused on the mission, although I conceded that vomiting was likely in my future. I rolled down the window as far as it would go and inhaled as deep as my lungs would allow. I repeated this a few times until the queasiness began to simmer down. The wind that whipped through the rear of the vehicle woke Adam from his slumber.

"Morning!" Mohammed said with a hint of sarcasm.

Adam just looked at him, puzzled, like he'd been awake the

whole time. "How long until we reach the reserve?" he asked. "I can't wait to stretch my legs."

"We'll be crossing the Tanzanian border in just a couple miles, and then it's not too far from that point. But when we get to the border, just let me do all the talking."

As we approached the Namanga border, the mountains began to increase in size in all directions, but more to the east, with moist clouds hugging the base, making the vegetation lusher and denser. Stark-white fluffy clouds, billowing but dry, blocked the tops of the peaks from view, keeping me guessing as to our proximity to the great mountain. But I knew we had to be close, based on my map.

We soon approached the border, which was more contemporary than I had anticipated. It had a small but modern structure with a red tiled roof, and instead of an armed guard, as I had expected, a man who looked half asleep was sitting in a chair, waiting to greet us. He stood and came to the window, speaking cordially with Mohammed in an African language that I did not recognize. After a couple minutes, we were allowed to continue, heading south along the two-lane route. Rolling hills and winding turns led the road into increasingly beautiful terrain. As we passed a few small villages, I spotted a few lodges for tourists who had come to experience rural Africa and enjoy the wildlife, which was depicted on several signs along the road. I took out my binoculars just in case we spotted something from afar.

Up in the distance, I noticed signs for the town of Arusha. As we drove through, it reminded me more of Nairobi than some of the other remote villages we had passed along the way, albeit a much smaller and poorer version. There were shops and stands, eateries, a hospital, and even a lush green park. A man in traditional, colorful African garb who looked like a farmer was leading his herd of brown-and-white goats through the town as we passed by. It made me think of the goat meat I had sampled just a day prior. My stomach's unease was now being subtly replaced by a low, rumbling growl.

I was thrown off course when we turned left at a stop sign and headed east, away from Arusha. I distinctly remembered that the reserve was west of Arusha, towards the Serengeti.

"The reserve is to the west, Mohammed, no?" I asked.

"Indeed it is," he replied. "Your sense of direction is keen. But you boys want to see Kilimanjaro, don't you?"

"Absolutely! I nearly forgot. My hunger is starting to get the better of me."

We drove past Arusha National Park, which I could see off in the distance. I took out my binoculars and peered through the lenses for a few miles, adjusting for optimal focus and feeling like a common tourist. But I didn't mind; it was an adventure, after all, not solely a mission.

The car suddenly pulled to a stop along the road as Mohammed cried, "Look!"

I wasn't sure what exactly he was referencing, as the acacia groves were only thickening. But through a small cluster of trees, I spotted a herd of nearly twenty black, brown, and grey wildebeests, tails flipping, grazing on the lush grass beneath their thin, tapered legs. It was fitting that one of the first creatures we came across was one of the main attractions on safaris, and one that was relied on to feed so many others.

"Damn, that's incredible!" Adam said.

I wasn't sure why he said that. He didn't have binoculars, and I wondered how he could see any detail.

"You're not looking," Mohammed said to me as I was scanning to see if I could spot something else—a zebra, perhaps.

"No, I see them," I said, the binoculars still lightly pressed to my eyes.

"Not the wildebeests," Mohammed said. "You'll see plenty of those where we're going. Look up and to the right!"

I had become so fixated on spotting wildlife that I had forgotten why we headed east in the first place. I panned up to the sky, high above the trees in the foreground, and there it was, standing tall, basking in a pinkish late morning glow, so high that clouds could barely reach the top. Kilimanjaro, in all its glory. I just sat in silence and admired as Adam did the same. It was truly a magnificent spectacle, and I pondered what it must have looked like before it blew and formed its plateau-like top.

"Beautiful, isn't she?" Mohammed asked.

"Beyond," Adam replied, as I was still looking at the intricate nuances of the mountain through the binoculars. I lowered them and nodded, almost unable to speak.

"Kilimanjaro is a dormant volcano over nineteen thousand feet high, the highest peak in Africa," Mohammed told us, "but its last eruption was over three hundred thousand years ago. Much of its glacier ice cap has melted over the years, which some scientists attribute to the warming planet. Others say it's because of deforestation creating more arid conditions. But I'm just glad there's still some ice near the prominent peak of Kibo. You see it?"

"Oh, yeah!" I said, peering through my binoculars once more.

"Three peaks make up Kilimanjaro: Kibo, Mawenzi, and Shira, with Kibo being the tallest and Shira the smallest. But Mawenzi has the most pointed peak. There are a lot of facts I could tell you about Kilimanjaro, but the legends are where it gets really intriguing," Mohammed said, like he'd given the speech a thousand times before.

I didn't hear him for the first ten seconds or so as my mind started to wander while I remained fixated on the massive peak. I recalled the legend of the frozen snow leopard in the opening of Hemingway's *The Snows of Kilimanjaro* and imagined one crawling around the rocky crevasses.

We exited the car for a proper view as I tuned back in and noticed Mohammed waving his arms in the air with zeal. He was recounting a legend as we stood by the side of the road, our chins high, admiring the sight that brought so many to Tanzania each year. Some had conquered the great mountain, and some had perished trying, while others like us simply gazed at its beauty, hoping to find wellness and perhaps inspiration in the healing power of the natural world.

"You see," Mohammed continued, recounting the folklore as if the mountain were alive, "Kibo and Mawenzi were close partners, until one day, Mawenzi greatly offended Kibo by throwing away a gift of embers that Mawenzi claimed had burnt out. This made Kibo very angry, and he beat Mawenzi mercilessly until the mountain was degraded. It is now referred to as the Scarred One."

I did not interrupt Mohammed or question the tales, for he seemed to have such passion when acting out the legends of Kilimanjaro, or Kili, as Mohammed called the mountain for short.

"Now, that may sound silly to Westerners such as yourselves, but there are many locals who believe wholeheartedly in the lore of Kili."

I shot a look at Adam and then up at the mountain before returning my focus to Mohammed as he continued.

"The *Wakonyingo*, as the tribesmen tell it, are mountain dwarfs with oversized heads who live in caves deep beneath Kili's slopes, and they prey on those who bring negative spirits to the mountain. Many die attempting to climb Kili each year. Perhaps the *Wakonyingo* have a hand in their demise. You can decide for yourselves. Scientists have confirmed the existence of pygmies that once roamed the mountain, so sometimes it's difficult to distinguish between legend and reality. Some even believe there are hidden elephant graveyards filled with ivory. Perhaps an archaeologist will make a valuable discovery one day."

We thought about Kili and what it must have meant to people of the past. We stood in silence for a few more minutes and snapped countless photos, as well as mental images, before getting back in the vehicle and heading in the opposite direction towards the reserve, grateful to Mohammed for bringing us to see the revered mountain.

As we headed back west, I turned and stared through the glass at the shrinking mountain, thinking about its beauty, about its lore, and what it symbolized for the people of region. It was striking, truly a wonder of the Earth, and one I was thankful to witness. I could not take my eyes away until it retreated behind the blanket of mist that seemed to seep from its base. I set my head gently against the window, closed my eyes, and tried to recharge, if only for a few minutes, as I assumed the reserve was our next stop, and I wanted to be rested and alert. I could hear traces of dialogue between Adam and Mohammed as I faded in and out of reality. I could feel the turns of the terrain and the bumps in the pavement, which kept me from a more thorough snooze. But perhaps the anticipatory anxiety of what was to come played a more substantial role.

"Joe, you awake?" Mohammed asked. "Did we lose you for a moment?"

"I think I dozed off."

"We'll be at the reserve in less than thirty minutes, and as I was telling Adam, we'll get you introduced to Captain Stewart, so you can get situated and be ready to begin your work. Sometimes, he likes to throw his people into the fire to see how they respond, so you have to be ready. Must be his military background."

"That works for me!" I replied, trying to act tough, but completely lying. "You ready, Rorbach?"

"I was born ready," he replied.

And I knew he was, which gave me comfort.

As the two-lane route meandered westward through the

changing terrain, I began to see signs indicating that not only were we nearing the reserve, but we were soon to be in the presence of some of Earth's most sought-after wildlife, in its natural habitat, even if restricted by the boundaries of a reserve. Signs for the Serengeti raced past the car as quickly as I could feel adrenaline racing through my veins. Not only was I thrilled to see creatures like giraffes and rhinoceroses, but my instincts told me that at any moment, we could be in the midst of a pack of lions, uncaged and on their own turf. An entire range of feelings, from exhilaration to dread, whipped through my body, heightening my senses. I pulled out my binoculars just as Mohammed was telling us that we were coming up on Lake Manyara National Park. But they weren't necessary. As we made our way around a bend in the road, a vast, deep blue lake appeared, and the famous black-and-white-striped pattern appeared no more than fifty yards from the vehicle. A herd of zebras were grazing on the vegetation scattered across the rolling land, as if they hadn't a care in the world. I was admiring their artistic hides, which reminded me of a faux-fur rug my mom used to own, when Mohammed pointed to the left and diverted my attention.

"Look," he said. "Over there. In the water."

"What are those?" Adam, who didn't have the best eyesight, asked about the distant grey humps breaking the surface.

"Hippos!" I exclaimed, seeing their ears flicking about through the binoculars. White long-necked birds that looked like cranes were perched on their backs, drying off. I handed the binoculars to Adam so he could get a better look.

"Wow, those are massive animals!" Adam said.

"Yes, and don't get too close, because their jaws are some of the most powerful in the animal kingdom, and when on land, they are sneaky fast," Mohammed told us.

"Are they poached for anything?" Adam inquired.

"Not like the elephants and rhinoceroses," Mohammed replied. "But speaking of rhinos, I know where a small herd usually hangs out about halfway between here and the reserve. Maybe ten miles or so."

We snapped some final photos as the vehicle pulled back onto the highway, and Mohammed continued his duties, not only as a driver, but as a tour guide as well.

"The current state of the rhino population is as sobering as the elephants', if not more so. Certain species are nearly extinct."

"Like the black rhino, right?" Adam asked just before I did. It surprised me that he even knew that.

"Yes, exactly," Mohammed said. "In the last half of the twentieth century, black rhino populations dropped about ninety-eight percent. There are only about five thousand left, but conservation efforts have helped recently. Other species in Africa, like the white rhino, are slightly more numerous, with numbers around twenty thousand or so, mostly in protected reserves. But that only relates to the southern white rhino. The other subspecies, the northern white rhino, is on the brink of extinction, with only a few left on the planet."

"They're poached for their horns, aren't they?" I asked. "It's considered an aphrodisiac of sorts in Asian countries, I read."

"That's correct," Mohammed replied. "The rhinoceros is poached for nothing more than its horn, because of its perceived sexual enhancement properties in Eastern countries like China, and especially in Vietnam. But the horn is made of the same material as a human fingernail, and it does nothing of the sort. But sometimes what the mind believes, the body will feel, and as a result, rhino horn fetches over a hundred thousand dollars per kilogram, making it more valuable than gold, with each rhino horn weighing between one and three kilograms. And much of the poaching is done in Kenya and Tanzania."

"Big business," I said.

"Very big business, just like with tusk trafficking," Mohammed replied.

We pulled off the highway and drove down a dirt road into a small open valley with few trees, but endless grasslands. We hopped out of the car once more and walked a short distance for a better view. Near a lone acacia tree, under an endless blue sky, stood a group of rhinos, three adults and two adolescents. Grazing and ignoring the sear of the burning sun, they seemed at peace, except for two of the larger adults with seasoned horns, who were squaring off in a playful duel—not actually charging each other, just practicing for when it mattered.

"They are protected here in this particular reserve," Mohammed told us. "But that doesn't mean they're safe. Much of the poaching actually happens on the reserves. They are such expansive areas that poachers have little trouble breaking in. And as you guys can see, the animals graze out in the open, making for easy targets. I wish they wouldn't, but that's where the desired grasses grow. And as strictly herbivores, they require a lot of grass for survival. Did you know rhinos can live up to forty or fifty years? If they aren't poached, of course."

We listened to Mohammed and his obvious fervor for the animals of Africa as we took mental notes and a plethora of pictures. We could've stayed and admired the prehistoric-looking creatures for much longer, but time was a factor, as we were supposed to arrive at the reserve in the early afternoon. So, we hopped back in the vehicle and made our way thirty more miles west, until we reached the place we'd be calling home for the foreseeable future.

The dirt road entrance to the reserve was lined with dozens of tall, white-barked trees that resembled eucalyptus, a common variety back home. The trees gave way to an open, dusty lot, and we exited the vehicle, thankfully for the final time. It had been a long day and a long journey, but a memorable one. Mohammed walked us to what appeared to be the main office building. It was a light grey single-story structure with a few small windows and a door right in the middle, with wings on both sides.

"I'll introduce you to Captain John Stewart, and then I have to be on my way," Mohammed said as he tried to open the door, but the handle failed to turn. "Oh, it's locked. They must be out on a mission. But there is usually someone here at the office, regardless."

He cupped his hands around his eyes and peeked through the window next to the door.

"We were supposed to meet here at two p.m.," Mohammed

said, visibly irritated. "I wanted to introduce you, but I have to pick up someone else in Nairobi this evening, and I must get back. I'm sorry. Do you think you can wait here on the steps? They should be back soon."

"I don't see why not," I said.

"Wonderful," Mohammed said. "And it's been really nice meeting you boys. I thank you for helping our cause, and I wish you nothing but success. But be cautious when you're out in the bush; it can be a rough place for the untrained. Listen to the captain; he will guide you. And remember to always look him in the eye."

We thanked Mohammed for the splendid sights and even better stories as we shook his hand. Then we watched him drive away, trailed by a cloud of dust.

I looked at Adam. He looked at me.

"Well, here we are," I said.

"Yep—and only us," he replied as we sat on the wooden steps, chuckling anxiously.

We sat there, waiting. The compound was quiet and devoid of any life, which was not what we had expected. We reflected on what had led us to the doorstep of an empty building on this dry, desolate property. I thought about the lion that had taken my daughter's life. I thought about the gun and then the boulder that nearly took mine. We talked about what the future might reveal, but at no point did we wish we hadn't made the journey to Africa. It had already been enlightening, and the mission hadn't even truly begun.

Nearly an hour passed, and my rear end was falling asleep

on the rigid steps, forcing me to stand and stretch. I looked to my left past the wooden barracks, across the large open grassland with a few scattered acacias, bordered by low, rolling hills that seemed to go on for miles. I admired the beauty, wondering how often elephants came to graze in the valley, and how close they came to where we were standing.

As I daydreamed, I thought I spotted something off in the distance, but it was too far for my eyes to register. Then it disappeared.

"You hear that?" Adam said.

"No, but I saw something out there," I replied, pointing. "I couldn't tell if it was an animal, or a human, or what."

"Wait… Listen carefully," he said.

After a few more seconds, I began to pick up a rumble, and then I noticed a plume of dust, growing in size as it got closer. The rumble became more of a hum, which I finally recognized.

"That's a vehicle approaching," I said to Adam.

"More than one, it sounds like," he said. "And they're coming fast!"

The trail of dust was now swirling behind what we could make out as three beige safari-style SUVs, very similar to the vehicle in which we'd arrived. We stood and watched as the caravan became more and more visible as it barreled towards us. The vehicles were not traveling on any sort of paved or even dirt road, but racing across the natural terrain, trucking through bushes and toppling small trees with obvious urgency. Neither I nor Adam knew if the people inside the SUVs were from the reserve, or poachers coming to loot the place while it was temporarily deserted. Still, we watched and waited, pretending to be guardians, in case it was the latter—not that we were capable of handling the situation if indeed it was a band of poachers.

The convoy approached in great haste. Dust permeated the dirt lot, to the point where we could barely see the vehicles that came to an abrupt stop just thirty paces from where we stood nervously watching and waiting. But I was certain that I was more anxious than my bold friend, who may have actually been eager to encounter whoever would jump out of the SUVs. I began to choke on the dispersion of particles as we heard several doors slam in succession, one after another, followed by frantic shouting from what sounded like close to a dozen people. One voice was more prominent and authoritative than the rest. The dust cloud was thinning now, and images could almost be identified.

"You three, take him to the infirmary!" the commanding voice exclaimed, with a thick, proper British accent. "The rest of you, get everything set up faster than you ever have before. We're going to save this man's life, dammit!"

A group of several men and one woman emerged from the cloud, and it became clear that they were the antithesis of a team of poachers. They were led by a wide-bodied, authoritative man whom I instinctively knew to be Captain Stewart, followed by three people carrying a wounded man on a primitive wood-and-canvas stretcher that looked like it had been assembled from old tree limbs. The middle-aged African man was wailing in agony, and as they rushed past us, we were able to see why. He was naked above the waist, with thick gauze wrapped tight around his abdomen, soaked in bloody red. A few drops fell near my shoe as they passed and climbed the three rotting stairs, nearly ripping the front door off the hinges as they hurried through. Seven people raced by—eight, including the man on the stretcher—not one of them so much as making eye contact with us as we watched the chaotic scene unfold.

Banging and clamoring could be heard through the walls as a constant, frantic yelling escaped through a cracked window. Adam and I could not tell exactly where in the building they were working, but we knew one thing: a man was dying, and his people desperately didn't want him to. We looked at each other. Adam's expression was different than the one I imagined I was wearing; he looked eager to jump in and help. I felt more like jumping in a plane and going home. But I knew that was just the fear in me—the fear that had always consumed me in dangerous situations, the fear that crippled and restricted life. But I knew we had a job to do. *I* had a job to do. I had to overcome myself. I knew that the man on the stretcher would not be the only bloody, dying creature I would see on this continent. Thus, I took a deep breath and tried to calm my nerves.

Before I could speak, Captain Stewart stormed out the door. Six stomping steps later, he was in front of us with a stern look in his eye. "Are you two sightseeing, or are you going to get the hell in there and help us save this man's life?"

Without any introduction, I knew who he was, and he knew us. And I remembered what Mohammed had told us about the captain, so I looked him straight in the eye, stood tall, and in military fashion, said, "We are ready to help, sir," even though I was the furthest thing from ready.

He looked at us with tentative approval, and as we raced into the building, I remembered something else Mohammed had said. He was not kidding: the captain liked to throw people into the fire, alright—and it was a scorcher.

# SEVEN

They worked on him for hours, but the man they affectionately referred to as Jafari was succumbing to the bullet that had ripped into his midsection and lodged in his liver. Although they were able to remove the slug, ultimately, Jafari had lost too much blood. As I stood by his side in horror, holding blood-stained towels while watching him take his final breaths, vivid, excruciating memories of Lily's death nearly made me turn away. But I simply couldn't. He was gripping Captain Stewart's mighty hand, staring deep into his eyes, until his body gave up and went limp—but not before he summoned the will to whisper a final message to the captain: "Thank you."

There was no way Adam or I could have known the all-encompassing effect of those two words that seeped from Jafari's lips, but we would soon come to learn that he had been one the most beloved figures on the reserve, and his loss was significant and would be felt.

A few hours passed as an awkward quietness crept over the reserve. No one said much, other than a little back-and-forth about what they were to do with the body. Captain Stewart was too distraught to even remember that we were there and that we needed to be directed to our living quarters. So, Adam and I decided to wander around the reserve to clear our heads and get familiarized. We walked around for about an hour, making our way across the flat and dry golden grasslands and into the rolling hills, feeling the brush change beneath our feet. We hiked through the thorny vegetation, examining the bark of the foreign, exotic tree varietals and noticed a few orange wildflowers that sprung up from the parched terrain. But all the while, we couldn't stop thinking about the man who had just died. Neither of us knew what to say, so we walked in silence, allowing nature to fill the void.

Dusk was approaching, and we could see the main office in the distance as we made our way back. Off to the left, in an open area surrounded by six small wooden barracks, a roaring fire crackled. Its flames illuminated the faces of two men standing nearby. I immediately recognized the stocky, round shape of Captain Stewart, who was waving his hands while sternly talking to a man we had assisted in the infirmary, but did not formally meet. We didn't want to interrupt, so we pretended to be admiring the flames as we approached.

"Should we wait 'til they're done?" I asked Adam, hoping the captain wouldn't hear.

"After what happened today?" Adam said. "I would."

"Quite the first day, wasn't it, boys?" Captain Stewart stopped us with his penetrating voice as we stood near the fire.

Adam and I nodded and shook the captain's powerful, callused hand, but we did not know what to say and didn't want to say the wrong thing. Again, we looked him directly in the eye, as we were told, while he sized us up.

The captain was a short, thick-framed man with meaty legs and perhaps the largest forearms I had ever seen. He had fair skin and not much more than a few strands of hair on the crown of his head, and I pegged him for somewhere around fifty-five years old. He had intense bright blue eyes and an unmistakable chin.

The captain broke the silence. "Well, aren't you going to say anything?"

"Oh, sorry. I'm Joe, and this is Adam. It's great to meet you, sir. We're still in a bit of shock, but we're really excited to be here and to help as much as we can."

"Yes, well, we could certainly use the help. I'm glad to have you gentlemen here. But you don't have to call me 'sir'; I'm not a real captain anymore. You can call me John, or Captain, or Captain John, but not sir."

"So, you really were a captain?" Adam asked him.

"Yes, in the British military. But that was decades ago; I'm a civilian now. I've been doing humanitarian work here in this region since I was forty, but the title stuck, I guess." The captain grabbed two nearby logs and tossed them into the fire, sending sparks high into the dimming sky. "I like to test newcomers when they first arrive," he said. "But today wasn't quite what I had in mind."

"We are really sorry for your loss," I said solemnly.

"Thank you," the captain replied. "This will not be easy to get past, but eventually, we'll have to. We've had two people perish previously, but Jafari was my first mate on the reserve. He'd been by my side since the beginning. He was the one who got all of this started many years ago. Elephants were in his soul. And now his soul lives among those whom he was unable to save. I don't know how we'll get by without him, but somehow, we all must pick up the slack—which is why it's even more important that you two are here." I could see his eyes welling up a bit as the fire's glow lit up his rosy cheeks. "I have a lot to do to prepare for the ceremony, which will be right here in three hours. Jafari loved goat stew, so I gotta go see how the prep is coming. But let me show you to your barracks."

"Did you say goat stew?" I asked the captain, but didn't wait for an answer. "I thoroughly enjoyed the goat I tried for the first time yesterday."

"Oh, good, that would make Jafari happy."

He led us past four old wooden structures that could not have contained much more than one room and perhaps a washroom. When he opened the door to ours, I realized it did not even contain that. It was a room no bigger than fifteen by fifteen feet, with two tiny cots and a small wood-burning stove.

"This is where you guys will be sleeping. I know it's not much to look at, but the two gentlemen who were here before you liked this room because it's close to the outhouse. I'm sure you will find it satisfactory. We have extra blankets if you need them, and wood to burn for the stove, but it doesn't get too cold this time of year, so you should be alright."

I looked at Adam, and this time, even he looked perturbed. But we didn't let the captain see. I wasn't sure what exactly we had expected anyway; we were on an African reserve in northern Tanzania, not at a Four Seasons resort.

"So, what do you say we meet back by the fire in a few hours, and I'll formally introduce you to the team, yeah?" uttered the captain as he turned and walked out the door, noticeably somber in his gait.

We sat on our two stiff cots, which seemed better suited for adolescents, our backs to the wooden walls. The only light came from a red plastic lantern placed on an old tree stump that served as a nightstand between the cots. We sat there in silence, both thinking the same thing: what the hell were we doing? Our thirst for adventure—and in my case, redemption—might have outweighed what we could actually stomach. But we both had our reasons to stand in the face of adversity, and we both knew it. So, we did not complain. We did not gripe. We didn't even speak. We just sat there and absorbed the day's events. Adam may have even dozed off, perhaps to regroup for the next undertaking. I think we both knew we were in for the adventure of a lifetime. But a question lingered in the back of my mind: would it end up costing us our own lives? Only time would tell. And if it wasn't at the hands of poachers, these deadly hard cots just might kill us, I thought to myself, chuckling and waking Adam in the process.

He looked over. "You wanna go back out by the fire? It's not like it's all that warm in here."

"Yeah, let's go," I said. "People will probably start setting up soon. But don't you think it's odd that they're having the memorial the same day that Jafari was killed?"

"Of course I do," he replied. "But we're in the middle of Africa. Folks do things differently here. And who are we to question their rituals?"

We went back out to the fire and sat on the end of a hand-crafted wooden bench, one of four making a square around the pit. The fire was fading, so I boldly grabbed two more logs and tossed them on. We could hear people working in the main building, and I wondered why the captain didn't ask us to help set up for the ceremony. But I left it alone. Adam and I sat there and conversed about what it had been like to watch a man die. I didn't want to admit it, but I was shaken up inside. Adam, however, seemed immune, almost as if he had seen it before. And perhaps he had; he had nearly killed a man himself.

"Do you think we'll die on this excursion?" I asked him half facetiously.

"We all die at some point," he answered with grave seriousness. "The only thing that matters is how, and more importantly, why."

We sat in silence as I digested Adam's unexpectedly profound words, watching the flames and feeling their heat. The concept of death was nothing new to me. I had thought of it often throughout my life, but not much in terms of its nobility. My thoughts quickly made their way to my daughter and the nuances of her once vital, perfect face. It didn't take long before I remembered why I was sitting on this bench in the middle of a foreign land in the first place. Adam was right: the *why* mattered.

My thoughts were interrupted by footsteps shuffling through the dirt behind us. I turned to look, and a silhouette was all I could make out. As the steps approached, the glow from the fire presented a man with a warm but hardened face.

"You fellas doing alright?" the man asked, with a lovely British accent, much thicker than the captain's.

"Yeah, just enjoying the warmth, waiting for further instructions," I said.

"A brilliant fire, isn't it?" he asked as he extended his hand first to Adam, then to me. "Hello, I'm Aaron. The captain told me to come out here and check on you both, and I wanted to introduce myself."

We shook his hand and exchanged names. He was a friendly but serious-looking man whom I pegged as about the same age as us, with a short, dark beard, the same length as his slightly receding buzz cut. He stood no more than five-foot-ten, and I could tell from his grip that the man was well built. I wasn't sure what to say, and Adam was being oddly reserved, so I said the only thing that came to my mind.

"I… *We* are very sorry about the loss of Jafari. He seemed very important to you all."

"Thanks, yeah, he was indeed," Aaron replied. "I've only been here nine months, so I didn't have the same kind of connection with him as the captain or some of the others, but he was certainly important. He was a founder of this venture, along with the captain. He will be missed, I'm sure. But I come from a line of work that's not unaccustomed to losing men on a mission, so I may handle things of that nature a little differently than most."

"Military?" Adam chimed in.

"Yeah, mate, I spent eight years in the British military as a Royal Marine."

"Wow!" I said. "I bet you've seen your share of catastrophe."

"You have no idea, mate," he said warmly.

"So, how did you end up here?" I asked him.

"Emmm, well, the reason I'm here is twofold, really," he replied. "The captain wanted to hire someone with a military background to teach his men on the reserve the proper tactics to combat the enemy, which in our case are poachers, as I'm sure you know. The folks here didn't have much formal training, but I will say, they are excellent trackers by nature. The other reason I'm here is random chance, I suppose. I met the captain after about a year in my new line of work, post-military."

"And that was?" I asked him.

"Fighting Somali pirates," he said with a big smile.

"No, really, how did you guys link up?"

"Dead serious, mate, yeah," he said, still grinning.

"You fought *pirates*?" Adam asked him. "That sounds like a good old time!"

"It was a bloody rush, indeed," Aaron replied. "Yeah, we were in between missions, picking up supplies in Mogadishu, when I bumped into the captain. He was British, I was British, so we had a bit of a chat, one thing led to another, and the next thing you know, I agreed to come work for him on this beautiful terrain."

He paused for a minute and then continued before we could ask him anything further. "Tracking pirates isn't all glamor though, you know," he said with charm and some dry British wit. "Long days at sea, sometimes weeks before we actually encountered the enemy. But once you do, it's wild, wild stuff. I'll have to tell you about it sometime. To be honest though, this job is much more rewarding—but far more dangerous."

"More dangerous than fighting pirates?" I asked, a bit shocked.

"Way more dangerous, mate. You see, we had guns on the ships, and if there's one thing I know how to use, it's guns. I was a sniper in special ops as a Royal Marine. But here's the kicker: the captain doesn't like guns. So much so that he doesn't allow them. So, we all go out into the African bush, tracking poachers who are fully armed, and we have to try to outsmart them *and* somehow try not to get shot. But as you saw today, that's not always feasible. Maybe after the loss of his first mate, the captain will change his mind about guns. I doubt it though."

I was trying to collect my thoughts while envisioning a confrontation with a poacher armed with an AK-47 as I tried to scare him away with a knife, at best.

"It's quite the challenge, and a bit frustrating, but I guess you could say it makes me more diligent with the methods I teach the folks here," he continued. "But when you actually save an elephant from—"

Five people heading towards us from the main office interrupted Aaron. There were four men and a woman, and all appeared to be native Africans. Two of the men were carrying a large metal pot, which was placed on a grate that hovered above the fire. Bubbles quickly made their way to the surface of the dark, thick reddish liquid inside. No one spoke much. Finally, after some momentary awkwardness, Aaron introduced us.

"Team," he said as they continued to stare at the fire, deep in thought, "this is Adam and Joe. They have come to help us in this bloody fight. And after today's tragedy, we could surely use it, couldn't we?"

The four men looked at us and grinned, nodding in moderate approval, but not necessarily acceptance. I was waiting to shake hands, but it didn't seem customary. The woman gave us a quick glance, but withheld a smile. I gave a timid wave as Adam ambivalently said hello.

"Gentlemen," Aaron began, introducing the team from left to right. But I could not remember anyone's name, let alone spell them in my head, and I figured I would learn them in one-on-one conversation at some point.

A door opened, and out came more people, one of them being the captain. They were carrying a long, folded table, chairs and two lit lanterns, which aided our view in the progressive darkness. They propped the table near the fire with the lanterns on each end as they approached and made a ring around the blaze.

"Helluva day, team," the captain said, his voice cracking even more than the fire.

Everyone looked up. Some appeared to have tears lingering in their eyes, especially the captain, as well as the lone woman.

"First, I would like to say thank you to everyone here for all that you did today," he began. "Today was one of those days we all dread, but we must understand and accept the realities of the business. And that business is protecting animals from harm against people who have no reservations about gravely harming them or us. It is the sacrifice we make. You all did everything you could for Jafari, both in the bush and in the infirmary. And I appreciate that. So would he, if he were still here. So, in his honor, let's enjoy his favorite meal, goat stew, knowing he is looking down upon us."

Tears trickled their way down the cheeks of a few, and the woman—Ashi, one of the names I did pick up—let out an audible sob.

"Oh, and in case you haven't already introduced yourselves, these two gentlemen are Joe and Adam," the captain said, pointing in our direction.

Again, a few people looked up and solemnly smiled at us. Some waved hello, Ashi being one, and a few just kept staring deep into the fire, clearly wishing their comrade was still with them. I didn't know the inner workings or relationship dynamics, but Jafari's death appeared to hit some harder than others. Regardless, there was a genuine sense of loss among all on the reserve.

I went over to Aaron to ask if I could help prep for the meal, but everything was nearly ready, so I went over to the table and sat. A few people went back inside and brought out other bowls that I assumed were side dishes to accompany the goat stew. I could not peer inside the covered dishes, but the aromas that seeped through the cracks were inviting. It was hard to think about food after the exhausting day's tribulations, but I was interested to see if the meat was as delectable as the street goat I'd sampled in Nairobi.

I looked over, and Adam appeared to be deep in conversation with Aaron—probably about killing pirates, I imagined. Aaron was crouched with an imaginary rifle pressed to his right shoulder, his left hand extended, holding the air gun for precise aim as he squinted one eye and looked through the invisible scope. By the way his face lit up when the imaginary gun fired, his former title of sniper was beyond believable.

I soon got tired of sitting and didn't want to be thought of as the guy who didn't help my first day on site, and no one was coming over to chat. So, I went over to the fire, where a very thin man who looked about forty was stirring the enormous iron pot resting above the flames, its contents submerged and hidden. The deep reddish-orange broth simmered as I leaned my head in and inhaled thoroughly until my nose was filled with a scent I had never smelled before—a scent that activated my stomach's brain.

"I'm sorry, I didn't catch your name," I said to the man, extending my hand. "I'm Joe."

He switched the ladle to his left and awkwardly shook my hand, as if he hadn't done it much. "Abasi," he said quietly as he returned his attention to stirring.

"Sure smells good," I said, not knowing what else to say.

He looked at me and nodded. "Do you eat goat where you come from?"

"No, rarely do you see it on a menu," I replied. "But I tried it for the first time yesterday in Nairobi. It was quite flavorful!"

"Just wait until you taste this stew," he said. "It's just about ready. You see that nice color? Jafari would've approved."

People were shuffling in and out of the building where I presumed the kitchen to be, bringing more dishes filled with sides, as well as plates, bowls, and spoons, setting them on the table. One by one, they began to sit, so I took that as my cue that dinner was near. I signaled to Adam to come over, and we sat at the far end of the table. Abasi grabbed the large pot from the grate and placed it on a rusty barrel near the table that served as a stand. Steam rose to the sky as the bubbling began to slow. The captain came over once everyone was near the table, grabbed a large pair of tongs, and addressed the group once more.

"Thank you all for the preparation of this meal. In Jafari's honor, we eat."

Some looked up to the sky and whispered a prayer, and the rest watched the captain. I too observed, wondering why he needed tongs to serve goat stew, when the ladle seemed much more apt. He positioned himself in front of the simmering pot and bent at the waist, his pointed nose nearly touching the metal, and took a sustained whiff of approval. Then he dipped the tongs down deep into the pot, latched onto the mystery ingredients at the bottom, and carefully lifted them to the surface. For several seconds, I couldn't tell what it was, but then it became grotesquely clear; the eyeball gave it away.

A head emerged from the pot as the captain set it on a wooden cutting board in the middle of the table. Severed halfway down the neck, a hornless goat's head, with its mouth open, rested not far from where I sat. I stared, speechless, my eyes as wide as saucers like I'd seen a ghost, fighting back the contents of my stomach that were suddenly in my esophagus. It had never occurred to me that goat stew would contain the actual head of a goat. I covered my mouth to make sure nothing spewed out onto the table as I looked at Adam, who seemed not only comfortable, but eager to sample. I thought about excusing myself, but didn't want to disrespect the group, especially since it was a ceremonial dinner.

The captain grabbed a foot-long blade from the table, propped up the head, and with one firm press, crunched through the skull, splitting it into two symmetrical halves, exposing none other than the creamy-white soft tissue inside the cranium. I sat speechless and mortified, flashing back to my stay in the hospital before running my fingers over the lengthy scar on the back of my head. I had never even seen brain fragments before, let alone sampled them. The captain kept carving, trimming and scooping until there was a pile of various edibles that had been relinquished from the skull. The muscle that surrounded the bone was separated and cut into tiny pieces, along with the brain matter, and dumped back into the simmering pot. A final stir was made, and the signal was given by the captain to dig in.

Everyone around the table looked eager to fill their bellies after the long day, but whatever appetite I might have had vanished into the darkness that fell upon the reserve. I wasn't fully aware of my face, but it felt like my eyelids were glued open, my mouth permanently ajar in horror. I didn't want to be rude or offend my new colleagues, but I certainly didn't want to hurl all over their plates either. So, I stayed silent and tried not to be noticed.

A team member whose name I did not recall stood up with his bowl in hand, but he was stopped by the captain.

"We have two new guests, and as you all know, it's customary to allow them the first serving. Adam, Joe . . . please enjoy."

My rear end was affixed to the wooden bench as Adam casually stood up, grabbed his bowl and the ladle, and took an unabashed scoop, like it was a tailgating chili cook-off. He sat back down directly across from me, as I could feel everyone's eyes impatiently turn to me.

"Joe, you're up," the captain said.

But my body would not move. I felt like passing out—or worse, I felt like trading places with Jafari.

Somehow, I made my way over to the pot, taking slow, calculated steps, stalling, trying to figure out how I could get out of the situation, but my mind was too cluttered. So, I took the ladle and stirred, slowly, trying to differentiate between muscle and organ, but it was too dark, and my attempt was futile. I scooped a timid helping into my bowl, praying that I had avoided any brain matter, and shuffled back to my seat. One by one, the rest of the team began to fill their bowls and returned to the table. One of the team members recited an African chant that I assumed was a prayer, as most of the other members joined in. Finally, everyone started eating their stew, as well as what looked like root vegetables. Adam dove right in like he was devouring a juicy filet mignon, his favorite meal.

Abasi, who was sitting to my right, looked over and could sense my hesitation. "Here, take this," he said, grabbing a piece of fluffy, aromatic bread from the table and handing it to me. "My wife,

Ashi, taught me this trick. Believe it or not, I struggled at first to eat this stew as well. The *chapati* helps soften the first few bites."

"Thank you," I said reticently, not even trying to pretend that I was fine. I took the foreign bread Abasi handed to me and warily dipped it in the stew. The flavor of the broth was intense, with a multitude of aromatic spices hitting my palate all at once. I couldn't say that I didn't find it at least somewhat flavorful. I used the bread as a scooper and brought to the surface what appeared to be meat, accompanied by a purplish root, and took a bite. This time, the texture was familiar, like the goat meat I'd so enjoyed the day before in Nairobi. But I knew that it was only a matter of time before brain matter snuck its way into my mouth.

"Pretty tasty, I must say," I uttered, noticing that Adam was nearly done with his bowl. "You cook a mean stew, Abasi."

"Ashi did most of it. I just tended to it over the fire."

I smiled at her, grabbed a wooden spoon, and scooped another bite—but this time, I noticed some of the soft, white tissue that resembled pasta. If only it were the Italian staple I so desperately wanted it to be. But I couldn't delay any longer and felt obligated to sample the foreign ingredient. With my hand quaking, I inched the spoonful into my mouth, bypassed chewing, and gulped it all down. It was cheating, but I thought it might keep the food in my stomach instead of it ending up on Adam's lap. So, I dunked my spoon again and came up with similar material. After my relative success with the first bite, I felt safe to chew the second spoonful as I tried to take in the genuine flavor of the meal.

As it made its way down my esophagus, it wasn't long before

my body let me know I had made a terrible mistake. I had gone too far. My gag reflex kicked into high gear as I tried to suppress it, but my stomach was winning the fight.

"I think I'll get some more!" Adam said with enthusiasm. "Never thought I'd like brain so much!"

"Good, isn't it?" the captain chimed in from the other end of the table. "So, tomorrow, we will..."

I tuned out the captain as I suddenly noticed one of the two eyeballs floating in my bowl, and I couldn't hold it back any longer. As far as my stomach was concerned, the only place a brain belonged was inside a skull. I didn't want to upset anyone, but I was out of options. I sprang from the table and hightailed it to where I thought the bathroom was, but it was dark, rendering my search useless. I raced behind our barracks so that no one could see me, and I prayed they couldn't hear. I bent over, grabbed my knees, and braced myself. The stew, along with what felt like the lining of my stomach, came rushing out, splashing the dirt as well as my shoes. I felt like crawling into a hole, but I was too drained to move—which was fine, as I couldn't face the group anyway. I stumbled backwards and slammed my rear on the ground as my head ricocheted off the wooden structure behind me. I felt like dying, riddled with embarrassment. I closed my eyes—and somehow, fortunately for me, I passed out right there on the cold dirt.

TIME SKIRTED BY surprisingly fast over the next few weeks. The team warmed up to Adam and me, but more so to him I felt, which didn't shock me, considering his affable nature and how the first day had gone. When they had found me on the ground, out cold, no one was too upset or offended, or so I was later told. I must have blacked out after hitting my head, because I remembered nothing after falling to the ground, but I woke up the next morning in my cot and was told that Adam and a few men had carried me there.

We began our training with the team, which was still in the process of learning Aaron's advanced military tactics and strategies. Every morning after breakfast, unless there was a field emergency, the team would study in the classroom, a small, stuffy room off the main building. It had a chalkboard and rickety wooden desks that looked like they had been salvaged from a ransacked elementary school, but they served their purpose. The captain led the classroom sessions, mostly reporting intel to us that he had acquired regarding where the next poaching strike might take place, and which group or groups were likely to strike. He also mentioned general methods we would need to combat the enemy, but he left most of the tactical details of the operation to Aaron.

Aaron got Adam and me up to speed on the devices and new technology he was constantly updating to try stay ahead of the poachers, which was often impossible. Satellite tracking devices, infrared goggles for night searches, and long-range communication systems were some of the new pieces Aaron had implemented just before we arrived. Two armored military vehicles were supposedly on their way as well, but he was not sure exactly when, and he didn't seem to be holding his breath.

After reviewing operation plans and data, everyone would leave the classroom, throw on their battle clothes, and spend two hours in a simulated bush area that Aaron had chosen not far from the barracks, so he could simulate his methods in as close to a real-life setting as possible. We would all engage in reenactments of situations that the group had previously encountered, as well as those that Aaron believed would arise in future manhunts.

I became more comfortable in the group as the days went on, and finally learning everyone's names was helpful. Adam and I built a good rapport with several members of the team, which was good, as camaraderie proved key when tackling problems and challenges in the field. Most of them warmed up to us eventually, which surprised me; they were genuinely welcoming and happy to have our help. I felt that our passion and commitment were noticed and appreciated, but I learned that our dedication to the elephants could not compare with the way the rest of the team viewed them. It was true love. Similar to the way Westerners shared a kinship with canines, Africans seemed to harbor the same feelings for elephants.

One exception was Dota, who was a hardened, large, muscular man with a shaved head and two large scars on the left side of his forehead, and one that ran down his veined bicep. He was the only one out of the remaining nine who didn't seem to want us there. He was quiet most of the time, but when words did come out, they were brash. I thought perhaps he didn't trust us due to our light skin, as he treated the captain with the same callousness, but he wasn't exactly friendly with any of the others in the group either.

One afternoon, we were all out in the training area, and Adam and I were hiding under a thorny bush with Kintu, the youngest and perhaps most exuberant member of the team. We asked him about Dota, but Kintu was too new to really know all the reasons behind his harsh demeanor. He did mention, however, that he had heard Dota had had a hard life, and the scars it left on his heart were as permanent as those on his face. He made it clear that crossing Dota was not in our best interest.

That said, Dota was invaluable in the field. Whenever strength was a prerequisite, he was called upon, and he never disappointed. In our second week of training, Adam and I saw him not just cut down a large tree, but rip its sizeable trunk from the earth with his bare hands. And the rumor that swirled around the reserve was even more astounding. Several years back, Dota and the captain had stumbled upon an abandoned baby elephant, trapped on its back in a hole. It was said to have weighed around six hundred pounds, and they had no equipment handy, while the searing heat was depleting the baby. The hole was barely big enough for one man to wedge a leg in for a small amount of leverage. As the captain got the baby to wrap its trunk around his arm, he pulled, while Dota, with relative ease, lifted the baby off his back and out of the hole, where it could use its wobbly forelegs to escape the grave situation. The abandoned baby elephant was taken to a nearby sanctuary, but unfortunately, it had died within a year. Sadly, it was the weak one of the herd—which was the antithesis of Dota.

Adam was flourishing, adapting to the environment even better than I'd expected, which pleased me. Not that he needed any coaxing to come out of his shell from a social standpoint, but he loved the outdoors, and working in the rugged bush every day invigorated him. He seemed to relish the challenge of learning about various poacher tracking methods. Plus, it kept him far away from the perilous pulls of city life. He was especially fond of Aaron, working closely with him during drill time, and the two seemed to be developing a genuine bond, routinely laughing at each other's jokes when it was appropriate. Adam had a keen sense in the bush and was becoming a useful tracker, even receiving praise from some of the older men who had been at it since childhood. I, on the other hand, was not nearly as confident in my abilities, but I was enjoying the learning process, nonetheless.

Our first day of bush training was full of life-saving techniques. They were new to Adam and me, and they needed to be reinforced for the team as a refresher course of sorts—one that Aaron wasn't particularly pleased to teach a second time.

The first training day was a scorcher, following a random downpour the day prior. It was the kind of day where we could feel the heat of the soft red dirt through the soles of our boots.

Aaron walked six paces away from the group, stopped, turned, and ushered us over. "Okay, team, I know this is not new to many of you, but it is new to some, so let's refresh," he said, pointing to the prints made by his shoes. "Due to the spongy nature of the dirt, these tracks stay fresh for how long?"

"Forty to fifty minutes," Kintu answered with pride.

"That's right, very good," Aaron said. "So, when we see a track like this, we know that the poachers are fairly nearby, but we don't know in which direction. So, we must immediately separate and spread out three hundred and sixty degrees to begin the search. As you know, it's imperative that we catch them before they get to the Mombasa Highway, where they can easily blend in with the locals."

I would later learn when studying a map of the region that the Mombasa Highway that ran through Nairobi was the highway we had briefly taken with Mohammed before heading south to the reserve. Poachers loved it because it was a direct route to the eastern coastal town of Mombasa, where they could quickly load their trophies onto boats, get paid, and return to the bush for more.

Next, after we reviewed hand and arm signals for stealth tracking, Aaron grabbed a few tourniquets from a nearby bag and showed the group how to properly tie one. He used Dota as the guinea pig. Tying one correctly seemed simple enough, but it was the speed that was paramount. He told Dota to walk twenty yards from the team.

"Bang!" Aaron yelled, extending his arm towards Dota, as if shooting a fake gun. Dota fell to the ground.

"Don't just stand there; that man's dying!" Aaron exclaimed in frustration.

We all rushed over to simulate the rescue effort.

"Aren't you guys forgetting something?" Aaron asked before we made it halfway. "The tourniquet, perhaps?"

There was no time to get sour or feel stupid. I took the initiative, feeling competent enough to tie one properly. So, I raced to the bag, grabbed a tourniquet, and rushed over to Dota. I tied it around the correct portion of his massive thigh with what I believed to be just the right amount of tension.

"Very good, Joe, quick learner," Aaron said appreciatively. "But the time you guys took to realize what was happening, all while forgetting the equipment, could cost another man his life. This has to happen much faster! Jafari lost a lot of blood before we got to him. Time is of the essence when someone gets shot."

We practiced drill after drill until we had it all down. I appreciated the challenge the bush presented and fully understood that adversity nourished growth. I knew that preparation was a large part of the conservation process, as fieldwork in the merciless bush was what would ultimately keep more elephants alive with their tusks intact. Nonetheless, I personally relished the classroom work. I was keener on our daily briefings, as I had always been more of an academic type.

Lunch had just finished—another delicious meal served by Ashi, the designated cook—and the whole team waited in the classroom for the captain to arrive. There had been a lull in the number of incidents over the past few weeks, which was especially welcome in the wake of Jafari's death, and it also allowed Adam and I to focus on training and getting up to speed. Only a few small groups went out in the field for herd monitoring, as there were no recent tips about poaching in the immediate area. But the previous night, the captain had called for us all to be in attendance for the following morning's meeting, as he had some fresh news to share.

The classroom was an old modular office, similar to something you would find on a construction site. It was cramped and bland, but had numerous maps of the continent, country, and region, all of which bore scattered multicolored pins with red yarn attached, like military battle plans. The room was sultry, and I began to feel moisture seeping from the skin above my brow. I could tell it was going to be a hot one, and unfortunately, air conditioning didn't exist anywhere on the reserve. Fans provided only minor relief.

We were all conversing and speculating about the captain's news—all except for Rukawa, the elder statesman and the wisest of the group. Besides Jafari, Rukawa had been working with the captain the longest. He was in his late fifties, but looked much younger. He rarely spoke, but when he did, the words were often prophetic. His eyes were squinty and mystifying, and as I looked over, something about them led me to believe that something substantial was brewing.

The captain stormed in and slammed his coffee down on the desk, spilling a few drops on an unrolled map. He paused and looked at all of us before speaking, gathering his thoughts and composure, while making sure all team members were present and attentive.

"I just got word from our friends to the south that there has been another killing of two large bulls, which were reportedly too busy dueling each other to fight off their killers," the captain said. "Apparently, a female got away."

"When did this occur?" Abasi asked.

"Last night, it appears."

"The attackers are long gone by now," Rukawa said.

"I'm sure you're right, Ruk," the captain replied. "But we must go investigate. We'll have to put training on hold. Everybody meet out front. We leave at noon. Abasi, you and your wife can stay and guard the reserve. We should be back by nightfall."

Abasi and Ashi nodded. "We will have a meal ready upon your return," she said.

"Great, thank you," the captain replied as the team began to depart the meeting room. "And Kintu, tomorrow I would like you to take Joe and Adam over to the sanctuary."

"You got it, Boss."

"What kind of sanctuary?" I asked Ashi as the captain walked out the door.

"An elephant sanctuary," she replied. "Orphaned baby elephants, actually. And you'll be introduced to the amazing woman who started the operation."

"Wonderful!" I said, trying to control my excitement. I had never interacted with an elephant that wasn't in an enclosure, let alone a baby.

But as thrilled as I was to go to the sanctuary, I could sense that Adam was looking forward to our first actual mission in the field. I hardly felt ready for active duty—we had only been training a few weeks—but I was keen on testing myself at the same time. Adam seemed born ready. I recalled what our driver Mohammed had told us about the things we might see, as if Jafari's death wasn't a rough enough introduction.

We drove to the site in two of the three beige Land Rovers, which had been upgraded with military-grade tracking systems since Aaron arrived. Adam and I rode with Aaron and Dota in one, and the rest of the team rode with the captain. It was only about thirty-five miles south, but it took close to an hour, as our vehicles could only penetrate the dense acacia grove so far until we had to set out on foot for the final mile or so.

Dota grabbed a large blade that resembled a machete, but a portion of it was serrated for sawing through branches. The grove was so thick that the midday sun could barely reach the ground beneath my feet. Trunks and limbed canopies extended as far as the eye could see. We walked single file behind Dota, who led the way, cutting our path. The underbrush was dry and crunchy beneath my feet, and every few steps, what felt like thorns scraped my exposed calves. Despite the heat, I regretted not wearing pants, like some of the more seasoned team members. I blocked out the pain, but images of what we might see upon our arrival at the destination kept flooding my mind. I tried to prepare as best I could. Deep breaths, in and out, one after another.

"The poachers are likely long gone, but keep your guard up. The female and possibly her calf may have returned to check on her mate," the captain said in a low tone. "And if she comes back, she'll be furious and hostile. Lions may be watching from the bush as well, so eyes peeled, everyone."

"My coordinates say that we're almost right on top of the site," Aaron said, looking at a tracking device.

Up ahead, the grove thinned, and the sun's rays began to erase the shaded ground. And then, just like that, the forest gave way to vast open nothingness, a perfect oval of empty terrain, with an oasis in the center—a pachyderm family's lifeline. A paradise it certainly was, but a safe haven it was not. The watery refuge that drew the animals was too exposed, and it was easy to see how a poacher could use the canopy as stealth cover.

As we walked toward the scene, two grey bodies became magnified with each step. The ground squished beneath my boots, the water that flowed from the highlands in the distance altered the texture of the usually firm red clay.

"*Tembo,*" Dota turned and whispered to us as he pointed toward the dead animals. Adam and I recognized the term, as the team had often used it in place of "elephant" during training.

We walked toward them cautiously, constantly turning our heads back to the dense grove to see if we were being watched or followed. I quickly understood why Aaron was so dismayed about the captain's no-gun policy. If poachers were setting a trap for us, we would be defenseless, like sitting ducks. Fending off lions or even hyenas would be no picnic either. But we didn't hear anything suspicious, just the scavengers cawing from high in the trees.

As we approached the carcasses, I didn't know what to expect, but I feared the worst, and my stomach let me know. A violent wave of nausea once again took over my insides, which only amplified with the smell of rot and death that intensified as we drew near. I gagged and felt my breakfast working its way up my throat, but I had to do everything I could not to let the team see my weakness again, especially after the goat head stew incident.

Just yards from the majestic creatures that just a day ago had been roaming the land on which we marched, I could see their lifeless bodies toppled over, their forelegs partially submerged in the bloodstained water. I pictured them relishing this source of life, playing, quenching, spraying, before a bullet or a dart had darkened their world; we did not yet know which. One had two legs draped over the other, almost in a protective pose, but we still could not see their heads or any tusks as we inched closer. A massive ear of the nearest male was blocking our view. And then suddenly, after a couple more timid steps, I stopped dead in my tracks, my insides churning. I realized why the most recognizable features of an elephant were not evident: they were no longer attached.

Aaron casually pointed about twenty yards to our right, as if he had seen this many times before, as if it were customary for poachers to hack off the trunks and discard them. I had just figured that the killers would saw off what they came for near the base and be on their way. I couldn't have been any more naive. The tusks were so valuable that they wanted it all, even the portion deep in the head cavity, well beneath the surface.

As we made our way to the other side of the bodies, images beyond my worst nightmares emerged, with flies and meat-eating bees feasting on the gruesome scene. If it weren't for the shape of the bodies and the unmistakable ears, we would barely have been able to determine the species that lay before us. There was no face. There was no trunk. And there certainly were no remnants of tusks. On both creatures, the faces had been ruthlessly hacked off with a blade, and not in one fell swoop either. There were no clean cuts. Instead, shreds of flesh and fragments of bone littered the space where the front of the head used to be. The wounds were so raw that the blood red I had expected was replaced with a cocktail of fleshy pink and white. Aaron explained how poachers often sawed as far back as they could until they hit the hard skull. They had done so in this case, but on the animal closest to us—the one that had tried to cover the other—I could see an eye that had been spared and was somehow still open. It was large, deep brown, and beautifully lashed, and I imagined it was looking right at me, although I was sure that was just my mind going haywire. The lifeless eye spoke to my soul, as if to say, *"Why is this happening to us? Please make them stop!"*

I could barely continue to look, but at the same time, I couldn't turn away. I was surprised that I hadn't yet vomited. Perhaps the scene was somehow *too* harrowing; I had never seen anything so brutal and vicious. My heart pounded, and my body surged with adrenaline. I couldn't understand how people could do such a thing to any living creature, let alone something as special as an elephant. And it didn't seem necessary to mutilate the creature in order to get to the tusks, but they wanted it all, and compassionate killers they certainly were not.

"Well, they got all the white gold they came for, didn't they?" Aaron said, as if reading my mind.

"They used a dart too," Dota said, pointing to the neck of the elephant closest to us.

"Sure did," the captain acknowledged.

"Goddammit!" Aaron exclaimed. "I can't stand it when they do that!"

"Why?" I asked.

"Because sometimes the poachers will start sawing through the flesh before they even shoot the tranquilized animal. I've heard stories of them letting out a low, rumbling cry as the blade enters their skin, but they don't wake, because of the powerful sedative. But you know they feel it."

"That's heinous," I said, shaken.

"It's monstrous is what it is," the captain added. "Alright, men, we've seen what we came to see. Let's take photos of the crime scene and head back."

As we reentered the forest, I tried to stay in the present, but my mind kept drifting back to the evil I had just witnessed. It wasn't like seeing a dead deer carcass on the side of the road that had been hit by a vehicle. There was something calculated and premeditated about it that blended with the violence and gore to make it truly unforgettable. I recalled what Mohammed had said on our drive to the reserve. He was deadly accurate: witnessing such things could change a person.

I hiked along in a daze, right behind Adam, and didn't even notice that the sun once again began to caress the ground as the limbs above us thinned. We were nearly back to where the vehicles were parked when Aaron, followed by the captain and Dota, halted and threw up a hand signal that we had learned meant "stop." A momentary pause followed as they lowered their hands.

We all crouched as Aaron pressed his finger to his lips and pointed to the left, about thirty yards away.

Behind a thick wall of brush and several young acacias, a rustling shook the leaves. Poachers likely wouldn't announce their presence, a lion would be equally covert, and a full-grown elephant could not go unnoticed. I began to wonder if it was the female that had fled the scene. Aaron motioned for us to find cover behind the nearest tree as he and Dota crept up on the brush from both sides. Aaron disappeared behind the acacias, but we could see Dota creeping in, gripping his blade in a defensive pose. But as he drew near, his body straightened, and he casually dropped the blade to his side. He just stood and stared as we waited for a signal. Finally, Aaron hollered from behind the trees, "Gentlemen, come quick!"

As we approached, most of the members of the team did not seem surprised, but I couldn't believe what I saw. Timid and scared, disoriented and malnourished, the smallest baby elephant I could have imagined wobbled around in the brush before us, nearly toppling over with every movement. It was a beautiful little female, with not long to live, her eyes glossed over but wide open, as if she had seen a ghost. She had possibly witnessed the murder of her mother, and as elephants were creatures with deep, vivid memories, an event like that could scar them for life.

"We must get this baby to Olivia's, and quickly," Rukawa stated in a grave tone.

"Correct," Aaron replied. "Joe, you and Adam go grab the stretcher from the vehicle, as fast as possible."

We rushed back to the vehicle, opened the back gate, and unrolled the large, thick canvas stretcher that had been hand-made by the captain, sporting two large dowels three inches in diameter, cut from an acacia tree. It took two people to carry, and I wondered how in the world we were going to get a five- or six-hundred-pound creature on it and back to the SUV. Then I remembered that Dota was with us.

Hurrying back to the team, I couldn't help but wonder who Olivia was. Such a soft, feminine, beautiful name... Even in times of emergency, the animal instincts in me could not be suppressed.

"Who do you think this Olivia is that Aaron mentioned?" I asked Adam, the dowel bouncing on my collarbone with each brisk step.

"I think it's probably the woman who runs the baby elephant sanctuary that the captain said we're going to visit soon," he replied.

"Ahhhh, yes, good call, I nearly forgot!" I said. "I'm excited to meet this woman."

"Or any woman, for that matter!" he said with a humorous tone.

Huffing and puffing, we passed off the stretcher to Dota, who seemed to have no problem holding the entire unit by himself.

"Okay, fellas, listen up!" Aaron called, getting everyone's attention. "As you all know, we can't tranquilize a baby because the drugs are too potent, so we have to do this the old-fashioned way. Everyone assume your positions. Joe and Adam, you mates have never done this before, so just take note of the procedure. Once she's on the stretcher, come help us carry her to the vehicle."

"Will do!" I said as Adam nodded.

"Okay, on the count of three…" Aaron began. "One … two … *three!*"

Aaron threw a black towel over the baby's head, darkening her world to lessen her awareness. Dota, Kintu, and the captain wrestled the elephant to the ground as gently as possible, while Aaron kept her head from banging on the dirt. She was too weak to put up a fight. Perhaps she had given up—or maybe she somehow knew she was being rescued. The rest of the team, minus us newbies, placed the unrolled stretcher against her back as she pressed up against it on her side.

"We will actually need you fellas. She's one heavy girl," the captain said to Adam and me.

On one more count of three, the entire team flung her legs over onto the canvas and scooped her on. Using all our manpower, we carried her several hundred yards back to the vehicle. Even Rukawa pitched in, who was wiry and strong for an older man.

"Man, I hope she fits," Kintu said. I was thinking the exact same thing.

"I think we have the width, but we'll need to open the back," the captain said, folding down the back row of seats.

We opened the rear, and everyone gave a shove with all our might, sliding the baby into the oversized SUV.

"Well done, everyone!" the captain said. "Now drive to the sanctuary like your pants are on fire!"

With our seats sacrificed, Rorbach and I were instructed to ride in the back with the baby, which bothered me not at all, despite the cramped quarters. Just being close to her made me feel like the whole journey was being validated. The goal was to save elephants, but also to find ourselves, our purpose, our meaning. I looked at Adam. He looked back at me. I could tell he was on my wavelength. We were connected in this moment, on the same mission. I wanted to look at the baby, but for her protection, the towel was still covering her face, so I placed my hand on her back instead. I knew she was still alive, as her lungs expanded and contracted against my palm, but her breaths were rapid and short. I was no expert, but I could sense that this animal did not have much time.

A RARE MONSOON PASSED THROUGH, turning the dirt a deep, fiery red. The low-lying hills that surrounded the plains sent the welcomed water cascading through the valley, nourishing the desperate vegetation and providing relief to many animals that called the reserve home. Just a few miles from camp was where the streams collected, creating an oasis and a gathering of creatures that would make any safari lover envious.

It was necessary to investigate the populations that migrated to the watering hole, not only to inspect the health of the various herds, but also to search for any poachers looking to make an easy kill. As the clouds parted and gave way to the beaming blue sky, Kintu drove Adam and me out to inspect. With binoculars in hand and eager to view the spectacle, we maintained our distance, scanning the entire area, especially the outskirts, where the bush could easily conceal a poacher. All appeared clear as my focus kept returning to the animals. I had never seen such a sight, such harmony, and all I could hear was nature. Every herbivore one could imagine had come to bathe and quench their thirst in this precious necessity of life, from hippos to zebras to wildebeests and impala, as well as warthogs, and as many varieties of birds as I had ever seen, all gathered together below the towering watch of the graceful giraffes. And the elephants, which were healthy in number, were of course the main attraction.

As I tuned back into the conversation Kintu was conducting with Adam, I heard him say that on infrequent occasions, where the life source gathered in such abundance, even lions and hyenas, two of the main foes of all grazers, could be seen drinking side by side with their prey, as if calling a temporary truce. However, no predators were at the party—not yet, anyway. We jotted down our approximate tallies of the herds as instructed, scanned one final time for poaching activity, admired the scene for several more minutes, and eventually made our way back to our vehicle.

"Pretty incredible, huh?" Kintu said as he opened the driver's side door.

"Man, that is worth the price of admission!" I replied as Adam agreed from the back seat.

"Typically, I like to observe for much longer, but I was told to take you guys to the sanctuary," Kintu said.

My ears perked up.

"Where we dropped off the baby a few days ago?" Adam asked.

"Correct."

"And where Olivia is?" I asked.

"Well, she is the founder, so, yes," Kintu replied somewhat sarcastically. "The captain wants you two to have a proper introduction, since the rescue effort was so hectic and didn't allow for it."

"Sounds good!" Adam said.

I held my breath. I didn't want Kintu to know that since I had first seen Olivia amidst all the chaos, I couldn't get her out of my head. I wasn't sure if it was because I hadn't interacted with a woman besides Ashi in what felt like eons, or if it was simply because of her undeniable beauty. I felt sweat forming on my forehead as we drew closer. I was going to find out, whether I wanted to or not.

We gently pulled into the sanctuary, trying not to disturb any of the animals on site. I did not see any from the entrance, which was lined with beautiful flowers of all colors and varietals. I could not tell if they were wild or had been planted, but wild was my guess, as they were scattered at random on both sides of the dirt road.

I was feeling overly anxious as I stepped out of the SUV, and I knew it had to be about formally meeting Olivia. And before I could even tell myself to take some deep breaths, the door to a long, one-story wooden structure opened, and out walked the very reason for my nervousness.

"The cap-captain must have told her we were coming," I stuttered, sounding more like Adam than myself.

She walked out of the building with confidence, like she was on the runway, one foot neatly striding in front of the other as her hourglass waist shifted to one side and her flowing dark brown ponytail swayed to the other. She had bush clothes on, but she wore them impeccably, unlike us, as if she'd had them perfectly tailored to her body. Her skintight beige pants, accented with brown boots, matched her loosely buttoned fitted top that went just past her belly button, all highlighting her jaw-dropping figure. Despite her obvious beauty, I sensed modesty in her face as she approached. She had a welcoming dimpled smile that grew the closer she came while her tanned olive skin illuminated as the sun's rays crept over her face. She was taller than I remembered, standing at least five-foot-seven, and she didn't look a day over twenty-eight. But something told me she was closer to thirty-five, just based on her confidence and comfort with herself. I also couldn't imagine a younger person running an elephant sanctuary in Africa.

"Hi, guys!" she said as she extended her slender hand towards Kintu.

"Olivia, always a pleasure to see you!" Kintu said. "These gentlemen are our two new colleagues in the fight."

"So nice to meet you both," she said with the sweetest female voice one could imagine, coupled with a uniquely pleasant accent that I struggled to pinpoint. "It's so great to have more people on board. We sure could use the help."

As she shook our hands, first Adam's, then mine, I couldn't believe the silky softness of her skin, and I couldn't take my eyes off her full, naturally pinkish-red lips. My nerves kicked into high gear, and I could barely get any words out at all. Luckily, Adam took over.

"Great to meet you," Adam said with admirable poise. "So, how's our girl doing?"

Olivia looked confused until she realized he was referring to the baby elephant. "Oh, you mean Nepasha!" she replied. "It was really touch and go when your team brought her in, but she has stabilized in the last few days. Still a little disoriented though. It's a process, but I think she'll make it. She's so sweet."

"That's outstanding!" Adam said. "We worked hard getting her here!"

"You named her Nepasha?" I asked, and she nodded. "What a great name," I said, making her smile.

And then I couldn't believe what spilled from my mouth, which I was clearly not in control of. "Almost as lovely as Olivia," I said.

Her naturally rosy cheeks turned a deeper shade. She didn't know what to say and looked at me with a puzzled expression. I immediately regretted being so forward, but it was more of my subconscious at work than anything else.

"It matches my olive skin, so I guess it works," she finally said, alleviating the awkwardness.

"Really, Joe?" Adam chimed in, looking at me like I was off the reservation.

Luckily, Kintu changed the topic. "We are so happy she made it. Can we see her?"

"She's actually undergoing a rehydrating treatment today, but I'll show Adam and Joe around the sanctuary so they can meet some of the others, and hopefully Nepasha will be fully integrated next time."

"Perfect," Kintu said as we all walked around the main building.

We went through a wooden gate to the rear of the property, where several corral-like enclosures were set up, presumably to separate certain animals from the others. Beyond the enclosures was open land, scattered with acacias for miles, similar to our reserve, but even more abundantly. I did not know how much of the land was Olivia's to use, but it seemed like a natural environment for baby elephants to feel somewhat secure while adjusting to life without their mothers.

Olivia led us through a corridor that separated two pens, and I started to hear the unmistakable sounds of young pachyderms just around the corner. I looked over the railing, but could not get a good visual, and as excited as I was, I had a hard time keeping my eyes off Olivia as her ponytail danced around in a mesmerizing fashion. I felt guilty for not having my head fixated on the elephants, but I was a man, and it had been a while since I had been around a woman like Olivia. My instincts were no less guiding than a baby elephant's, or so I told myself.

As she strode along, Olivia explained how she had built the structures and why it was necessary to separate certain elephants from others during the healing process, citing medical reasons as well as emotional barriers. She was a natural tour guide, looking back at Adam and me, flashing her brilliant smile as she spoke so passionately about her project—her "baby," as she called it. I was all in, and I hadn't even seen one animal yet.

"Okay, guys, are you ready?" she said as we stopped by an

outdoor sanitizing station. "We don't want to spread any harmful diseases to them, so we always wash before entering."

"How many are in there?" Adam asked as he sanitized his hands. "It sounds like a dozen!"

"Only five right now," she replied. "But you're right, they make so many different noises that it can sound like a whole herd!"

"Can't wait!" I said as she opened the gate.

In an instant, five adorable baby elephants of various sizes, some looking closer to adolescents (but no less cute), rushed over to Olivia, trumpeting incessantly and caressing her arms and legs with their trunks as if she were their own mother, and I had no doubt that that's exactly how they viewed her. I was amazed at how jovial they all were, considering what they had been through. Once they were done greeting their surrogate, to my surprise, they all came rushing over to the three of us with their ears flapping, tails flipping, and trunks prodding curiously in the air, but a tad more cautiously than with Olivia. However, I was shocked at how relatively trusting they were with us, recalling Nepasha's timidness when we had rescued her.

"They're so friendly!" I said as I reached out and touched the smallest one's wet-tipped trunk. "You've done some amazing work with these animals."

"Well, thank you, Joe," she said. "I couldn't be happier with how they're adapting. Of course, not all rehabilitate at the same rate, as each one has experienced different levels of trauma. It can take a while for some, and some never do fully accept their new life. But for the ones that do, I'm able to develop a special bond with them. I'm just so grateful that they accept me."

Two of them that appeared to be female were warming up to Adam, who seemed to be relishing the moment. Kintu had two more engaged, but I was drawn to the tiniest and most docile baby.

"This one is so sweet. Is it a girl?" I asked Olivia.

"She is, yes," she replied. "That's Sasha. She's one of the youngest, just two months old, but she's adapting so nicely. A little hesitant, but not wary of people, like some of the others. I hope Nepasha does as well as her, but she seems a little more traumatized.

"You're a natural, Joe!" Olivia continued with a smile while I gently rubbed Sasha's trunk as it curled and uncurled. "She likes you. She might even doze off!"

Sasha eventually dropped to the ground and rolled on her back like a dog, her enormous feet splaying in the air.

"Look at that one go!" Adam said as one of the larger babies with Kintu began running joyfully around the enclosure.

"He loves to tromp around, but be careful. If he hits you, you'll feel it," Olivia warned.

"I can't believe how well adjusted they are," Adam said. "I thought they would have more emotional issues after what they've gone through."

"Oh, some definitely have their struggles," Olivia said. "Some are so scarred that they stop eating and die from malnutrition or starvation. Those are hard times around here, but it's the unfortunate reality, and we deal with it the best we can."

"I can't imagine," I said. "But it's nice to know that the work we do out in the field pays off for some."

"Many!" Olivia said warmly. "If it weren't for Captain Stewart's operation, there would be little need for the sanctuary. I am so very grateful for the work you all do."

"The pleasure is ours, believe me," I said. I thought I noticed a tear forming in her eyes as she looked at the elephants, then at the ground, then back up at me. I didn't know what to say, but I was relishing the connection that I was sensing between us.

But before I could confirm my intuition, the walkie-talkie attached to Kintu's hip killed the moment.

*"Kintu! Kintu, come in!"* Aaron's voice blared through the speaker.

Kintu held down the button. "Yes, I copy."

*"We have a situation developing. You, Adam, and Joe need to leave immediately. We got word of a poaching operation in the area that's supposed to unfold before dawn. It's game time, mate."*

"Copy that, on our way!" Kintu replied.

An all-too-familiar shot of unwanted adrenaline coursed through my veins as I anticipated a potential real-life gunless battle with the enemy. Adam seemed ready though, quickly thanking Olivia and beating everyone back to the vehicle. I was the last to depart the sanctuary. I stood there with Olivia, motionless, awkwardly wondering if she could sense my fear, but also wondering if she could sense my desire to see her again. I wanted to tell her that I would rather stay with her and help with the babies, but I knew we had a duty. It was the reason we had ventured to

Africa in the first place. And as I looked into her deep blue eyes, I saw a new motivation for making it back alive. I simply had to see her again.

"Joe! Let's go!" Adam yelled from the front.

"You be safe out there, Joe," Olivia said with affection. "You gotta come back another time and see how Nepasha's doing."

*If she only knew*, I thought to myself, shooting her a parting smile as I raced out the gate. With her unforgettable face stamped in my mind, two words kept ringing in my head: *game time*.

# EIGHT

We drove across the still terrain in the early morning hours, before the sun could light our way. After a long night of strategic planning, as well as some disagreements between members on which approach to take, we finally felt ready to set out on the mission—a mission I knew could cost someone their life, as it had for Jafari.

Everyone was called to duty besides Ashi, who again stayed behind. She had gone on missions before, and she was more than capable, but Abasi had mentioned that he hated worrying about her out in the field, where bullets showed little mercy and didn't recognize gender. So, everyone was supportive of her prepping the meal for our scheduled return.

We rode over the parched land as our two Land Rovers made their way north towards the highway. I could feel the impact of the boulders and shrubs beneath the floorboards as I went over the details of the captain's meeting and the subsequent strategy laid out by Aaron the previous night. However, I had already forgotten most of it, as I couldn't get Olivia out of my mind. Her long, flowing hair. Her sensual lips. Her soft, sweet voice. The way she walked. Real danger was on the horizon, but all I could hear in my mind was the name *Olivia*. Maybe she was the real danger.

The sky above the distant hills began to lighten as the morning drew on. I peered out the left rear window, but still couldn't make out many images. My breath fogged the glass. The cabin was silent. Perhaps everyone was pondering what would happen when we confronted the assailants. I managed to scour up the captain's discourse from the back of my mind, hoping that Aaron, who was driving our vehicle, would reiterate the mission protocol along the way.

A neighboring reserve had gotten word that the most successful and most feared poaching unit, the Black Mambas, were planning an operation about sixty miles to the north, where a large herd was known to roam. They alerted the captain immediately to bolster the size of the squadron. However, I wasn't sure how much assistance we could actually provide, as the captain still had a no-gun policy even in the wake of Jafari's death, much to the team's dismay.

The Black Mambas—or Mambas, as they were colloquially known—were named after one of Africa's most deadly snakes. They were a ruthless group of poachers that tallied up the most tusks of any group, living up to their name. They were militant and efficient in their approach, using some sophisticated weaponry and communication devices, and they were typically in and out of a crime scene before any rescue groups could arrive. But the Mambas had been relatively quiet as of late, focusing their attention on larger-scale operations. The group was well funded, which was why they were so aptly equipped. Funded by a terrorist cell that operated out of Somalia, they shipped their goods to the coast, where they were put on ships and hauled to certain Asian countries where demand was ripe.

I noticed Adam's leg shaking next to mine. "You're not nervous, are you, Rorbach?" I asked him.

"Nervous?" he echoed. "More like anxious ... and ready."

It was a silly question. I should've known; Adam didn't get nervous. I was the one who got nervous. I had no idea how we would engage armed poachers without being killed. But I had to trust the captain's judgment. What choice did I have?

"I'm just getting tired of—"

Adam was interrupted by the captain coming through the two-way radio. *"Aaron, come in. Do you read me?"*

"Loud and clear, Cap."

*"When we get to the highway, cut your lights. The sun should be up by then,"* the captain said over the crackling speaker. *"We should remain as inconspicuous as possible. And when we get five miles out from the target, we need to pull over and go over the plan one more time."*

"Roger that," Aaron replied.

I pressed my temple against the chilled window and pondered what we were going to do if we caught the killers in the act. We had rehearsed various tactics the previous night, but I hadn't slept a wink, and my mind was hazy. I peered out the window as the visibility began to improve. Everything was still, with not even birds flying about in the cloudless sky. I imagined a herd off in the distance, a family grazing in the morning mist, peaceful and content. A pothole in the neglected road jolted our vehicle and ended my reverie.

"Sorry, what were you saying?" I asked Adam.

"I was saying something?"

"Yeah, you said you're getting tired of something?"

"Oh, yeah. I've been getting really sick of all the crap in the world," Adam said.

"Me too. But what are you referring to, exactly?"

He paused and gazed out the window for several moments. Then he turned back and stared me right in the eye with a look that was part rage, part determination, and part resignation. It was obvious that he was subduing a fire burning deep within, and had been doing so for a while. I wasn't really sure what might come out of his mouth that Aaron and Kintu would not only hear, but cringe at.

"The evil, bro," he said, still staring intently. Finally, he blinked and looked straight ahead. "I'm sick of seeing man destroy the land … the animals … his fellow man. I know it will never stop, but this adventure has fueled me. We came here to make a difference. We came here to fight. It's about time we start getting some trophies of our own. And if risk comes with that, then so be it."

I didn't know what exactly he intended, but I knew for certain that he was serious. My eyes locked with Aaron's in the rearview mirror, and I could tell he'd heard what Adam had said. His expression was one of approval, not dismay. He liked Adam. They had developed a soldier-like bond during our brief time at the reserve. They had a similar fearlessness and a sense of duty. And even though Adam had never been in the military, he had a strong moral compass, which was one of the main things that drew me to him.

"We're almost to the highway," Aaron said. "We'll all pull over and check the satellite imagery, see if we can pinpoint their exact location. We won't be far from where the tip suggested they would be. If I'm correct, they'll be in a popular open area of the Catawaba Reserve, where a large herd of twenty and their revered matriarch roam. There's a small reservoir to the south-west of the territory, which I'm guessing they will be near. It's close to the highway, so we'll need to circle around and come in through the bush, if it isn't too dense. That should give us some cover."

We soon arrived at the main highway, and the sun was creeping over the low, distant hills, illuminating the vast openness. Luckily, there were not many vehicles on the road yet, but we pulled off a few hundred yards into the dirt behind some brush to conceal ourselves the best we could. We got out of the SUVs as the captain flattened out a large map on the hood of his vehicle. Aaron set up the satellite devices, and he and the captain checked the coordinates, assessing whether their prediction was correct. The technology we used could show movement, and it was up to us to determine whether it was animal or human. The images were fuzzy, small, and colorless, but we relied on Aaron's and the captain's military experience.

It turned out that the tip we'd received was more or less

accurate. Aaron and the captain spotted movement in the Catawaba Reserve, which was about ten miles north. But based on their dialogue, I could tell there was conflicting information.

"As I suspected, there's the herd in the southwest corner," Aaron said. "But nothing out of the ordinary. They're behaving like grazing elephants typically would."

"I agree," the captain said. "Then what's that a few miles to the northeast?"

They weren't positive and began studying the imagery more closely.

"It almost looks like nothing out of the ordinary, but I'm seeing faint traces of movement, which could be consistent with poachers at work," Aaron said.

"There!" the captain said with zeal as a moving object entered the screen. "That's them!"

"Yeah, that's definitely a vehicle approaching," Dota said.

"But the herd is over there, behaving normally," Kintu chimed in. "That wouldn't be the case if they were carving up one of their family members."

"Very true," Aaron said. "But they're obviously working on something."

Just as the captain was getting ready to tell us to move out, the radio unit in his vehicle sounded off. He reached in through the window and somehow squeezed his upper half in to respond. We couldn't hear exactly what was being said on the other end over the background noise, but the captain seemed pleased when the exchange ceased and he wiggled back out, his extra-large shirt catching on the door handle. I'd feared we were going to have to pull him out.

"That was Jemba from the Meruwa Reserve," the captain announced. "As I mentioned in yesterday's briefing, they're going to join us today. They see the same activity from their post, but they aren't certain what's going on either. They're much closer and are viewing it through binoculars deep in the bush, but they have yet to get a clear view. He said he'd spotted three vehicles, but we'll have them out numbered. We'd better hurry. Everyone, move out!"

As we rushed back to our SUVs, I kept asking myself a question that finally spilled from my mouth: "What the hell are we going to do once we engage them?"

"The captain always comes up with a plan," Aaron said. "But the dynamic has changed in our favor."

"How so?" Adam asked.

"The Meruwa team doesn't play by the same rules we do," Aaron replied. "They don't have the same limitations. They're fully armed."

With sufficient sunlight illuminating the road, we turned off our headlights and crept back onto the highway, trying not to stir up dust clouds behind us. As we headed west, away from the rising sun, I felt my adrenaline spike, accompanied by a fresh bout of anxiety. I looked over at Adam, and as predicted, a sense of calm was draped over his face.

We traveled a few miles until Aaron pulled off the main highway onto a dirt road, following the vehicle Dota was manning.

To the left was a beautiful expanse of lush green grass, perfect for grazing. It was obvious why so many animals instinctively gathered in these places, but it made them sitting ducks for those that intended on doing them harm. To the right was tree-lined, dense bush terrain skirting the edge of the reserve.

We passed a herd of wildebeests grazing off in the distance, at least thirty in total, with seven zebras accompanying the feast, necks bent to the ground, ears flicking about, foraging for breakfast. Everything seemed so tranquil. I tried to pretend that a similar serenity was enveloping our vehicle. Then the captain came over the speaker.

*"Aaron, come in,"* he said. *"Do you see what I'm seeing?"*

"Well, Cap, if you're talking about the grazers we just passed, yes. But they're kind of a dime a dozen, wouldn't you agree? They were a nice treat though!"

*"This is no time for jokes!"* the captain fired back. *"Look through your binoculars, about a half mile further."*

"Okay…Grab those binoculars on the floor there, Joe, and tell me what you see," Aaron said to me. "Hang on a minute, Cap, back in a jiffy."

I found the case on the floor, removed the binoculars, and pressed the cold plastic to my eye sockets, adjusting for clarity. I saw the herd we had just passed, but couldn't find anything else but open grasslands with dense forest in the background.

"The captain doesn't have all morning, does he, mate?" Aaron said with sarcasm, but his British charm always softened the harshness. "Spot anything?"

"No, not yet," I said. But just as Adam was reaching over to grab them from me, I found the source of the captain's concern. "Wait—yes, I got it. There's a large herd of about twenty elephants, mostly adults and adolescents, with a few babies. No one seems startled. They're just going about their business, calm as can be."

I rolled down the window to get a clearer view. It was such a beautiful sight that I didn't want to relinquish the binoculars, but Adam finally grabbed them and had a gander, leaning over my lap.

"Captain, we got the image," Aaron said into the speaker. "Just a happy family of elephants, it seems."

*"Doesn't that strike you as odd?"* the captain asked.

"Well, considering we're looking for poachers who we were told might be in the act of carving off one of their mate's tusks, it does, now that you mention it." Aaron had a way of sounding nonchalant about everything.

*"Exactly,"* the captain said. *"What's odd is that our target is a couple miles further. Turn into the bush, drive slow, and try to stay inconspicuous."*

Aaron, followed by Kintu, looked through the binoculars to confirm what we saw before our view was obstructed as we turned into the bush. It was loaded with tall but skinny acacias, an elephant's favorite meal, although they preferred the lower-hanging fruit of the shorter varieties. Luckily, the trunks were thin enough that we could navigate through, plowing over the underlying brush.

"If they're not messing with the elephants, what else would they be doing here?" Adam asked.

"Rhinos," Aaron and Kintu replied in unison.

"As I think I mentioned during one of the training sessions early on, rhino horn is even more valuable than ivory, and certain species of rhinos are truly on the brink," Aaron said. "I hope we get there in time, if indeed we are correct."

"Yeah, our driver who took us to the reserve told us all about the perceived medicinal value of the horn in Asian countries," I said.

"Right, right," Aaron said. "People will pay a lot to try to cure impotence, I suppose. It's an uphill battle, isn't it?"

"It's a bunch of horseshit is what it is," Adam blurted out, and again, I saw the intensity in his eyes.

"I second that," Kintu said. "Rhinos are sweet creatures, contrary to what people think. To lose them would be devastating—equally as devastating as losing the elephants. They're ancient! They kind of remind me of the prehistoric days, when dinosaurs roamed the earth."

We all nodded as the cabin went silent, and all we could hear was the crunching of branches beneath the tires and an occasional limb scraping the side panels. The bush was getting thicker, and there were no dirt roads. We couldn't travel more than ten miles per hour. I kept envisioning the killers in the act of sawing off a rhino horn while we were stuck at a snail's pace in the never-ending bush.

"I hope the other team is already there, wrecking the poachers' party," Aaron said.

"The captain made it seem like they were close," Kintu added. "According to the coordinates, we should be approaching their team shortly."

I looked out the window to see if I could see any activity in the grasslands to our left, but only slivers of sunlight made their way through the wall of vegetation. But that kept us concealed, which was vital if we were going to somehow sneak up on them. I wasn't confident, however, as our trampling vehicles were anything but silent. Hopefully, they were out of earshot. The uncertainty of the moment was ratcheting up the tension, and I could feel the blood pulsing through my veins. The slow crawl through the terrain was agonizing.

Finally, a light flashed three times up ahead.

"There they are," Aaron said as he redirected to the right slightly, following the captain and Dota deeper into the bush towards two beige military-grade, Hummer-like trucks. The windows were tinted black, and it was impossible to see how many people were inside. We drove up behind the two vehicles, forming a single file line of four, so that if we were seen, the enemy wouldn't be able to definitively tell the size of our squadron.

The captain opened his door and got out while we waited for instructions. He quietly made his way over to the first truck in the line to greet the driver, whom I understood to be the leader, Jemba. He stepped out of his vehicle, and the two men embraced for several seconds. Jemba was a large man of African descent, dwarfing the captain, who was strong and sturdy himself, despite being short in stature. The captain might have been thicker in the trunk, but Jemba was as tall as a tree, and he appeared strong as an ox. He reminded me of Dota, but taller. I could see his muscular arms below the rolled cuffs of his dark green military-style uniform.

After quickly looking at a map that the captain had spread out on the hood, they both pulled out their scopes simultaneously. They stood there in silence for at least thirty seconds, peeking through a gap in the trees to the open field several hundred yards in the distance. I could not see any poachers through my window, and the trucks in front of us blocked our view of the direction in which the two men were looking. Appearing satisfied, they lowered their scopes and began conversing. My window was cracked, so I extended my neck as far as it could reach and eavesdropped.

"I'm glad you're here, Jemba," the captain said. "Thank you for coming. I didn't think there would be so many of them. And because of the position of their vehicles, we can't even determine the exact number of poachers, but it looks like at least eight."

"You know I care just as deeply as you, John. I just wish we could've got here sooner," Jemba said.

"Yeah, the poor rhino is gone, but that doesn't mean we have to let them leave with what they came for," the captain said. "But it won't take them long, so we must act quickly. Did you see that pride of lions off to the left under the acacia grove? They're probably waiting to devour what's left behind."

"I did," Jemba replied. "It would be nice to leave a poacher or two behind for their dessert."

"Couldn't agree more," the captain said as he gave a little grin, then gave the arm signal for us to vacate our vehicles. Jemba did the same.

We all got out, at least fifteen men in total, and greeted each other. The others were very polite, but serious, and more militantly attired than our team. No one was smiling. They had all donned the same dark green uniform Jemba was wearing, with matching short-billed combat hats. They gave off an aura of competence and professionalism, which I was sure made Aaron and the captain feel more confident. It sure made me feel better. Perhaps what stood out the most, however, was the rifles that were slung over each of their backs. They weren't flashy new AR-15s or AK-47s; they were older, wood-butted weapons, but scoped. Historically, guns made me nervous. But the guns Jemba's team carried ironically put me at ease, because despite us going over numerous possible battle plans, I didn't know how in the hell we were going to attack the poachers without them.

"The enemy appears to be at least eight, but could be as many as twelve," said the captain, who was allowed to lead the operation. I noticed a reverence about him in the presence of his other colleagues. "We have sixteen men, thanks to your team. Everyone, take out your binoculars and monitor the target. We don't have much time. Jemba, do you still have the smoke launchers?"

"We have two in the truck," he replied as we all dug through our packs and took out our binoculars.

"Good, I think we'll need that diversion," the captain said. "Do you agree?"

"Indeed, I do. Otherwise, we'll be spotted firing from the tree line, and shots will come racing back in our direction before we can seek proper cover."

I pressed the binoculars to my eyes and panned the open

plain through the trees that were interfering with my view. I suddenly spotted the vehicles and some men working on a large grey mass. Some were standing, and some were working closer to the ground, but I could not make out many details of the operation. I looked several hundred yards to the left and found the acacia grove that the captain and Jemba spoke of, and there lay six lionesses, looking patient and regal, but hungry. The face of the lion that had snatched Lily flashed through my brain. I had a hard time taking my eyes off them, for I saw the same look on their faces that Leo had worn that fateful day. I couldn't believe I was standing in the middle of Africa, staring at a pride of lions, the very creature that had taken my heart and ripped it to shreds. A part of me wanted to grab the gun from Jemba's shoulder and shoot them all, but my bitter, foolish notion was replaced with clarity as I returned my eyes to the scene of the crime.

"Everyone, listen up!" the captain announced. "Jemba and I have decided we're going to use a diversion method, so let's make our way to the tree line. Grab your gear and follow me, single file."

"Ubota, grab the launchers," Jemba told his second-in-command. "Team, make sure your weapons are loaded and ready to fire."

We were led by the captain, followed by Jemba and then Aaron. I still wondered what our strategy would have been if the Meruwa clan with all their weaponry weren't with us, because it sure felt like a potential suicide mission. But perhaps the captain had known all along that he could count on them. I trusted the captain; we all did. But that didn't keep my heart from feeling like it was about to leap out of my chest. I looked at Adam, who was a few feet ahead of me. He had a genuine smile on his face.

We were nearly at the edge of the cover provided by the dense grove and underlying brush when the captain stopped and addressed us. "This is as far as we can go without alerting them to our presence," he said. "Although I am directing this mission, Jemba and his team are going to take over, as they're armed and we're not. We're going to be their eyes and ears."

Jemba looked warmly at the captain, as if to say, *"It's our pleasure, brother; we're all on the same side in this fight."*

Then the captain continued. "Okay, team, use your binoculars and find a tree with enough girth to shield yourself. Expect bullets to be fired in this direction once they realize where we are."

I found ample cover about thirty yards from the front as the rest of our squad did the same. Jemba addressed his team in his native language as they positioned themselves much more vulnerably near the open terrain. He designated two of his men to be the operators of the smoke launchers, signaling them to drop to one knee and remain as covert as possible. The rest of the men with rifles staked out their own posts, made sure they were locked and loaded, and pressed the weapons against their shoulders as they located the target through their scopes. We all had our eyes locked on the perpetrators. I was able to see two of the men on their knees, sawing with a large blade, and I knew we didn't have much time before they would be leaving with their valued prize. They were all dressed in black, which I thought was an odd and perhaps arrogant choice, as it made them the antithesis of camouflaged against the golden terrain. Clearly, they took their Black Mambas title seriously.

Out of the corner of my eye, I noticed Adam vacating his sheltered position and darting towards the front, where the captain was staked out a few feet from Jemba, who was directing his men.

"Adam!" I called out as loud as I could without yelling, but there was no reply. "Rorbach! Get back here!"

It was quiet, but I couldn't quite determine what Adam was so adamant about as he approached the captain, so I used my binoculars to read their lips.

"I appreciate the enthusiasm, son," the captain was saying, "but there's no way I'm letting you run in there without a gun— and as you can see, we don't have any. We're needed as backup on this mission."

Adam appeared to plead his case, as there was a bit more back-and-forth that couldn't be deciphered. But eventually he gave up and found another tree near the front, obviously dejected. I returned my eyes to the captain, who raised his binoculars back to his eyes as Jemba motioned for the smoke launchers to be fired on his signal. I looked back at the captain, who was suddenly raising and lowering his binoculars, squinting each time, doing double takes in what appeared to be disbelief.

I focused my binoculars to get as clear a view of the target as I could. One man was still working on the animal, while another stood up and was partially facing in our direction. I looked at the captain once more. Anger was clearly seizing control of his face. I looked back at the target, trying to discern exactly what it was he was so stirred up about. Right as my eyes locked back on the scene, a man walked out from behind a vehicle and approached the man standing by the head of the carcass. He was an olive-skinned man who walked with a superior leadership swagger. He had a coarse black beard, dark aviator sunglasses, and short, choppy black hair. He looked so familiar, but I just couldn't place the face. I wondered if the captain was sharing the same perplexity. I knew the smoke was about to be launched, and we were running out of time before chaos ensued.

The man's black shirt was partly unbuttoned, showing his upper chest as he turned ever so slightly in our direction. I held my binoculars as steady as I could to keep the image from oscillating, but my heart was racing, and I couldn't steady my hand completely. I focused just long enough to pick up dark ink in the shape of what appeared to be a curved blade that made its way towards his neck. His beard hid the totality of the tattoo, but I knew I had seen it before. Then the man slowly removed his glasses, and that was the final confirmation. I knew those steely, evil eyes.

"Adam!" I blurted out in a loud whisper, pointing at the target as he turned my way. "That's Ahmed!"

Just as Adam peered through his binoculars, I lowered mine and returned my eyes to the captain five feet to his right. All of a sudden, in what seemed like slow motion, the captain, whose face was now a mask of undeniable rage, dashed over to Jemba, who was still standing with one hand in the air, the other holding his binoculars, waiting for the right moment to give the signal.

The captain spoke sternly to him, but I couldn't pick it up. But whatever he said was convincing. Jemba lowered the binoculars and allowed the captain to snatch the rifle from his shoulder so he could strap it over his own. He moved to the left and a few feet forward, standing erect as he jammed the butt of the rifle into his shoulder, closing one eye and peering through the scope with the other. I hustled the binoculars back to my face, and amidst the panic, I struggled to relocate the target. I finally homed in on the two men, who were still in discussion. That's when I heard Aaron's plea.

"Cap, no!" he cried.

It was too late. A vociferous bang echoed off the trees as the bullet flew from its metal chute. I immediately lasered in on Ahmed, the expected target. Startled, he crouched down, but the dark-skinned man he was speaking with did not; he collapsed to the ground. Blood squirted from his neck like a busted garden hose as he lay limp. Ahmed didn't even bother to check on him, while all the visible men dove for cover behind their vehicles as Jemba lowered his right hand. The smoke grenades were away.

There was no time to wonder why the captain, who was so averse to using guns, had taken a man's life, but I knew everyone was thinking the same thing. For the next several seconds before the poachers' visibility vanished, a cascade of return fire came our way, piercing the trees that provided shelter. Some bullets sounded like they were ricocheting as if in a pin ball machine, placing us all in grave danger. When the gunfire paused, Jemba ordered his team to retreat back to their vehicles. The captain, who still had the rifle in his grasp, also scampered back behind the trucks to speak with Jemba. Then, for reasons I could not explain, the captain beckoned Adam to race over to the trucks.

"Adam!" I hollered as he booked on by, ignoring me.

"I'm ready, Cap!" Adam shouted.

"Where the hell is he going?" I yelled to Aaron, who was behind a nearby truck.

"Hell if I know, mate!"

And just like that, the two vehicles revved up with Jemba, his crew, and Adam inside, making their way through an opening in the foliage, barreling directly into the plumes of smoke.

I still had my binoculars clenched in my hand, now soaked with perspiration. I placed them against my brow, which was also drenched with sweat. The vehicles were about halfway to the target, taking an indirect route, around the direction of the gunfire. Suddenly, for a few brief moments, the rapid popping intensified, until a quiet again fell upon us, and the only remaining racket was off in the distance. I positioned myself so I could get a clearer view. Out of the cloud of smoke came a cloud of dust from the rear left. The poachers were in retreat.

When Jemba's squad finally arrived at the scene a couple minutes later, the smoke was beginning to dissipate. The first truck pulled up next to the bodies. Jemba and a few men got out, but Adam wasn't one of them.

"Look!" I said to Aaron. "The other truck is chasing after them! Pretty sure Adam's in there!"

"Well, he always said he wanted to fight, didn't he?" he replied.

I didn't respond. It was a rhetorical question anyway.

"Everybody, back to the vehicles!" the captain called out. "We gotta get out there and back them up!"

Just as we were packing up, a low, pained groan came from behind some bushes. It was Kintu.

"Kintu, you hit, mate?!" Aaron asked.

"Think so, boss," he replied as we scurried over to help. "Went in and out, I think. Just a flesh wound. Hurts pretty bad though."

Dota hurried to the SUV and grabbed the first aid kit. He disinfected the wound in Kintu's lower right thigh and rapidly tied a proper tourniquet. Aaron and Dota carried him to the vehicle and placed him in front, reclining the seat.

"You were lucky not to end up like Jafari, mate," Aaron said as we tailed the captain's vehicle, racing to meet Jemba and the rest.

"Not out of the woods yet," Kintu replied, grimacing.

As we pulled up, the dust and smoke had mostly cleared, and the team was gathered around the bodies, assessing. We joined them as Kintu stayed put. The rhino was sprawled out, eyes closed, with a bloody, hornless face and a gunshot wound drying near its belly.

"Looks like they got away with the horn," Aaron said as we circled around the body.

"Maybe not," the captain said. "Jemba's men are in pursuit. Hope they get to them before they hit the highway."

"Adam as well," I added.

The captain nodded. "We got a prize too," he said to Aaron, pointing to the lifeless man lying in a puddle of his own blood.

"Yeah, I see that," Aaron replied. "What the hell was that about? Thought we had a no-gun policy, yeah?"

"You don't recognize him?" the captain snapped back.

"Perhaps if his face wasn't caked with blood." Aaron's dry wit never failed.

"The man who killed Jafari?" the captain asked with a rhetorical tone.

Aaron stood there motionless, head tilted, staring at the body, assessing what he could of his face. "No shit!" he shouted in amazement. "Brilliant recognition from long range, Cap! But it doesn't really change the fact that our anti-gun policy not only put us all in danger today, but probably cost Jafari his life! Bloody hell, Kintu is in the car with a bullet wound to the leg! Perhaps this no-gun thing should be revisited?"

The captain just stood there, his face turning tomato red. It looked like he wanted to smack Aaron, but he settled himself before boiling over.

"We will revisit that when we get back," the captain said, gritting his teeth. "It's not fair if I am willing to violate—"

"Gentlemen, please!" Jemba chimed in. "We have a crime scene to examine here."

The mood was tense, but the two men shelved their quarrel for the time being. Everyone followed Jemba's lead and crouched around the carcass, looking for any useful evidence left behind, analyzing the snout where the horn used to be to determine the method of removal. The smaller horn was left intact. We had obviously interrupted the operation when the bullet pierced the neck of their comrade.

"Black rhino," Jemba said.

"Yep, pointed upper lip," Aaron said.

Rukawa whispered something to Dota and the captain over on the other side of the dead animal, but it came out so soft that I couldn't hear. Instead of asking Ruk to repeat his comment, I turned to Aaron. "So, did you guys see Ahmed?"

The captain stopped in mid-sentence and looked at me curiously. "What exactly do you know about Ahmed, Joe?"

"He was standing right over there," I said, pointing near the man the captain had blasted in the jugular.

"Yes, we know, mate. We saw," Aaron said. "But how do you know his name? We haven't mentioned his name to you in our meetings yet."

I began to realize that the tone they were using was driven by suspicion, as if I were involved in some sort of espionage, infiltrating their operation. I couldn't blame them; how else would I know Ahmed?

"Adam and I met him in Nairobi on our way here," I said apprehensively.

"What do you mean, you met him?" the captain asked, an uncompromising look in his eyes.

"We met him in his Moroccan restaurant. We had some time to kill," I replied, realizing that my choice of words was casting even more suspicion on Adam and me.

"Joe, Ahmed is the head of a massive poaching organization, not a restaurateur," Aaron said, trying to be less harsh.

"Well, that may be, but he owns a restaurant in Nairobi as a side hustle; that I can tell you for certain."

"Maybe that's where he launders all his money and meets with the terrorists," the captain said softly to Aaron, not intending for me to hear.

"What terrorists?" I asked. "You mean his poaching unit?"

No one answered. No one spoke for several seconds, like they didn't want to disclose anything. Finally, Jemba, who appeared ashamed of the captain's inaccurate presumption of my guilt, responded. "Ahmed uses his poaching operation to fund certain terrorists in the region," he began. "Ansar-Somalia is a medium-sized extremist group that executes bombings and killings in East Africa. They've been dormant for a couple years, but we suspect plans are in the works. Seven years ago, there was a bombing on a promenade in Sudan, killing dozens. They use the blood money appropriated by the Mambas to fund their operation, utilizing the coastal areas of Somalia for exportation."

"He knows all this, Jemba. He's one of them, remember?" Aaron said with a big smile as he looked at me. "Just joking, mate."

I did not smile back.

"Sounds like we need to take a trip to Nairobi in the coming weeks, gentlemen," the captain said. "Alright, let's finish our examination and get the hell out of—"

Jemba's radio blared. *"They reached the highway. We lost them, boss,"* a voice said. *"We're on our way back."*

"Copy that," Jemba muttered, his upper lip contorting in a snarl.

We photographed the bodies and scrounged up any useful evidence, thanked Jemba and his team for their assistance, got back in our vehicles, and headed back to the reserve. Aaron drove, while Kintu grimaced and moaned in the front seat, the pain from the gunshot wound obviously intensifying. I was distraught and alone in the back. Somehow Adam had ended up riding with the captain, who I assumed wanted a full, fresh debriefing on the chase. And as much as I wanted to know what had gone down on Adam's Wild West escapade, I was fine with the extra space, as I was emotionally spent. I kicked a leg up on the empty seat, turned sideways, placed my head against the window, and drifted away, much deeper than I would've predicted following a gunfight, ignoring the door handle stabbing me in the spine.

My dream was scrambled, but vividly psychedelic. I found myself in the center of a hut in the shape of a teepee. But instead of it being made of hide, dozens of gargantuan bloodied tusks leaned against one another, and a smoldering fire in a dug-out pit in the dirt released smoke through gaps in the top. And instead of wood, sharp, slender fragments of tusk acted as coals. An African shaman appeared, hovering, suspended in the air above the flames, waving the smoke towards his nostrils, inhaling before it escaped through the hole. His face, which looked exactly like Jafari's, was dripping with blood, and a rhinoceros horn protruded from the crown of his skull. He began reciting a trance-inducing mantra as I sat on the cold dirt. I closed my eyes for a moment, and even though I didn't speak his language, subconsciously, I knew the meaning of his spiritual chant.

Then the ground started to tremble, and the embers in the pit began to dance violently. It had all the feelings of an elephant stampede directly outside the structure. Death seemed inevitable, yet somehow I sensed that I was far from reality and would ultimately be spared. The shaman picked up a sharp fragment from the fire, cut open my shirt while still reciting the mantra, and began carving into my chest just below the skin's surface, so that the outline of the image stained my skin red. But the only blood that oozed was that from his face, landing on my bare feet. I felt no pain, just an odd sense of calm.

When the ritual was complete, his ceremonial chant started to wane. I peeked down at my chest and read the carved letters upside down: T U S K.

The shaman cupped his hands, capturing plumes of smoke and releasing them under my nostrils, as if freeing butterflies. I began to have visions on top of visions. I looked up at the top of the hut as Lily appeared, watching over me from above, only her hair was no longer a long, glowing blonde, but a shorter light brown. But I knew that face; I would forever know that face. Two pieces of tusk from the fire appeared in her palms, but she was impervious to the scorch of the heat. She extended her little arms to me, but I couldn't touch her hands or the seared ivory. Then she dropped her arms to her sides and gradually withdrew the offering. What was she trying to show me? I desperately wanted to know.

The shaman then grabbed two pieces from the fire, and as he and Lily both hovered above side by side, they began clacking the fragments together. *Clack! Clack! Clack!* One after another in total unison. I wanted so badly to stay in the trance; I had to know what Lily was trying to convey. But as the sounds grew more distant in my dream, they intensified in my consciousness, keeping the same rhythm and pace. Lily and the shaman began to evaporate into thin air, like mist from a crashing wave.

As I opened my eyes and transitioned back to reality, the jolt of the SUV settling into park ensured that my dream was over. Disoriented, I stepped out, looked towards our barracks, and found the true source of the clatter. Adam's arms were raised high over his head, with a piece of wood affixed to the end of an axe, hammering down on a chopping block over and over again until it split. His face was stained with rage. I wanted to know why, but was too unsettled to ask, so I walked in the opposite direction towards the kitchen. I thought about the bizarre dream. I thought about the shaman. I thought about Lily.

And then it hit me like a slug to the chest, just as the log crashed onto the block for the final time. Hunting poachers wasn't meant to be my mission after all; that was Adam's mission. Saving elephants had many different faces. That's when Olivia's soft, alluring face rushed back into my mind.

ADAM AND I DIDN'T SPEAK much for the next few days, despite sharing the same quarters. It wasn't for lack of desire, at least on my part. He was just giving off the vibe that he did not want to be approached. There was an intensity about every move he made and everything he said following the shoot-out. I knew generally what had taken place and wanted to ask him about the minutiae, but I decided to give him space, because that's what his demeanor demanded.

When we weren't in briefings or in the field training for the next encounter, I spent a lot of my downtime with Kintu, aiding him in his recovery from the gunshot wound. He was coming along nicely, infection-free, and when he no longer needed the bandages, I promised I would help him with his rehab, as I had a lot of experience in that area from old baseball injuries. I enjoyed my time with Kintu—more than he realized, most likely—and I was mentally checked out of the fighting mode needed to maintain an edge in the bush. He told me about his mom and dad, how he had grown up in unrelatable poverty, living in a mud hut in his early years, and how his younger sister had died from malaria when he was only nine. They owned no cows, the symbol of wealth in his village, and just to acquire water, a trek of twelve miles had to be made, shoes and socks being an afterthought. I found his stories fascinating and was embarrassed about sharing my first-world problems, which paled in comparison. But he didn't see them in that light. He was equally interested in the unknown, as a big, modern city in America was as foreign and mysterious to him as mud huts and malaria were to me. I told him about Lily, about losing her, and how the whole adventure in Africa had begun. Kintu was an empathetic soul, and because I was the same, I could tell we had a strong bond when conversing about the deaths of our loved ones. We could connect in ways that Adam and I could not, simply due to our innate personalities.

I divulged to Kintu how I was experiencing a change of heart over my role in the fight to save the elephants, without making him think I was quitting and returning to the easy life in the States, because that wasn't the case. I just felt a change was needed. He understood to some degree, and he urged me to tell the captain what I was thinking sooner rather than later, as he said the war against Ahmed would only intensify, and soon.

For the entire next week, I thought about my plan day and night, and how to tell Adam and ask for the captain's approval. I wasn't even sure if it was a viable option, but I knew it was one I had to pursue. My feelings were only growing stronger by the day. Following yet another delectable meal under the stars, served by Ashi, I decided to tell Adam and the captain the following morning. Both conversations gave me an anxiety that I could feel in my bones. For some reason, I felt shame and guilt for wanting to alter my mission. But in my eyes, I wasn't totally abandoning the mission; I was merely shifting its focus. I would still be helping the elephants. However, I would be abandoning my friend, and my gut knew it.

I tossed and turned that night as I prepared to break the news at dawn's arrival. We always woke just as the sun peeked its rays over the mountain range in the distance, not just because it was the captain's policy to get the engine revved up early, but because the tiny holes in the wooden walls allowed the sunbeams to creep into our quarters.

The next morning, Adam and I walked to the kitchen to grab our customary java, and although it was much needed to kick-start the morning, it only added to my jitteriness. All was quiet on the walk back, until I broke the silence.

"Hey, Bach, what do you say we take a little stroll around the reserve?"

"What for?" he replied. "It's kinda brisk this morning. Plus, we start simulated weapons training with Aaron in forty-five minutes. Isn't it killer that the captain changed his stance on us having guns?"

I thought about his ironic choice of words before answering. "Well, that's related to what I want to discuss with you," I said.

"I knew you wouldn't be in favor!" he exclaimed.

"No, it's not that. I was just as perplexed as you, when bullets were flying past our faces, that we didn't have any proper means of protection. Here, just walk with me for a few minutes."

He agreed, and we set out towards the western perimeter of the reserve, where dozens of yellow-billed oxpeckers were chirping their hearts out in a grove of baobab trees that we often used for training. I tried to gather my thoughts, but my mind was distracted by the unforgettable and unique shape of the baobabs. With their colossally wide, smooth grey trunks that branched only at the very top, high above the ground, they had a truly unmistakable appearance, as if from an alien world. As I began to lose my train of thought, I switched my focus back to the conversation.

"You wanna go home, don't you?" he asked. "I could tell something was up after the whole shoot-out."

"I wouldn't call it a shoot-out," I snapped, feeling somewhat attacked. "The shooting was predominantly coming from one direction, from where I was standing."

"Not from my vantage point! I was hanging out the window of the truck, firing at their windows and tires! I took dead aim at Ahmed's skull, but I missed. It was a goddamned rush, I'll tell you that."

"Yeah, I heard. It's so crazy that Ahmed is behind all this. And it sounds like there will be more encounters for you in the near future. Don't the guns come in next week?"

"Sure do! Aren't you pumped?"

"Not at all. See, this is what I'm trying to tell you. This is *your* fix, *your* vice, *your* thing. Not mine."

"What the hell are you talking about?"

"I thought I wanted to come protect the elephants by killing poachers, but that was just the fire in me burning after Lily died. Turns out, I only want to protect the elephants."

"But to protect the elephants, you gotta kill poachers, no? Or am I missing something?" he asked with notable sarcasm.

Silence fell upon us for several seconds before I answered.

"You do, yes. But I don't want to. I'm not a killer. I don't even really like guns. This whole experience has been very eye-opening. And what a journey it's been so far; I'm so glad we came. But I need to take this in a new direction."

More silence ensued before the words would escape the safety of my mouth. "Later today, I'm going to ask the captain if I can work primarily with Olivia at the sanctuary."

"You're going to *what*?"

"I'm going to ask the captain—"

"It was rhetorical! I heard you the first time!"

"I'm sorry, man," I said lamely.

"You're sorry? Is that supposed to make me feel better?" He paused for a moment and reined in his emotions before continuing. "Let me get this straight: you bring me on a one-way trip to no-man's-land to live in a shack with no air conditioning, eat the heads of goats, and chase after terrorists with flashlights, pocketknives, and binoculars—only to leave to go hook up with some woman?"

He had a point. I paused for a moment and thought about what he'd said, but what came out when my mouth finally opened didn't help matters. "You got a pocketknife?" I asked.

"Really?! I embellished, you numbskull!"

"Okay, look, I apologize. And you're right, I can't lie: this *is* partly about Olivia. I can't stop thinking about her. And I don't know if there's anything there, but I have to find out. But this is also about the elephants. Call me a softy and a sissy if you wish, but I'm more a nurturer than a killer, more lover than fighter. You have your thing, and I have mine. I want to help take care of the orphans, if Olivia even needs the help. And moreover, we were both lost souls when we agreed to board that plane, searching for something, anything to give us meaning and direction. I didn't force your hand then, and I'm not forcing you to stay now.

I'll even give you whatever money I have left if you want to leave. But something tells me you're not going anywhere. You and I both have unfinished business. It's just different business, that's all."

As he processed my rant, I noticed his face softening ever so slightly. He didn't speak, just gave me a halfhearted nod and headed back to the compound. I trailed behind in silence, as there was not much more to say.

While gazing at the puffy cumulus clouds hovering just above the horizon, I couldn't stop my mind from wandering as I began to think about what I was going to say to Olivia, and especially to the captain. I started to feel silly for entertaining a new plan in my head without even knowing if an opportunity existed. But for some reason that I couldn't explain, my gut was telling me that I was on the right path. But I was dreading the conversation with the captain. For the rest of the walk, I thought about my words. I needed to choose them wisely. So, I took the long way back to the compound, gathering my thoughts and attempting to absorb the calming sounds of nature. They had little effect, however, as I was even more hesitant to divulge my idea to the captain than I had been to Adam. I didn't want to let him down.

I made my way to the wooden porch fronting the main building, thinking of Jafari and the helpless feeling I'd had the day he was rushed up the steps and into the infirmary. Through the screen door, I heard the rattling of pots and pans as I picked up the aroma of cooked meat. I tiptoed in, unsure if the captain was in his office, until I heard his bellowing tone on the commanding end of a call. I didn't want to interrupt, so I went and said hello to Ashi, who was singing under her breath in her native tongue, preparing the team's favorite, boar and eggs. But her usual warm smile was replaced by a look of apprehension. When I asked her if anything was amiss, her words said no, but the lines in her face screamed the opposite. I assumed it was about the increased tension with the Mambas and the heightened danger that Abasi could soon face. Or perhaps it was about the weapons that were well on their way. But I decided not to press the issue, and instead, I complimented her cooking, as it smelled truly delightful. She smiled ever so slightly as we both stood there, unsure about what to say next.

Just as a tinge of awkwardness was creeping in, the barking from the captain's office at the end of the hall grew faint. I smiled at Ashi, organized my thoughts, took a couple deep breaths, and gently knocked on the door that was cracked open a hair.

"Yes?" he said. "Come in."

I walked in so timidly that I could hear every creak in every floorboard with each step. But with my shoulders back and chin up, I was still trying to convey as much confidence as possible.

"Oh, hi, Joe. To what do I owe this pleasure?" he asked, his British formality shining through.

"Well, Cap, there's something that's been on my mind that I wish to discuss with you," I said, pulling out the rickety chair on the other side of his old brown desk. "Is this a bad time?"

"I always have time for my men, Joe, you know that," he said, and I felt my guilt amplifying. "I just got off the phone with Jemba. We're trying to put together a reconnaissance mission to learn more about Ahmed's operation. The information you gave us about his restaurant could prove invaluable. I think that's where he launders the money."

"Yes, but Adam and I just stumbled on him by accident, Cap," I noted, trying to downplay our significance.

"It's not just that. You boys have integrated very well and helped the team tremendously."

I felt like just thanking him and walking out, as the guilt was becoming increasingly unbearable. But my desire to alter my path superseded the shame I felt, and the words leapt out before I could change my mind.

"Well, that's what I wanted to talk to you about, Cap," I said, taking a long pause and a couple more deep breaths. "I am really grateful for you letting us join the team, and I've learned so much in these past few months. It's been an enriching experience all around so far." I took another deep breath and made sure I was looking him directly in the eye. "But I really feel that there is another way for me to aid in this rescue process—a way that suits me far better. I don't know if she needs the assistance, but I was wondering—with your permission, of course—if I could begin transitioning to the rehabilitation side of things over at the sanctuary."

He took a moment to ponder, which felt like forever. His eyes began to glare and squint, and I thought I saw anger developing in his face, but I couldn't be sure. I braced for a verbal lashing.

"With Olivia?" he asked with surprising gentleness.

"Yes."

"It's funny you should ask, because just a few days ago, she mentioned to me that with the recent increase in poached adults, she's seen an influx of orphans lately, and she's thinking about bringing in more help."

"Interesting," I said, trying not to sound too excited.

"And after you guys met her, she also told me that she was hoping you could come by again sometime and help her with the baby we brought her—which is not like Olivia. She's very self-sufficient. You must've made quite an impression."

"Really?" I said, struggling to keep my enthusiasm under wraps as my palms began to sweat. "Yeah, we seemed to have a good interaction, I suppose."

"But my quandary is, Joe, our operation is really picking up steam here, and with the rifles coming soon, the more trained men we have on board, the more effective we'll be. To be perfectly blunt, we need you here."

"I respect that. I do. But that's a part of what drove my decision to ask you. You see, although I feel like our lack of weapons left us completely vulnerable out in the field, the battle with the Mambas reinforced something that I've always known about myself: my instinct is to shy away from guns. At the same time, I know how needed they are in this arena. But I just don't feel very comfortable around them. And after observing the wonderful work that Olivia does with the orphans we bring her, I feel like my abilities would go much further over there. That's where my heart is, Cap. Respectfully, I would like to ask you to reconsider."

He squinted at me with his hardened eyes, as I could almost

hear his wheels turning. He didn't look angry, just pensive, but I was not confident. After he took a few sips from a crimson coffee mug resting on the corner of the desk and adjusted his glasses, he finally spoke. "Okay, Joe, I can tell your heart is in the right place. And being a military man, I know the importance of having people in the right positions, so that the totality of the mission can succeed. And I'm sure seeing Jafari shot and bleeding to death the first day you arrived didn't help matters. I'll give her a call and see if she does indeed have any needs. But I can't guarantee anything. And if she doesn't, I hope you'll reassess your stance. We will really need you as we prepare to go after Ahmed."

"Thank you, Cap, I really appreciate it," I said as I felt my heart rate soar. "I hope to be a tactical part of the process regardless, even if it's from the sidelines."

"I hope so. I'll give her a ring and let you know what she says."

I rose from my chair, shook his vise of a hand, and turned to walk out of the office with a reinvigorated gait. But before I opened the door, I had one more question that had been eating at me.

"Hey, Cap, what made you change your stance and grab the rifle off Jemba's arm?"

There was a lengthy pause, and he stared directly into my eyes before speaking. "Instinct," he replied as a wry grin crept across his face.

# NINE

Minutes felt like hours and days felt like weeks as I waited for word from the captain in regards to Olivia. It was partly because I did not want to be a part of the new culture that was to be centered around the rifles that had just arrived, but even more than that, I couldn't wait to see Olivia again. My desire was building with each passing day.

Luckily, I only had to suffer for a few days without knowing. And when the answer came back affirmative, I was over the moon. I was to report to the sanctuary the following morning, the one caveat being that I would still sleep in my barrack on the reserve at first, which was fine with me, as it would make me feel less guilty for abandoning my friend. Fortunately, the captain had an old four-wheeler ATV that I could use for transportation; otherwise, the eight-mile round-trip trek might have become overbearing on foot. But if I could see Olivia every day, no distance was too great.

The ATV was easy to operate, and the captain provided a map, since I did not recall the exact route to the sanctuary. The main road was the most convenient, but it was quicker to cut across the open terrain, and since I had the perfect off-road vehicle, I chose the more exploratory route. Adam was not around to wish me well, and I didn't get a chance to tell the rest of the team I was changing objectives, but I was relieved that the captain was supportive of the move.

I rode over the dry, cracked terrain that hadn't seen rain in several weeks. I was oddly composed, considering I was alone in the middle of Africa, heading to work with a woman whom I was completely enamored with, but barely knew. But I trusted my intuition, and it was telling me that I was headed down the proper avenue. So, I kept on riding until I reached the point where I could see the acacia grove off in the distance, where I needed to veer south until I came to a dirt road lined with eucalyptus, which led right to the front gate of the sanctuary.

I approached the wall of acacias that provided some shade from the blistering rays overhead, riding as close to the grove as possible. The old screeching engine drowned out any birds that might have been singing in the treetops, so I slowed to a stop, turned off the vehicle, and swigged from a canteen I pulled from my pack. As anticipated, fowl of all shapes and colors dotted the limbs of the grove. I had some time before I was to report for duty, so I admired the spectacle for a couple minutes before pulling out my map to ensure that the road was up ahead.

As I studied it, the rapid, continuous chirping that flooded my brain started to wane as my ears began to pick up a rustling coming from the low-lying brush nearby. It was too dense and shaded for me to identify anything concrete, but my mind began to panic, as whatever was shuffling about did not sound petite. I did not rule out a lion, but I figured a giraffe couldn't be concealed. A rhinoceros was my best guess, based on the movement of the brush and the emanating sounds. Whatever it was, it was time for me to go. I started the obnoxious motor, losing any chance of remaining covert as I alertly made my way towards the road, giving myself space from the brush just in case. I could no longer hear the crunching noise over the engine, but I no longer had to. My eyes confirmed the nightmare as a bull elephant stepped out from the shadows just thirty yards in front of me. I halted immediately, but did not kill the engine as I stared into his scathing amber eyes.

He was massive, his tusks much longer than I was tall, his ears flapping in haste, and I knew he was sending a warning signal. He picked up his front right leg and slammed it back to the earth, shaking the ground, sending a dust cloud into the air that was close enough to taste. Bulls were known to charge if encroached upon, especially during mating season. He had a sizeable chunk missing from the top of his left ear, leaving me to wonder if it had been at the hands of poachers, or if fighting was simply his forte. I had learned that elephants, despite their mass, could easily outrun a human. The only possible thing in my favor was the ATV, but I wasn't too confident in that either. As the stare-down continued, I couldn't help but be awestruck by the sheer magnificence of the animal before me, standing so authoritative and regal. Thus, instead of devising a plan, I just sat there on the vehicle, mesmerized like a deer in headlights, hoping he would retreat into the woods.

Instead, he doubled down, and my heart rate spiked. He trumpeted violently and stood on his hind legs, making his trunk appear thirty feet high from my seated vantage point, and I had a vision of one of his ivory spears piercing through my abdomen like goat meat on a stick. I was not intent on finding out the accuracy of my premonition, so I gently put the ATV in reverse and nudged backwards as deliberately as the vehicle would go, keeping my eyes locked on the bull's every move. To my amazement, my retreat seemed to calm him some, as his ears began to drape and soften while the stomping ceased. He lowered his trunk, and a look of truce crept over his face as he let out a deep rumble and meandered back to the forest. I gasped in relief, wiped the sweat from my brow, turned left, and darted toward the road, where I should've gone in the first place. It had been an extraordinary encounter, and a fortunate one.

My watch revealed that I was going to be late for my first day working with Olivia, but at least I was alive to apologize. I hoped she would excuse my tardiness, if she even believed my tale.

It had been over a month since I had last visited her place. The lane to the entrance was lined with luminous pink, yellow, and purple flowers of several varietals that freshened the air as I slowly drove into the dirt lot, where only one other vehicle was parked. A bright white fountain stood in the dead center of the courtyard, surrounded by eucalyptus that framed the small, tan wooden house. The fountain was a tad taller than I was and had an elephant trunk for a spout, which trickled water into the bowl below. I admired the sculpture for a moment before I approached the front door, wondering if Olivia was going to come out before I knocked, as she had the previous time, but I detected no movement coming from inside. I tapped on the door, and as I did, a rush of nerves coursed through me like I was in high school again, showing up late at my date's house for the prom. I half expected a father in a bathrobe with a scowl and a shotgun to open the door. I took a deep breath and told myself that I was just there to assist with the operation. But my subconscious knew that was a partial lie at best.

No one came, so I rang the elephant-shaped bell, pulling down on its tusks. Still no sounds. Was it the right day...?

I stepped off the porch, walked to the right-hand corner of the house, and looked over the fence. For an elephant sanctuary, it was awfully quiet. No pachyderms were in the main enclosure, and the gate was locked. I decided to walk around the back of the property, where I had not yet been, to see if anyone was around. I peered through the metal fence and saw a large dark brown barn with red trim that I assumed could house stalls, but I could not see in. I picked up on a docile trumpet or two and knew that at least some of the babies were inside. Twice, I called out to Olivia to alert her to my presence, but no one responded.

Then out of nowhere, someone or something tapped me on the shoulder. My hands clenched the metal fence, and I could've sworn my soul jumped straight out of my skin as I spun around.

"Hi, Joe," Olivia said with a soft smile. "I'm sorry, I didn't mean to startle you."

"I'd like to say that you didn't, but I'm good!" I said, trying to play it off while catching my breath. "Where did you come from?"

"There's a trail that leads into the woods right over there. I guess I've become skilled at walking with a silent step. I had to go investigate, because last night, we received word of a pack of hyenas a few miles north."

"Oh, wow. Their powerful jaws could probably chew right through this fence, I bet," I said, saving the story of the bull elephant encounter for another time.

"Probably could," she said in her angelic, high-pitched voice. "A couple of them could easily kill a baby. I've even heard about a pack taking down an adolescent male. But enough about that; it's so great to have you on board!"

"Thank you! I am really thrilled to have the chance to work with these special animals," I said nervously, trying to conceal the fact that she was also one of the special creatures with which I was so enamored. "I'm so glad you needed the help. So, where are the rescues now?"

"They're having their breakfast in the barn with Udokwe. I'll introduce you to him. He's wonderful, and incredibly dedicated to the babies. You'll like him a lot. C'mon, we'll go through the front gate."

She turned and led me around the enclosure. I had to force myself to walk faster, because the trailing view was as traffic-stopping as I remembered. Her light beige shorts hugged her hips to perfection. I felt guilty for looking, but I simply couldn't resist.

"So, how many rescues do you have now?" I asked her.

"We just released two to a nearby family, so we now have seven, which is slightly less than usual."

"Well, that's good, right?" I asked. "That means you're doing a good job of rehabilitating."

"Well, yes and no. Sometimes we fail, and they pass away, as was the case with Lucy last month."

"Oh, I'm sorry," I said.

"Don't be, it happens. It's unrealistic to expect to save them all. But I sure wish we could. If there's one thing I've learned, it's that you have to try to keep your emotions out of it as much as possible, or the job becomes impossible. But you do get attached, so it's easier said than done. Let that be your warning."

We kept walking through a chain-link-fenced corridor with a crushed gravel walkway that separated the barn from the training pen, where I had first been introduced to the rescues. I was thinking about what Olivia had just said, when suddenly, I was dumbfounded and halted in my tracks. On a crooked wooden post that appeared to be an old acacia branch about as tall as Olivia, an arrow-shaped sign pointing to the barn was nailed to the top, forming a cross that read LILY's WAY.

"Is something wrong, Joe?" Olivia asked, unlocking the hefty latch to the massive sliding barn door as the elephant sounds strengthened.

I didn't know how to respond. I didn't know if something was wrong, or if it was astonishingly right, but I took it for the clear sign that it was. I told her nothing was the matter, smiled, and walked inside, trying to ignore the highly unlikely synchronicity.

The barn was vast, with a dirt floor, a vaulted ceiling, and several stalls that looked just like horse stalls, but twice the size. Udokwe was gently bathing one of the babies in a separate designated washing stall, while two others were contentedly munching on a breakfast of twigs, leaves, and stems. The one being given a bath was considerably smaller and presumably younger than the other two, and I wondered if any of the three was Nepasha. But I remembered that she had a distinctive ear with a significant piece missing towards the top, and none of the three in the barn shared that feature.

"Udokwe, I'd like you to meet Joe," Olivia said. "He's going to be working with us every day. He and his team are the ones who brought us Nepasha."

I extended my hand as his face lit up when he heard her name. He had a gleaming white smile, with immaculate teeth, and soft, compassionate eyes. "It's nice to meet you, Joe," he said in perfect English as I shook his slender but strong hand.

"Good to meet you as well!" I replied.

"I want to thank you for bringing that sweet girl to us. Don't tell the others, but I think she's my favorite," he said, half cupping his hand over his mouth, as if he didn't want to offend the other three in the barn. The one he was washing gave him a trunk tap on the back.

"I'm so glad she pulled through," I said.

"It took her a while, but she made it, and now she's a fixture around here," Olivia said. "We just adore her. It'll be a rough day when we release her to a family."

"I can imagine," I said. "So, who are these three? None of them appear to be Nepasha."

"This one is Sasha," Udokwe said, gently running water over her back. "Those two down there with their trunks poking through the gate are Simi and Debo. They're both young males and love being washed too. Look at them! They can hardly wait. It'll be your turn in a minute, you two, be patient!"

The furthest one, who I thought Udokwe said was Debo, began to trumpet with more vigor.

"What are we going to have Joe get started with this morning?" Olivia asked Udokwe.

He thought for a moment, put the hose down, and chuckled under his breath. He could hardly answer as she stood there waiting.

"What is it?" she said, now chuckling with him.

"He has come at the wrong time," he said, now laughing a bit harder. He could barely get the words out. "It looks like he's on poop duty."

Olivia stopped laughing, trying not to spook me off the lot. I began to frown at the prospect of shoveling elephant dung, but I didn't want her to know, so I acted like I was ready to get my hands dirty.

"Alright!" I said. "How hard can it be? I've had dogs."

They looked at each other as if they knew a secret of which I wasn't aware.

"These are elephants, Joe. They eat like you wouldn't believe," Olivia said, as I looked over at Debo and Simi, their trumpeting replaced by spirited gorging on branches.

"You see?" Udokwe said, still laughing. "Always eating. And what goes in…"

"Must come out… Yeah, yeah, I get it," I said, still not smiling. "Well, let's get to it."

Olivia led me out of the barn, again passing by the Lily's Way sign. Udokwe waved and said he would come see how I was getting along after bath time.

"Hey, look on the bright side, you'll get to see Nepasha and meet the rest," Olivia said.

"Very true," I replied. "I'm ready to tackle whatever you need me to do. That's why I'm here. I just want to be part of the operation."

She didn't respond, but instead looked at me with a sweet grin that told me I had struck a chord.

We opened the gate to an enclosure that dwarfed the training area where I had first been introduced to the orphans. It was nearly as large as a football field. Four elephants were at the far end, but when they heard Olivia open the latch, they came charging towards us, which diverted my attention from the mounds of feces that I knew had my name on them. I wanted to ask Olivia about the meaning of the Lily's Way sign, but I figured it wasn't the right time. The elephants hit the brakes just in time before knocking us over. They began circling us, trunks flying and flopping all around, playfully inspecting us. I searched for the missing piece of ear that was distinctive to Nepasha, but before I found her, she found me. She wasn't as timid or shy as she had been during our previous encounter. She draped her trunk all over my light beige T-shirt, streaking it with fresh mud, but I didn't care. It was so refreshing to see her again, alive, well, and thriving. She was smaller than the rest, but appeared to nearly double in size when she stood on her back legs, letting out an exuberant trumpet, and she genuinely seemed to be smiling. She trotted around, shaking her head wildly with her trunk in her mouth, before cozying up next to my leg as I stroked and patted her neck.

"She remembers you!" Olivia said.

"I was hoping she would. I'll never forget the day we found her, left for dead, and brought her to you. It was one of the most rewarding days I can remember."

"I guarantee she remembers you saving her. There's no memory like an elephant's," she said, trying to corral the other three for an introduction.

"Who are these other spunky creatures?" I asked as Nepasha curled her trunk around my right knee, keeping me planted.

"She's protective of you! That's so cute! She doesn't normally act that way. She's the reserved one of the bunch."

I bent down and whispered in her ear, stroking her trunk as she began to loosen her grip. "We go way back," I said, a tad arrogantly, but Olivia could tell I was being playful and chuckled.

"These two sisters are Kioni and Mukami, and that big boy over there is Jomo," she said.

"He's got some tusks growing in already!" I said, pointing to the four-inch ivory protrusions below his confident amber eyes.

"Yes, he's a little older, and the biggest one we have. He's going to be a handful as he continues to grow."

With Nepasha still locked on my knee, I introduced myself to the other females, but Jomo had too much energy to come say hello, stomping and charging around as young males tend to do.

"So, what was it like the day you rescued her?" Olivia asked, delaying my scat pick-up, for which I was thankful.

I paused for a moment and looked towards the cloudless sky as gruesome images returned to my mind. "Well, it was an emotional day, to say the least, both good and bad. Everything people told us we would feel out in the field, I felt. The unconscionable killings and the grisly visuals were even worse that I could've ever imagined though… I mean, what they do to these poor creatures to get their tusks is beyond inhumane. It's pure evil."

"It is to us, but not to them," Olivia said. "It's taken me a long time to understand that. Without a doubt, they could be much more humane, but to them, it's just hunting, a sport that's practiced all over the world. And to them, it's not only a sport for trophies; they do it to put food on their tables and feed their families. Most of the poachers live in inconceivable, desperate poverty. I'm not trying to justify it, and I hate it with every fiber of my being, but I've come to understand it a bit better."

"Yeah, I've definitely considered it from that angle. But for some reason, it makes me no less angry," I said.

"We share the same sentiment there," she said. "So, you found Nepasha near the two adults that were killed?"

"We did, yeah. We were just about to get in our SUVs when we heard something rustling in the nearby bushes. She was so weak and feeble... I thought she was going to perish for sure. But you pulled through, didn't you, girl?" I asked Nepasha, gently stroking her trunk just below her eyes as they began to close, the sides of her mouth lifting to form a little grin.

"And now she's thriving, thanks to you and your team," Olivia said.

"No, she lived because of us, but she's thriving because of you."

Olivia blushed and looked down at Nepasha, not knowing how to accept the heartfelt compliment, so I changed course.

"But that was the amazing part of the experience. Getting to see the atrocity that produces orphans, and then getting to save an orphan in the same day was a full-circle feeling. And when I had my hand on her back in the SUV, that was the moment I was truly thankful that I came to Africa. And now I'm thankful to be here working with you."

Again, Olivia blushed, more noticeably this time. She was about to speak when Jomo came rushing in, bumping Kioni out of the way, trumpeting nonstop, and killing the moment.

"Okay, okay, Jomo!" Olivia said. "I know you're hungry, but you get a wash first. You're filthy!" She turned to me. "I'm going to take them into the barn for bathing and breakfast while I let you get to it." Then she began to walk away, the elephants in tow.

"The shovel, bags, and can are over there behind the wall. Try to cover the entire lot; they poop everywhere."

"Will do," I said. "But you forgot one."

Olivia turned around and saw Nepasha still clinging to my side. She stood there for a second, smiling, and she looked as if tears were going to form. "That is so sweet. She really likes you."

"I guess I made an impression," I said as Olivia's warm, beautiful smile diverted directly to me.

"You definitely did," she said, holding my gaze. "She can stay with you. I'll come get her after we wash the others."

I scanned the field and saw countless mounds of dung that needed attention.

"Well, Nepasha, it's just you and me, girl," I said. "We're going to need a massive shovel, aren't we?"

I went over to the barn and grabbed a shovel that looked like it was meant for scraping snow off a driveway, not for picking up poop. But when I arrived at the first pile, I understood why. The mound was immense, though relatively odorless. It had a resemblance to cow manure, just more plentiful. Both animals feasted solely on vegetation, so I wasn't surprised.

We went from pile to pile, circling the entire enclosure, with Nepasha not leaving my side, sometimes wrapping her trunk around the shovel, grabbing it from my hands, but I didn't mind at all. She was not hyper, but very inquisitive and subtly playful. As the morning wore on and the sun began to bake the terrain, sweat started to roll down the sides of my forehead as I looked around at the golden hills that surrounded the property. Who would've thought happiness was shoveling elephant poop with an orphaned elephant? In that moment, I knew that I had made the right choice.

After about a half hour, we scooped up the last pile and began walking back to the barn, just as Olivia was coming out to get Nepasha for her bath. As soon as she saw Olivia, I felt her trunk curl around my other leg this time.

"Hey, how was poop duty?" she asked lightheartedly. "Did she let you get anything done?"

"Yeah, we had a good time. I taught her how to shovel the piles herself while I monitored. Very efficient."

"Very clever!" Olivia said as she laughed.

"Nepasha, are you ready for bath time?" she asked as I felt Nepasha's trunk curl more tightly around my knee. "Oh wow, she usually loves bath time! I guess you'll have to come help us! Good time for you to learn, anyway."

"I'm ready!" I said as the three of us went back into the barn.

As we entered, Udokwe was leading the four freshly washed young pachyderms back out to the yard. Through the door, I saw who I thought was Simi and Debo immediately engage in a dirt-throwing war, scooping up dirt and shooting it onto each other, making me wonder why we would ever wash them at all. Elephants loved water, but they also liked to be covered in dust, dirt, and mud, Olivia explained. The three of us washed the remaining orphans, Olivia allowing me to continue to forge the growing bond I seemed to have with Nepasha. She didn't like having soap on her back much, or especially near her face, but when the water flowed, the corners of her mouth turned upward, and I could tell that she was smiling again.

Not long into it, the trunks of all three elephants were swirling wildly in the air, trumpeting so much that I felt like I was in a concert hall. At one point, Nepasha gathered as much water as she could from the hose and sprayed it indiscriminately, soaking me in the process. But it was all in good fun, and it was getting hot anyway. Olivia and Udokwe laughed, as if that happened to all newcomers. But I didn't care; I laughed too, for I felt truly content to be here with them and the elephants. I did not miss working at the reserve much, but knew I had to go back in a few hours, which dimmed my exuberance momentarily. I did not want to leave Olivia; her presence was simply too enthralling. But I couldn't let her know that—not yet, anyway. I caught myself, on more than one occasion, getting lost in her alluring, almond-shaped eyes.

"All done!" Olivia said. "You all can go frolic and get dirty again out in the yard. It's just about lunchtime. Are you hungry, Joe?"

"Starving, now that I think about it," I said. "I've just been so engrossed with the elephants that I think I forgot!"

"We'll go inside and grab some lunch, and then it will be feeding time for the little ones," she said. "Some are still drinking milk, but most are eating a normal diet. And their food supply is getting low, I think, right, Udokwe?"

He nodded.

"After lunch, you and Udokwe can go into the bush and get more," she said. "Then you boys can get better acquainted."

Udokwe and I looked at each other and nodded simultaneously, though what I really wanted to do was get better acquainted with Olivia. But I had to stay on task; I knew that was the best way to make a lasting impression.

We made our way out of the barn, passing the Lily's Way sign that resurrected painful emotions as we walked into the main house. It was a small one-story house with a few rectangular windows and a pitched roof. The living room to the left of the entrance had a musty dark brown couch in front of a brick fireplace, with a rickety old chair opposite the couch. There was a small wooden table in between, and a beautiful painting above the fireplace of elephants grazing in distant golden fields. To the right was a small kitchen with cream-colored walls and a few light brown cabinets, an electric stove, and a small counter. A round wooden table rested in front of a window just beyond the doorway to the kitchen, where I assumed we would be eating. The house was dark and dusty, almost like no one had been living in it, which surprised me.

"You came on the right day, Joe," Olivia said as we entered the kitchen. "Udokwe made his specialties."

"It's not goat's head stew, is it?" I asked her warily.

"No, why?"

"No reason."

"We're actually vegetarian here, so there's no meat in the house," she said. "What are the dishes called, Udokwe?"

"We have *ndizi*, *bugali*, and of course, my favorite, *ibiharage*," he said as he opened a small rust-stained refrigerator that looked at least fifty years old.

"Sounds delicious," I said, not trying to dwell on the no-meat policy. "But what are they?"

"Well, *ndizi* is a fried plantain dish. *Bugali* is a white starch that looks like mashed potatoes, but doesn't taste like them. And *ibiharage* is a delicious kidney bean stew, cooked with onions and chilies."

"Sounds hearty," I said, not disclosing my distaste for onions.

Olivia and I sat down at the table while Udokwe heated up the food on the stove. I heard a swamp cooler kick on in another room, which I was grateful for, as I felt beads of sweat again forming on my forehead.

"So, Udokwe does all the cooking, huh?" I asked Olivia playfully.

"No, I have my specialties too. Maybe one day you'll get to try them, if you can hang around long enough," she teased back with a smirk. "What is an African woman without her recipes?"

"Fair enough!" I said. "So, what's your heritage, anyway?"

"I'm half South African, half Dutch," she replied as Udokwe set the steaming, intensely aromatic tray on the table, neatly divided into his three specialties. "My mother was South African, and my father was Dutch. I speak three languages: English, Dutch, and Afrikaans, the latter being the language the Dutch spoke during their colonial days in South Africa, and it's still spoken today."

"That's quite a background. But I noticed you mentioned your parents in the past tense?"

"She doesn't want to talk about that," Udokwe snapped, killing the pleasantries.

"Oh, I'm sorry. I didn't mean—"

"No, it's okay, Joe, you understood correctly," she said. "They're no longer here on Earth with me. They crossed over a long time ago. But they were wonderful people, and I miss them very much. Now, let's eat; you boys have to get to the bush."

I scarfed down the food, which was oddly sustaining, despite its lack of animal protein. But my body was certainly going to have to adapt to the new diet.

We talked about the elephants, their individual quirks and habits, and what day-to-day operations entailed. Attending to large animals' everyday needs sounded like grueling work, but I was excited and ready to dive right in; anything was better than being out in the bush with bullets whizzing by my face. Olivia could sense my enthusiasm. Udokwe? I wasn't so sure. He was cordial, but obviously also very protective of her. At times, he gave me looks that made me believe he could sense my full intentions. But I wasn't about to let that deter me. Fate was in control of my vehicle, and I was going to let it steer wherever it desired. Besides, my intentions were noble, even if Udokwe didn't approve.

We finished lunch and hooked up a large open-ended trailer to the back of the ATV, something that would be used on a farm to haul hay. Udokwe normally pulled it with a tractor, but the ATV was much faster. He threw a couple sizeable machete-like blades in the trailer, one serrated, as well as tree-trimming shears, and off we went to fetch dinner for the elephants.

The bush was less than two miles from the edge of Olivia's

property, but it felt like many more with me riding on the back of the one-seater, hanging onto Udokwe's shoulders. Somehow, we made it work, uncomfortable as it was.

The bush that pressed up against the lowland's golden foothills was dense and shaded, littered with several varietals of trees, some of which I recognized, like acacia and eucalyptus, and some that were foreign to me. The underlying brush was thick, and we had to plow our way through. Thorns, which I had become accustomed to, pricked the sides of my calves as we rode, drawing faint streaks of blood. Pants would've been by far the better attire.

"Use the blade to hack through when you can no longer walk," Udokwe said in his accented perfect English as we hopped off. "The freshest stuff is right over there. You want to look for leaves that are soft and green, and branches that aren't too thick. They're young elephants; they can't devour trees like their parents."

"I understand."

We spent the next hour trimming and cutting and sawing when necessary, carrying our loads back to the trailer parked about twenty yards away. My arms, which were also exposed, soon began to resemble my legs, and the wounds from the thorns began to sting and ache. Udokwe didn't say anything, but shot me looks like I was a stupid, unprepared American. We didn't speak much, and I was sensing more and more like he didn't fully approve of my presence, but I sought to change that.

"So, Udokwe, how did you end up here?" I asked.

He shot me a glare, pondering whether he wanted to engage. "I usually don't talk much when I work," he replied curtly.

"Oh, okay," I said as I sawed through a low-hanging limb, wondering if I had hit a sore spot.

"You really want to know? Or are you just making conversation?"

"No, I genuinely want to know. I enjoy learning about other cultures and where people come from."

He paused, stopped trimming, and reflected for a moment, staring at his blade as a slightly sinister look streaked across his face. "Are you familiar with the genocide in Burundi, Joe?" he asked, returning his blade to the branches on the ground, hacking with more aggression than before.

I began to regret my inquiry. "No, I don't think so," I replied. "I know about the genocide in Rwanda in the nineties."

"They are one and the same," he said. "They stem from the same evil. Do you know where Burundi is?"

I shook my head.

"Burundi is a country only a few hundred miles or so west of where we are right now," he began. "It's a small country that borders Rwanda. Most people are aware of the genocide that took place in Rwanda, but few have heard of Burundi."

"Yeah, there was actually a popular movie made in the US called *Hotel Rwanda*," I said. "Sorry, please continue."

"The war was between the Tutsis and the Hutus. They had political and socioeconomic differences, and they hated each other. My family was Tutsi. One day, when I was returning from town several miles away, I came home to find both my parents and my younger sister savagely murdered."

He stood in silence, palpably somber, staring at the ground. I didn't know what to say.

"They used a blade very similar to this one here," he said, pointing it in my direction. "The wounds were fresh, and I could sense that they weren't far, so I hid in the tiny shack we used for a toilet for over a day and a half. When darkness fell, I gathered whatever food and water we had left and fled east. I thought I would be spotted by Hutu militia and hacked up too, but someone or something guided me to safety. Part of me wanted to die, but something primal, something instinctual kept me fighting inside. But my story is not unique. I am not special. Over twenty thousand Burundian Tutsis were slaughtered. It was an ethnic cleansing."

"I'm speechless," I said. "I'm so sorry, Udokwe. I can't imagine. I…"

"Don't be sorry. You didn't kill them," he said with a crackle in his voice as the awkwardness only grew.

"Everyone goes through trying times, but some experience things no one should ever have to endure," I said. "I feel for your loss, Udokwe. You don't have to tell me, but how did you end up here with Olivia?"

"I made it all the way to Arusha, only by the grace of villagers who sheltered and fed me along the way. After a few months of just trying to survive in Arusha, I heard about a woman in Tanzania who was rescuing elephants. We had a family of elephants that lived near our home in Burundi, and a few used to come around and say hello. I had developed a bond with one of the young ones. Elephants remind me of the joy I used to have in my life, so I came here to see what it was all about. And as fate would have it, she needed help the exact day I arrived. So, here I am. Been here ever since."

"Amazing," I said.

"So, how did *you* wind up here, Joe?"

"Also fate, I suppose," I said, not wanting to relive my trauma as he just did. "But I do empathize with you. My daughter was killed."

He didn't say anything, but I could tell he was moved. He stopped cutting and looked up with his dark, mysterious eyes, and compassionately smiled ever so gently. And with that, I felt our relationship shift.

We didn't say much on the way back; there wasn't much to say. We unloaded the trailer that was piled to the brim as the sun caressed the golden hillside. The elephants came out from the barn and tromped around the lot, munching on the fresh vegetation that was put in a rusty bin behind the barn. Nepasha greeted me briefly, sticking her trunk out and touching my elbow, but she was too preoccupied with hunger to stay for long. I watched the animals parade around and play in the afternoon glow, feeling tremendous gratitude for the opportunity to work with such unique creatures. As I turned to head into the house to see if the day's tasks were complete, Olivia walked out to meet me in the courtyard.

"Good first day?" she asked, her wavy hair still damp from a shower.

"Indeed, it was! I thoroughly enjoyed it, thank you. I learned about Udokwe's story, which was pretty intense, but I think he may be warming up to me, so that will be good going forward."

"Oh, he told you his story, huh? He's had an unimaginable life."

"That's an understatement. So, is that all for today?"

"I think so. Are you coming back tomorrow?"

"That's the plan. Every day, eight a.m., right?"

"Good. Yes, that's perfect. Are you hungry?"

I was starving, but didn't want to wear out my welcome. "No, I'm okay, thank you. I'll see what Ashi fires up later tonight back at the reserve."

"She is such a sweet woman," Olivia said. "I've only met her a few times, but she's so authentic. I like her a lot."

But before I could agree, Olivia caught me by surprise. "You know, we have an extra room here with a cot, if you want to spare yourself the ride back," she said, leaving me stunned and momentarily speechless. If she only knew…

"Thank you, but I'd better not. It's been a successful first day, but I don't want to impose. But I look forward to what tomorrow has in store."

She thanked me, waved goodbye, and walked back inside as I rode away, thinking about how I could barely wait to see her face again. But my bliss suddenly turned to trepidation as I wondered how I would be received by everyone back at the reserve.

I approached the reserve as day bid its final farewell and gave way to the pale moon's evening prowess. I half expected to ride up to find everyone sitting at the fireside table, talking behind my back about what a quitter I was. But to my delight, the compound was quiet. A faint flicker illuminated the side window by the kitchen, and my curiosity superseded my hesitation as I crept up the creaky stairs, poking my head through the screen door.

"Hello?"

There was no response, only the kitchen light's continuous hum. I called out again. This time, a woman poked her head around the corner, clearly shaken up, as the whites of her eyes resembled saucers until she realized I wasn't a perpetrator. "Oh, hi, Joe," Ashi mumbled, looking relieved but aggravated. "I was in the back bedroom, reading. They didn't tell me you were coming back tonight. You frightened the devil out of me."

"I apologize," I said. "I didn't mean to startle you. I'm working with Olivia during the day, but coming back here to sleep in the evenings. For now, anyway. Where's the team? Are you okay?"

"They were supposed to be back by now," she said with obvious angst. "I've been worried for the last few hours."

"Where did they go?"

"I don't know exactly, but I know they went far," she said. "I overheard something about Jemba and surveillance of Ahmed. Abasi wouldn't even tell me."

"Hmmm," I said pensively, pretending not to know what they were up to in an effort to keep her mind at ease. "I don't know either, but personally, I'm kind of glad they aren't here. I feel like everyone is upset with me."

"Some of them are," she said, not holding back. "But I am not one of them. I understand why you wanted to go work with Olivia. I don't hold it against you. Ever since the guns arrived, the mood has changed. Everyone is acting more militant. It reminds me of the militias that used to control the land where I'm from. And Abasi is not a fighter. I fear something is going to happen to him, just like Jafari."

"I hear you, but everyone will be okay," I said with my best poker face, hoping she couldn't detect my uncertainty. "The captain and Aaron will have them well trained, I'm sure."

But I wasn't at all sure. Ahmed was a very dangerous man, and I knew they could've walked right into a trap.

"Do you want me to stay up with you?" I asked.

"I'm a grown woman, but thank you, Joe," she replied, still frowning. "It's good to see you though. There's meat in the fridge if you're hungry." She turned and went back to her room.

I grilled up some meat that smelled like wild boar, but I couldn't be sure. I ate it by the empty firepit near our barrack, visualizing a roaring blaze as my eyes began to droop. I wondered how Adam was doing, and what he would say to me in the morning, but my thoughts were becoming jumbled and unfinished. So, I stumbled into the dark quarters, kicked off my shoes, and fell face down on the tiny cot. It had been a long day, but a good one. All I could think about was Olivia, dreaming about her for what felt like half the night. Her soft, full lips. Her dimples below her high, rosy cheekbones. Her slender, curvy waist.

I couldn't wait until the sun allowed her to become my reality once again, but for now, I was content to dream.

I DIDN'T HEAR ADAM COME BACK, but his snoring certainly alerted me to his presence as the sultry, luminous morning entered the room through the cracks in the walls. It was just after 7:00 a.m., and I was due at the sanctuary in less than an hour. I could not wait to see Olivia again. She was my new drug. Adrenaline replaced the need for caffeine.

I rose from bed and quietly tiptoed to the corner of the room, slipping on my pants as I heard Adam stir. I did miss conversing with my friend, however, and just as I turned around to see if he was awake, he beat me to the punch.

"So, how's your lady friend?" he asked disingenuously, yawning.

"She's great. I love working with her . . . and the elephants. How are things going with the mission? Ashi was worried last night. When did you all return?"

"Pretty late," he said hesitantly, as if I shouldn't be privy to classified details anymore, but he couldn't control his enthusiasm. "Man, I tell you, I know it's not your brand of vodka, but it's a whole new ball game, having the guns! And not just any guns, but full-on modern assault rifles the captain scored. We were doing some late-night surveillance of a suspicious clearing in the middle of dense bush that we were tipped off about. I bet it's Ahmed's refuge. You wouldn't believe it, Joe. Impossible to describe. But hopefully, it won't be long 'til we put an end to that criminal."

"I sure hope you guys do," I said. "That would be a massive step towards conservation efforts in the region. So, is everyone upset with me?"

"The feelings are mixed... They're not really upset, but some are disappointed, and they don't really understand. I'm probably on that list. But it's all good, my brother. You gotta do what you gotta do, right?"

I nodded, albeit half ashamedly. "Well, you be careful, Bach. I don't want to hear about some American fighting for elephant justice gunned down by an assailant. It's a dangerous game out there."

"I'm aware," he said overconfidently. "We got this."

"I gotta run, but hopefully I'll see you all tonight for some dinner," I said, grabbing the keys to the ATV and stepping out the door.

"Hey, Joe!" Adam called out. "How's the little elephant we rescued, by the way?"

"Fantastic," I said with gratitude and a grin.

I had the route to the sanctuary almost memorized, and the ride was fortunately devoid of angry male elephants as I stayed close to the road. I pulled in right on time. Olivia was out front, bent at the waist, planting lavender and yellow flowers around the fountain, her long, tanned legs glistening in the radiant morning sun.

"Gorgeous!" I said with dual meaning as I cut the motor.

"You like them?"

"I don't just *like* them," I replied flirtatiously. "Where did you get them? There aren't exactly a lot of nurseries around here, as far as I know."

"Oh, you're a funny guy this morning, huh?" she countered. "No, I took a little walk into the hills and saw a patch of wild-flowers, so I dug up a few and put them in a moist pouch I brought with me."

"They're lovely," I said, recalling the strikingly similar colored wildflowers along the trail to Shady Cove, squatting next to her and using my hand to shovel some dirt her way, picking up her addictive scent. "I enjoy gardening myself. So, what's on the docket for today?"

"Well, in addition to the usual stuff, like feedings and scat duty, we're going to get our two young ones more acclimated with some training, similar to what their mother would have shown them in the wild. They have to learn these skills if they are to survive when they're released."

"Makes sense," I said as some exuberant trumpeting escaped the barn.

There were only three little ones in the barn: Jomo and the two baby sisters, Kioni and Mukami. Jomo was rolling around in the straw used for bedding as the other two were draped all over Udokwe, their trunks scouring every pocket for food. They were not too much older than infants and had to be fed constantly. I said hello to Udokwe, who seemed back to his typical, solemn self.

"Where's Nepasha?" I asked Olivia, but Udokwe answered instead.

"Out in the hole."

"'The hole'?" I repeated.

"Yeah, did you notice the depression in the earth towards the back of the lot yesterday?" he asked.

"No, I was too focused on the poop, I guess," I said with a little chuckle.

"We dug out the hole when the well was installed, and we fill it with water for the elephants once a week. The dirt is so dry and firm that the water has a hard time seeping into the ground, giving the orphans a chance to simulate a very critical part of elephant life: playing and bathing in water."

"I see," I said. "And it looks like these two are hungry for breakfast?"

"Indeed, they are!" Olivia said, heading out of the barn. "I'll go make the formula."

The two sisters were joined at the hip, mimicking each other's every move. Where one went, the other followed. They were hard to tell apart, but they both shared a distinguishing feature: massive heads that stood out compared to their still-growing bodies. They had soft eyes and curious trunks and still walked with a slight wobble.

"When these two were found, the men thought they were dead," Udokwe said. "They were curled up in the searing heat, with their eyes shut, next to their faceless mother. But they must not have seen the tragedy unfold, because they don't seem as scarred as some of the others."

"Wow, that's hard to even think about," I said, wondering if

Nepasha had seen her mother get hacked up. "They sure are sweet and playful for being so young."

"Yeah. But some, like Sasha and Nepasha, took much longer to come around," he said, as if reading my mind. "There were trust issues."

"Yeah, if someone mutilated my family, I probably wouldn't trust a human ever again," I said, forgetting for a moment that I was basically describing Udokwe's past.

Before I could apologize, Olivia walked back into the barn, holding two large metal canisters that were shaped like water bottles for cyclists, only much larger, and with a rubber nipple around the top. She handed one of them to me.

"Me?" I asked as Udokwe quietly sauntered out of the barn with his shoulders slumped and his head down.

"Yep!" Olivia said, Kioni clinging to her side, trunk squirming for the bottle. "You get to feed a baby elephant today!"

I was intrigued but somewhat nervous as we sat on an old, unstable wooden bench near the barn door. Olivia taught me how to angle the bottle ever so slightly downward, so that the babies could get all the liquid. The bottle had to be placed pretty far inside their mouths for adequate suction. But once they latched on, they were in heaven. Their trunks curled and calmed, and their eyes closed as they savored each drop of the nourishing con-coction. It wasn't real milk from an elephant, but they did not seem to mind. For a second, Mukami, who was a tad smaller than Kioni, gently rested her heavy head on my knee, still firmly attached to the nipple.

"You can stroke their foreheads as they drink," Olivia said, demonstrating. "They love that. It gives them a sense of reassurance, like they would've had with their mother."

I followed her lead and gently pet Mukami's forehead as she gulped down the liquid. Her skin was dry and cracked, with bristly little hairs sparsely scattered in no particular pattern. She appeared comforted by my touch, so I kept my hand moving up and down her face as I looked over and locked eyes with Olivia. She didn't coach me or say anything. She just gazed at me in a way that seemed to cross into different territory, away from a working relationship. Several moments passed, but her sweet stare persisted. I wasn't sure what to do or say, so I just kept my eyes deep in hers and smiled. Oh, how I wanted to lean in and kiss her—so much so that I nearly forgot about holding the bottle for Mukami. I had no idea whether or not my feelings were reciprocated, despite her face suggesting that perhaps they were. But I wasn't about to find out and potentially ruin my new situation—not yet, anyway. Luckily, Mukami helped break the silence as the suction ceased, and her trunk tried to reach into my shirt pocket to look for more food.

"No, that's all Joe has, sweetheart," Olivia said with motherly affection.

For a second, I had a flash vision of Olivia holding our child, but quickly snapped out of it, feeling completely ridiculous.

"Fun feeding them, isn't it?" she said as Kioni's bottle ran dry as well.

"It's quite an experience, I must say," I replied.

"You have a nice way with them, Joe. They respond to you. So, tell me, is it Joe or Joseph?"

I was amazed that she asked. No one had called me Joseph in years. She genuinely seemed to want to know me on a deeper level; otherwise, why would she have cared what my full name was?

"It's Joseph, which was my grandfather's middle name. He was a kind, charismatic Italian man, but he passed way too young, when I was just a teenager. I love the name, but I've always gone the easy route with Joe. Just plain ol' Joe."

"I like your name," she said. "Good, strong name."

"Oh, thank you," I said, looking down at the ground, attempting to avoid another eye-locking moment. I wasn't sure if I could resist temptation a second time.

"Should we go see what the others are up to?" she asked as she stood.

"Let's do it," I said, with more than half of me desiring to stay right there on the bench with her.

We met Udokwe and the rest out in the large enclosure under a green tarp canopy that protected the orphans' fresh skin from the scorching heat. I noticed sunscreen applied to their ears, except for Jomo, who had clearly been rolling around in the dirt all morning and was now covered in dust. Several of them were playing with plastic toys that a human toddler would enjoy, except Nepasha, who dropped hers and rushed up to greet me, as had become customary. Then she, Mukami, and Kioni said hello to each other, trunks intertwined in the sweetest encounter one could imagine.

"You give them human toys, I see," I said somewhat judgmentally, wondering if it violated the rules of nature and rehabilitation.

"They're social creatures, Joe, not to mention babies as well," Udokwe snapped. "They need to play, just like human babies do, to develop the motor and social skills they'll need in—"

"Sorry, I didn't mean—"

"No, it's fine," he said. "I'm sorry. I didn't get much sleep last night; the little sisters kept me up all night."

"They got you out of bed, huh?"

"No, I was in my bed, which is also their bed."

"You sleep with the elephants?" I asked incredulously.

"When they're real young, I often do. It makes them feel safe, as if their mother were still around."

"Wow, that's righteous of you," I said as Olivia stepped in to sever the tension.

"Yeah, we have them play with a variety of toys in the sanctuary to develop much-needed trunk skills," she said. "As you know, they use their trunks for just about *everything*. You see?" she said as Nepasha dug into my pants pocket on cue. We all shared a good laugh, even Udokwe.

The rest of the morning went well as we played with the elephants, teaching them different ways to pick up and move objects, while observing their interactions. Sometimes Debo, who was older and bigger than the rest, would seem bored and become too aggressive, so finally he got a time-out in the water hole, which I'm sure he preferred, splashing and spraying to his heart's content. The others eventually dropped their toys and ran over to join. Elephants could not resist water; it was their obsession.

The sun rose to its zenith in the hazy blue sky, and my stomach was gnawing with anticipation of lunch as we walked back towards the barn, the elephants still playing in the lot.

"They're having fun. Let's eat, and then we'll feed them," Olivia said, just before stopping in the middle of the lot, noticing something on the ground that reeked. "Udokwe, did you see this?"

He shook his head.

"One of them has diarrhea, and I bet I can guess which one," she said, striding back over to the elephants. She bent down and opened Jomo's mouth while simultaneously inspecting his eyes before bringing him back to us. He cried out the whole way.

"He's still teething, and I think he has a fever," she said. "I'm taking him into the barn. I'll meet you guys inside shortly for lunch."

I looked back at the group, where Nepasha's ears were propped fully forward, concerned about the well-being of her male companion.

"He's going to be fine," Udokwe said as we walked back to the house. "It's common when they're young."

THE REST OF THE DAY PASSED as briskly as the first, and the first month flew by even faster. I was so engrossed by the job, each day learning more and more about the operation and the elephants, their traits, their quirks, and their tendencies. But getting to see and work with Olivia every day was the icing on the cake. I began to develop a unique bond with all the orphans, except Simi, who remained guarded, with my gender being the reason, according to Udokwe. But I didn't buy that, considering Udokwe was no less male than me, and Simi was fine with him.

Nothing, however, came close to the bond that was forming between Nepasha and me. Everywhere I went, she followed. Everything I did, she mimicked. When I shoveled, she scooped dirt with her trunk. When I used the hose, she used her "hose." When I struggled to cut thick branches, she snapped them in two with ease. We were buddies; that's all there was to it. It was becoming difficult to leave her every day, as it was with Olivia. But Olivia and I were crafting a closeness as well, deeply conversing at times, playfully flirting when appropriate, but remaining more professional than I had hoped. I did take her up on the offer to stay the night in the guest room on a couple of occasions, as the job lasted well past the moon's arrival in the night sky.

I yearned to tell Olivia of my feelings, but just couldn't bring myself to utter the words. But I thought she knew. She had to. She was a woman with uncanny perception. But I was not going to let the assumed linger in the air for much longer. I had to confirm my intuition—but in doing so, I would risk losing her, the work, and Nepasha, and I knew it.

The third time I slept over at the sanctuary, about a month and a half into the job, I awoke to birds singing just outside the window in a group of kigelia trees that skirted the front of the lot.

A deep blue sky greeted me as I rubbed the cold from my eyes. It was Saturday, and a fine one at that. I wasn't sure what it was, exactly; perhaps it was the feeling of the wind dancing through the bedroom, but something told me that it was going to be a different kind of day. Whether that was good, bad, or something in between, I did not know. I had not been much of a morning person in the past, but I couldn't wait to see what the day had in store. Secretly, I hoped to spend it with Olivia. Our affection for each other had been effortlessly growing with reciprocity.

I slipped my legs into my pants and gathered my belongings as I made my way down the dusty hardwood-floored hallway that led to the kitchen. And there was Olivia, sitting at the table, reading, looking as brilliant as ever, her big blue eyes sparkling in the sunlight creeping through the window by the door. I stood in the doorway, caught up in the moment, just staring at her for probably way too long. When she finally looked up, I pretended to be searching my pockets for keys.

"Oh, here they are!" I said convincingly. "Good morning, Olivia. Reading anything interesting?"

"Morning, Joe!" she said with graceful cheer, showing off her perfect smile. "Just the pamphlet I get each month on the poaching activity in the region. Things are delightfully quiet this month after the surge over the last couple months. Did you sleep well? It was such a taxing day yesterday."

"I did, thanks," I said, wondering if the captain's expanded efforts were closing in on Ahmed's Mambas, keeping them at bay. "Sorry I had to sleep here last night; I'm sure you have things to do."

"I told you, anytime, Joe. I don't mind at all. It's nice having you here."

"Thank you, I enjoy being here," I said, turning for the door. "I'll see you on Monday, bright and early."

As I stepped outside and shut the door, breathing in the fresh, dry air, swinging one leg over the ATV, I heard the door creak open before I could fire up the engine.

"Where are you rushing off to?" she asked in her soft yet self-assured voice.

Before I could answer, she answered for me.

"I have an idea. How 'bout I make us breakfast, and then we go on a nice, long hike? We can search the area for any signs of orphans, and then, there's something I wanna show you. Unless you have to be back at the reserve…"

I tried to play it cool as my heart rate amplified, but my reply shot out like a cannonball. "No, they won't miss me! But are you sure you don't need a break from me? Too much of me can be addictive, you know."

"I told you I like having you around, didn't I?" she said, brushing off my playful arrogance. "C'mon, I'm going to cook something up."

WITH NOURISHED STOMACHS, we dressed for the bush and set out through the back gate towards the hills, where golden grasslands gave way to dense woods. I asked if Nepasha could come along as she watched us walk by, ears perked up, with an eager but confused look in her eye. Just as we stepped out of view, she let out her signature call, a long-winded, high-pitched trumpet followed by two abbreviated, vibrating rumbles. But Olivia said the others would get jealous if we only took her, and if we were to encounter an injured or dead calf, it could be traumatizing.

I was nervous yet excited as we ascended the hillside underneath the outer edge of the canopy. I wasn't sure if her proposed excursion was intended to be business or pleasure, but the latter was capturing my imagination as I watched her glide up the hill with ease. Her shape was mesmerizing: a diminutive waist, contrasted by round, full hips and toned legs, accentuated by her skintight beige leggings. She had a figure that would make an hourglass blush, and thus, I did not mind letting her lead the way, to say the least. But when she bent over to tie her shoelace, placing one foot on a pointy brown boulder along the path, I just kept trucking past her to keep from gawking. As I did, my jaw nearly hit the ground. She was truly a sight to behold.

The dynamic started out a touch awkwardly at first, almost feeling like a first date with its unusual quietness, but eventually, the easy, natural rapport returned. There was, however, something different about her demeanor that I couldn't quite place. But it was a good different—an inquisitive different. As we walked in and out of the bush, she instructed me on the things we should be looking for: fresh scat piles, elephant and human footprints, dried blood, or anything a poacher may have left behind. Oddly though, she seemed much more interested in studying me than teaching me. It wasn't long into our conversation before I sensed that her intentions were not just work related, which was exactly what I had hoped.

"You know, I just realized that in all the hours we've spent together in the past couple months, I've yet to learn where you're from," she said, catching up to me.

"Well, you've been too busy being an amazing mother to the orphans," I said as she smiled and looked at the ground. As strong and confident as she was, compliments tended to bring out her bashfulness. "I'm from the Bay Area in California. Do you know California?"

"Of course!" she replied. "I first learned about California being known for its world-class surfing, similar to my hometown."

"It's got that for sure! It's a stunningly beautiful state. Particularly, the rugged, picturesque coastline of the northern part is simply breathtaking. I wish you could see it."

"Perhaps I will one day," she said with a change in tone and a suggestive smile.

Was she flirting with me? I tried to pick up additional clues while continuing the dialogue.

"We have a pretty scenic coastline near my hometown as well," she continued.

"And where is home, exactly?"

"Just outside Cape Town, South Africa, in a somewhat rural area, with gorgeous green highlands and an abundance of wildlife."

"Ah, I've heard wonderful things about the beauty of your country. I assume that's where you found your love for animals?"

"Yeah, and especially elephants. They used to come graze on

our land quite often. But I do fancy the ocean too, which wasn't more than an hour away. Sometimes I miss home. Well, a lot of the time, actually."

"I can imagine," I said, watching her face turn reminiscent. "If you don't mind me asking, what were your parents like?"

"Well, my mother was a beautiful, strong woman who was born in Johannesburg, which is the largest city in South Africa, and that's where she met my father."

"Was he native to the region as well?" I asked.

"He was, yes, but his lineage came from the Netherlands. My great-grandfather came to Africa during the colonial period, when so many European countries had their hands in the continent's treasure chest. My great-grandfather actually fought in the Second Boer War. Are you familiar?"

"Actually, yes! It was a war between the English and the Dutch for the right to exploit the resources and people of Africa, right?"

"Wow, I'm impressed!"

"Don't be, I watch a lot of *Jeopardy,*" I said, expecting a laugh. But I quickly gleaned from her expressionless face that she had never heard of the American TV show, which should've been obvious, so I answered more candidly. "That was a dumb joke," I said. "I studied history in college."

"I see," she said. "I find history fascinating too."

All I could think about was how fascinating I found her, but I couldn't let her know just yet.

"I really like your accent," I said.

"Do I have a really strong accent?"

"A little," I said, hoping I didn't offend. "And a delightful one, at that."

"You like it, really?"

"I could listen to it all day, every day," I replied, shocked that I had let my subliminal thoughts escape my lips. But she didn't mind, just smiled, and again, her eyes fell to the earth.

"So, I'm assuming your dad was white and your mom was black?"

She didn't reply for a few seconds, still looking at the ground, apparently deep in thought as she negotiated a sizeable tree stump in our path. I was worried that I might have brought up a touchy subject.

"I was just wondering if your parents were interracial. I apologize if that's too personal. You don't have to answer."

"No, I was just thinking, I'm sorry," she said. "Yes, they were. I'm very proud of my mixed heritage. It opened my eyes to a lot of things growing up, especially as a girl coming of age during apartheid."

"I bet," I said, not wanting to press the topic unless she did.

"Despite his upbringing, I'm thankful that my father believed in the opposite of colonialist ideals and actually entrenched himself in South African culture, joining the faction that helped end apartheid, breaking from his ancestral tradition. We still have a lot of work to do as far as racial tensions go in South Africa, but 1991 was an important landmark in the nation's history."

"Nelson Mandela was an incredible man," I said. "He lived an incredible life."

"I don't know where my country would be without him," she said in agreement. "We all cried when he died a few years back."

"'I don't lose, I either win or I learn,'" I said, hoping she knew the famous Mandela quote. Luckily, she did, and she again seemed impressed with my knowledge of her country. "What was it like growing up during apartheid?"

"It was rough at times," she said as her facial expression hardened a touch. "I saw several people die in the streets, fighting for their right to simply exist. Fortunately for me, I'm light-skinned, which provided some privilege and protection compared to what others had to endure. But still, being treated like a second-rate citizen is truly a horrible feeling. It does make you stronger in the end though, I will say that. I am who I am today in large part because of what I experienced, even though I was pretty young."

"Well, I think who you are is pretty great," I said.

"That's sweet, Joe, thank you," she replied with reddening cheeks, and our eyes met briefly before she turned them back to the red clay beneath our feet.

"I have always maintained that the single worst notion a person can possess is to believe that another human being is inferior strictly because of the shade of their skin," I said passionately. "It's not only morally wrong, it's borderline evil."

She did not respond, but I could tell she felt similarly. She peered at me again, more deeply this time, melting my heart with her stunning baby blues.

"You're a different kind of guy, aren't you, Joe?" she said, holding my gaze.

"I just try to live by a strict code of morality and integrity, that's all," I replied. "I wish it came as naturally to others. If people would just treat others with kindness, love, and respect, societies wouldn't have half the problems they do. There is a severe lack of empathy in the world, that's for sure."

"For animals as well," she said, and I nodded in agreement.

We kept trekking over a crest and onto a moderate downward slope, neither of us knowing what to say for a moment. I thought about her heritage as I again admired her perfect golden-brown skin. I wasn't sure if I should extend the conversation, but she beat me to it.

"You've had problems with race in your country too, right?"

"Without a doubt! It started centuries ago, stealing people from West Africa and forcing them into bondage. The wounds from that original sin have never really healed. Many people in America don't like to think about or accept that history, so they just push it right out of their minds and sweep it under the rug. But racial injustice against black people is happening in every city, every day, even as we speak. The institution of slavery became the institution of segregation, which has evolved into the institution of prejudice, profiling, and imprisonment."

"You seem pretty passionate about it," she said.

"Yeah, I'm a pretty big champion for the cause. It makes me so angry when I think about it. Growing up playing so many sports, I had so many great teammates who were black. I got to know them, and I relied on them like a soldier would in battle. A bond and a trust were formed, and I thought of them as brothers. I could never understand how people could develop such hate for another group, folks they would never even meet. In the end, we're all the same inside. And the truth is, until we as a species learn to raise our collective consciousness, racial tensions will forever persist."

She smiled warmly, but didn't quite know what to say next. I could tell that she was comfortable talking about race and appreciated my sentiments, but I decided to change topics and ask her something that had been on my mind since I started at the sanctuary.

"So, I have a question for you—and don't worry, it's not about race," I said.

"Yes?" she said curiously, but with slight apprehension.

"What is the significance behind the Lily's Way sign outside the barn?" I asked.

Her face turned a touch melancholy while she paused for a few moments. "Lily was my favorite," she replied. "She was like Nepasha is to you. She was the sweetest baby girl. But she died before her third birthday from a rare disease. I tried so hard to save her, but she just grew so weak. It's hard to talk about, really. Why do you ask?"

I noticed a glossy film forming over her eyes as I took a deep breath and attempted to gather my own emotions. "I had a Lily too, spelled the same way. The sign startled me when I first saw it. I thought it was a sign from the universe or something."

"A sign, huh?"

"Yeah, do you believe in signs?"

"You mean like supernatural or spiritual signs?"

"Either or."

"I absolutely do. But hold on, mister, I want to know more about this Lily."

"Well, like your Lily, it's hard to talk about," I said. "But I'll try."

I stopped walking and inhaled all the elements I could to calm my system as the words struggled to form into sounds. But Olivia did not appear impatient, only comforting.

"She was my daughter," I said with a lump in my throat. "She passed away not too long ago. She was only five."

I stood motionless and stared off into the distance as flashbacks flooded my brain. Olivia, being the ever-nurturing force that she was, could sense my distress and took a couple steps towards me, placing her palm on my shoulder. Her gentle touch soothed my mind immediately.

"I'm so sorry, Joe. I thought you were going to say you had a pet named Lily. I had no idea. I…"

I knew she wasn't going to ask how Lily died, and a part of me wanted to tell her, but I didn't want the day to take a morose turn.

"Lily loved elephants. And one of the last things she ever said was that when she got older, she wanted to help save them."

"So, that's what led you here, isn't it?" Olivia asked astutely.

"How did you know?"

"Joe, I'm a woman," she said confidently. "You are finding yourself, your mission, your purpose through her vision, her memory."

"Damn, you're good. I suppose that's exactly what I'm doing."

She caressed the back of my shoulder one final time as we

just stood there for a few moments, the awkwardness no longer present. She looked deep into my eyes with sincere admiration as I locked onto her radiant blues. Time seemed to bend, like in an intoxicating dream, and in her eyes that reflected the color of the sky above, I could see the rest of my life. It was as if everything I had experienced in the past had led me to where I now stood—as if it were meant to happen. All of it. I yearned to kiss her, and I sensed that she knew, as she inched closer and closer to my face, gently biting her bottom lip. But something held me back—the same thing that had held me back for my entire existence: fear. And before I could give myself a pep talk, she smiled and backed away. I fought hard to not reveal any disappointment, but inside, I was kicking myself. Hard.

The sun was climbing to its apex in the bright blue sky as a few high clouds began to form behind us far in the distance. I couldn't discern if the increasing perspiration gathering on my brow was from the heat or the anxiety of the moment. Olivia turned and began walking up the rocky slope as I followed, wondering if I had just blown my chance, my opportunity—perhaps my only opportunity. Then she spoke.

"Well, we've searched for tracks enough today, wouldn't you say?" she asked, again flashing her mesmerizing smile. "C'mon, Joe, it's Saturday, and it's gorgeous out. There's something I want to show you."

With piqued interest, I followed, ascending deeper into the grove, which provided some welcome shade. We kept losing any semblance of a path and had to cut our way forward at times, but she knew the route perfectly, as if she had trekked the hill a thousand times before. Blisters were forming on the balls of my feet, and my back began to stiffen, but I did not complain. I briefly paused to pick up a black arrowhead-shaped rock that caught my eye before striding up the hill, energized by the adrenaline of anticipation. I would follow her just about anywhere she wanted to go.

We hiked for what felt like hours, but it was probably just a few miles. The foliage became ever denser, completely blocking out the light overhead as something resembling a trail appeared, leading to a dark and narrow entrance in the hillside. The temperature plummeted and visibility dimmed as we entered the rocky cavern.

"Watch your step," she said, interlocking two of my fingers with hers as she guided us through.

"Boy, it's dark!" I said as the luminosity behind us continued to wane. "I've never been in a cave before. How far does it go?"

She chuckled.

"Why do you laugh?" I asked.

"You'll see," she replied, gripping my hand with more vigor than before. I could feel the sweat from the rising heat between our palms. Her hand felt tiny in mine, and as soft as her cheek.

We didn't go too far into the narrow corridor before vibrant light that spanned the spectrum began to shine through up ahead, crisper with each carefully negotiated step. My pupils constricted as I regained my vision, still clutching her palm. My adrenaline spiked in anticipation of what the light would uncover when we stepped out from what I had initially thought was a cave but turned out to be a tunnel through the rocky hillside. I didn't have to wait long. What was revealed was one of the most beautiful things I had ever seen.

"Not too bad, huh?" she asked as I just stood there in awe, not realizing that she had slipped her hand from my fingers, resting it on her hip.

"Simply breathtaking," I replied, soaking it all in.

The gap in the rocky hillside from which we emerged opened on a blue oasis with a forty-foot waterfall, surrounded by a coliseum of light grey slabs of stone, lined with rusty-red streaks and lush green ferns at the base, intermixed with pink and white flowers reaching towards the light. The water cascaded courageously into a crystal-clear shallow pool below, illuminated by the rays above. The sediment created a glowing turquoise hue that left me at a loss for words. It was not something I imagined when I thought of the African bush. It was truly a hidden gem. I stood and marveled at the beauty so intently that I didn't notice Olivia making her way across the stony steps towards the falling water. Clouds of mist ricocheted off the waterfall, cooling my body as I began salivating at the prospect of my head being ravished by the continuous flow. But just as my body began to cool, a primal heat overtook me as I glanced to the right of the falls.

There she was, in all her splendor, making me as eager yet nervous as ever, provocatively stripping off her garments one by one, until she was left with nothing but a lacy bra and white underwear that accented and hugged her every curve. The beauty of the setting was surpassed only by the beauty of her. Although I tried, I couldn't peel my eyes away as she undid her ponytail and ran her hands through her wavy chocolate brown hair, peering at the pool below. She looked at me and smiled as the sun hit her face, making her way over the rigid rocks to the shimmering water. I stood motionless and watched as her tiny waist was submerged, and before I knew it, she was gone, frolicking beneath the surface, leaving me with a choice. She emerged on the far side of the pool, the water glistening on her body as she opened her eyes and seductively raised her index finger out of the water, beckoning for me to come.

In my mind, my pants were being ripped from my legs and tossed aside, but my body stood motionless. I had to keep reminding myself that it wasn't a dream, that I wasn't still in bed sleeping.

"You coming in or what?" she asked.

I snapped out of it just in time, before she gave up on me. "Of course I am!"

With my clothes thrown to the side and stripped down to only my black underwear, I submerged with confidence and felt the rush of electrons engulfing my senses. The water rejuvenated my being as I made my way to the top, wiping my eyes before opening them. And before I could say how sensational it felt, Olivia was swimming straight for me.

"Good, yeah?" she said, revealing her cute dimples.

"Spectacular," I said, hoping she sensed that I wasn't just referring to the water.

"I thought you'd like it," she said seductively, sticking with the coded dialogue.

She swam closer until she was practically in my lap, gently placing her hands between my shoulders and chest, one, then the other. Slightly below eye level, she gazed up at me with her large, sparkling eyes, rendering me powerless. She inched ever nearer to my face as I placed my hands on her perfectly rounded hips just below the surface. Her nose tickled mine as I picked up her alluring scent. She looked at my lips, then back up at me, teasing with every suggestion. Just as my lips were a tantalizing second away from hers, she withdrew, giggled, and slipped through my arms, back underwater, not returning for air. I caught my breath as I saw her head emerge at the edge of the falls, the water caressing her hair and running down the small of her back. She looked over her petite shoulder at the effervescent water, as if patiently waiting, inviting me over.

I surged through the water as if I were escaping quicksand, not wanting the moment to pass me by yet again. I appeared behind her in a flash, placing my hands on her waist, more convincingly than before, conveying to her that this time, I did not want her to slip away. I bent my head down to the slope of her neck and gently teased her skin with my breath. Our waists converged, gliding over each other like tectonic plates as I noticed goose bumps springing up on her round, supple breasts. I felt my blood rush, rerouting to the procreative parts of my body. She placed her hand on mine and squeezed as she turned to face me, the water from the fall dousing both of our flanks, beading down her silky-smooth golden-brown skin. I took my hands off her waist and placed them gently on the sides of her face, slowly moving my right hand towards her chin, sliding a finger over her luscious bottom lip, right before my lips found hers as bravely as an arrow. She tasted so sweet that I couldn't pull away. Luckily, she didn't want me to. She pulled me under the fall as we ignored the rush of the water spraying our faces, passionately kissing for what felt like an eternity. Instinctively yet tenderly, my left hand made its way from her face over her tantalizing breast before gliding back down her side, returning to her hips. She only kissed me harder. I wanted to pull her onto the flat, smooth slab of stone to the side of the falls, but I knew we should wait. There was so much exhilaration yet to come.

But I could never have imagined what was looming just over the horizon.

We exited the tunnel in a state of sheer bliss, not speaking, just sensing each other's elation over where the road might lead. There was a certain tranquility in the air, a stillness, with not a breath of wind. Again, Olivia took me by the hand, stroking my index finger ever so slowly, and I knew that what had taken place under the waterfall had changed everything.

As we descended the rocky hillside and made our way out of the woodlands, the dry golden basin below was all the eye could see for miles, with lone acacias scattered here and there. The hazy, faint outline of a mountain range far in the distance was one of the only things that gave a sense of depth and distance.

But between the mountain range and where we stood, the sky had taken on a different attitude. Thick layers of ominous dark grey clouds billowing towards the heavens had replaced the infinite blue dome. I released her fingers and pointed as we stopped and assessed.

"That's odd," she said. "Those clouds are very atypical for this time of year. And they look like they're in the vicinity of my property, right where we're headed."

"They look like they're carrying buckets of rain too!" I said. "We'd better hurry."

We descended another few hundred yards as we headed towards the shaded valley floor, when suddenly a deep rumble shook the terrain beneath our feet. Olivia looked at me with a fear that I had never seen before on her typically jovial face, but I didn't quite know what to make of it. And then it hit me: where there was thunder...

And before I could complete the saying under my breath, three blinding flashes shot down from the heavens, one much more radiant and elongated than the others. The concern on her face only intensified as I stood stunned by the powerful display of nature.

"This is not good, Joe," she said as she began to scamper down the hill, while I tried to keep up. Just as we reached the bottom, and before I could realize the true cause for her concern, a plume of smoke rose from a grove of trees about a mile or two in the distance.

"Joe, the elephants!" she cried, breaking into a sprint. "We've gotta get to them!"

With my heart pounding like a drum, I ran as fast as I could, ignoring my shoelace that had come undone. I couldn't believe what was happening. I had never considered lightning in a place that rarely saw rain, but in the rare moments when it did occur, the land was so incendiary that grave danger was never far away. It was clear that the Earth's climate was changing, and I knew that. The droughts were longer, the terrain was drier, and the fires burned hotter. I thought of Nepasha and all the others. My future was the sanctuary. My future was the woman running like the wind in desperate haste to my left. I was not going to let her down. I channeled all the clarity I had as beads of sweat dripped off my face, the smoke growing darker, thicker. I had to come up with something.

"We have to call Captain Stewart as soon as we get to the sanctuary!" Olivia said. "We may need all his people to help us transport the animals."

"Okay, but we're not losing your sanctuary," I promised, not knowing if my idea would work or if we would even get there in time. "I have a plan."

"You have a plan?" she echoed, with more than a hint of doubt in her voice.

"My dad used to volunteer for the US forest service when I was young. He dealt with a lot of disasters involving fire. He taught me several tricks to keep a structure from going up in flames."

My burnt lungs gasped for oxygen as we approached the sanctuary, but it was not from the smoke that permeated the air; it was simply from the rate at which we ran back to the property. But there was no time for rest. From atop the hill that bordered her land, we could see black smoke rising from a thick grove, and I could make out the orange glow of flickering flames in the treetops. There was a fair amount of parched, yellow-ochre grasslands covering the hills, but Olivia's land was fairly barren and cracked, not suitable for much vegetation, and thus, not ideal for fire, which aided our chances. But her house was made of wood, and the blaze on the hill was likely to spread rapidly, so we had to act fast.

"I'm going to go call the captain!" Olivia yelled, racing toward the house, but first stopping by the barn to check on the elephants, who were trumpeting like I had never heard before. "We need to get them all out of the barn!"

"I get it, but we have no time to round up the elephants!" I shouted back. "We need to act now! Send Udokwe out here immediately!"

I ran over to the hose that was connected to the well near the fence that walled off the training pen. I assessed its length. It was just long enough to reach the house, but not nearly long enough to make it to the other side of the lot.

Udokwe finally raced over to me, utterly distraught. "The elephants are going crazy!" he said. "It was the lightning. It was so close that it shook the barn!"

"I know, we saw while we were coming down the hill," I said. "Udokwe, go grab your biggest rake. I need you to rake the lot like your pants are on fire! Put any loose leaves, branches, or brush in piles near the well. Also, bring me a hefty pair of shears."

He did not seem appreciative of being ordered around, but he knew that now was not the time to argue. He ran to the barn and scurried back, handing me the pruning shears, then began raking like his life depended on it. Looking up at the malignant fire, I knew that it basically did. There were no trees on the lot, other than in the very front by the entrance, which was a godsend, as the fire would have a hard time reaching that far over bare terrain. But there were several hazardous desert-like bushes resembling tumbleweeds scattered throughout that needed to be removed. I raced around the property like I was trying to set a world record in an obstacle course, severing each one at its base. Then I soaked each branch and loaded them into the trailer that was attached to the back of the ATV, and I took them as far from the house and the burning hillside as possible. Finally able to catch my breath, I ran past the barn and could see the elephants nervously pacing around inside.

Olivia came out, flagging me down. "Nepasha is missing!" she cried, frantic. "I've searched the whole property! And the captain is out with the team on a mission! We're on our own, Joe!"

"What do you mean, she's missing?" I asked with elevated angst as my heart sank. "She's not a set of car keys! She's a two-ton pachyderm!"

"I don't know, Joe, but we have to find her!" A tear rolled down her cheek.

"We will, Olivia, I promise," I said, again making uncertain guarantees. "But right now, we have to fireproof this place. Try to get the elephants out of the barn; I have to hose it down. But first, I need to move several bales of hay from the barn to the back to create a resistance line."

I loaded up bale after bale and spread it out in a three-foot-wide barrier that ran the length of the lot. But I knew the hose wouldn't reach more than halfway, so I drenched half of the hay first before laying it down. Udokwe did a stellar job of raking the area and helped scatter the bales, and we added the soaked trimmings to the barrier. I looked up at the hill as the flames were jumping from one tree to the next, scorching the grasslands, filling the air with floating ash. I knew the fire would be at the base of the hill in no time, and we didn't have long. Udokwe found me a power wash nozzle that he kept in the barn, so I doused the structures as well as the surrounding ground to the point of complete saturation, to protect from flying embers.

Olivia came out and watched me toiling to save her sanctuary like it was my own. What she didn't know was that I loved it as if it did belong to me, so it wasn't a difficult choice. I could see the gratitude in her eyes, and the fear momentarily subsided as she rested her head against my shoulder. All we could do was wait. But as I saw the blaze leaping down the hill like an advancing militia, I knew the grove that extended for miles into highlands—the grove we had just come from—was in jeopardy, even if the sanctuary was spared. And I sensed in my heart that somewhere in the dense, threatened woodlands, Nepasha wandered, frightened and alone—again. Looking for Olivia. Looking for me. But we were at the mercy of the unbridled flames. We were at the mercy of the wind.

We stood and watched the fire slalom down the hillside, the heat growing more intense the closer the flames came. We re-soaked the structures and the barrier several more times, hoping the embers that flew above wouldn't find any fuel. But as the day waned, I realized there was not much more we could do. Fortunately, the wind appeared to shift to the north, away from the sanctuary and the forested mountainside to the west. I didn't know if it was a good time for bravery, but I knew I might not get another chance if the wind reversed course. I told Udokwe to man the hose as I ran into the house, grabbed some gear and a blade, and set out towards the trees for the second time that bittersweet day.

"Where are you going?!" Olivia demanded.

"I'm going to find her!" I said, trying to relay confidence. "I know she's in that grove up there."

"Not without me" she said. "Udokwe, protect the elephants at all costs. We can always rebuild the sanctuary."

He nodded.

We left through the rear gate, and it didn't take long before we spotted the mangled fence along the very edge of the lot that Nepasha had apparently destroyed in her panic, setting her free to roam. It was nearly impossible to elephant-proof a fence, due to their sheer strength. We hacked our way through the bush as smoke from the nearby blaze permeated the air, calling out for her at every turn, but she was nowhere to be found. We covered the whole grove, assuming she would not venture up the mountain unless it was a last resort. Crunching through thorny brush that scraped my legs with every step, I began to lose hope.

"She couldn't have gone far," I said.

"I don't know, Joe, they can move when they really want to," Olivia said. "She could be miles away by now . . . and in the opposite direction!"

"Maybe, but I just know she's here in this grove. I can feel it. I can't explain how, but I can sense her."

Dusk fell upon us without warning, and before we knew it, we could barely see twenty feet in front of us. The last place in the world a person would want to be after dark was in the dense African bush with no visibility, especially near an unrestrained wildfire.

"I want her back too, Joe. I do. But we have to get back. It's not safe out here. Elephants are smart; she may have already made it back to the sanctuary."

"She's here!" I snapped. "I know it!"

Olivia didn't seem to appreciate my irrational tone and fell quiet as she turned and began to head back. I knew I wouldn't remember the way out of the grove without her, so I decided that discretion was the better part of valor as I changed course, following her toward the tree line, jutting in front to help cut her a path, but I could barely see the shoes on my feet.

I couldn't believe we were giving up; it felt like a betrayal. We called out to Nepasha again and again, but heard nothing in return. We were cutting and stomping through dense brush and were nearly at the clearing, when suddenly, I stumbled as my foot ran into something large but soft—something foreign, yet somehow familiar. It was warm against my leg. Before I could get a closer look, that warmth began to curl around my leg like a boa constrictor, and for a brief second, an image of a massive snake flashed through my brain. Olivia was unaware and passed by me as I held my breath, bent down, and examined what was wrapped around my limb. I half expected something slimy, or something scaly, but as I grazed my palm over the familiar body, I knew exactly what it was. The tiny, bristly hairs played over my fingertips as my palm made its way to the base, where an open, dry mouth was struggling for air. I ran my hand over the thin cartilage I knew to be an ear, waiting for my eyes to better adjust to the darkness to make a positive identification. But it wasn't necessary. I knew it was Nepasha.

"We found her!" I shouted to Olivia as she whirled around in astonishment. "She must've been half under this big bush, but her trunk caught my leg like a snare."

"Oh, my goodness!" she cried, bending down to confirm. "Are you hurt, sweet girl? You frightened us!"

Nepasha rumbled so low and deep in her body cavity that I could feel the vibrations as my hand caressed her neck.

"It's too dark to assess. We just have to get her to her feet and get out of here," I said.

"Yeah, she seems a little weak," Olivia added. "I'm so glad we found you!" She kissed Nepasha's forehead.

The little elephant was hesitant to rise to her feet, leading us to think she might be injured, but we gently kept coaxing, knowing that an elephant moved only when ready. She finally caved after a few minutes of Olivia whispering in her ear.

The darkness only grew thicker as we headed for the edge

of the canopy, the land lit only by the subtle beams of the crescent moon overhead. We crept through the brush with our eyes peeled as they adjusted to the night, and I desperately tried to ignore the thorns that ripped through the top layers of my skin. It was too dark to cut us any sort of clearance. I admired Olivia's keen ability to negotiate the terrain, and of course Nepasha, who toddled between us, had little trouble. I bent down to feel the blood trickling down my leg when Olivia stopped abruptly, and Nepasha followed suit.

"Joe, do you see that?"

"I can barely see Nepasha three feet in front of me."

"No, look to your left, through the grove."

I focused my eyes and locked onto something strange that appeared to be around a hundred yards deeper into the trees. Pairs of bright fluorescent greenish-yellow speckles of light that blinked intermittently glared in our direction.

"I'm not going to tell you what those are, but we need to move—calmly but quickly," she said quietly.

She didn't need to. Despite the distance, I knew the sinister shape. They were eyes—hungry eyes. They could only belong to one species, the most regal of them all—the one that ruled the land on which we were trespassing. My heart was racing so fast that it skipped beats the entire way back. Out on the open plains, we were sitting ducks. If the lionesses had been sent by the king to fetch a meal, a meal they would have—and a multicourse one, at that. But for some unknown reason, we were spared. Guided by the scent of ash and the dimming glow that still speckled the hillside, we arrived at a home that had some-how remained intact.

Olivia stood next to the barn for a moment before taking Nepasha inside. The light from the barn lit one side of her face as she stared up at the smoldering hill. Another tear crawled down her face as she turned to me and gently raised her arms around my neck, embracing me for what felt like an entire minute. I could feel her appreciation through her fingers.

"Thank you, Joe," she said softly as she pulled away, leading Nepasha, who was still shaken, into the barn.

I didn't respond. I didn't have to. She felt the love and thank-fulness flowing through me as well.

It had been an exhausting day, but adrenaline was still cours-ing through my body. I took a shower to rinse all the grime and soot from my skin and crawled into bed, bypassing dinner. But I couldn't sleep. Images from the entire day flooded my mem-ory, from the lightening to the fire, to the steely, glowing eyes of the lions. But one image in particular kept me tossing and turn-ing: Olivia, standing beneath the waterfall, water careening off her immaculate physique.

I opened my eyes and realized that I'd never heard the floor-boards creak, as they always did whenever Olivia retired to her room. The light from the kitchen still reached under the door as I sprang out of bed and down the hall to see if anyone was awake.

I was hoping to see Olivia, but it was Udokwe who greeted me instead.

"Helluva day, huh?" I asked as he loaded some food from the fridge onto a plate.

He did not respond, did not even look at me; he just kept preparing his late-night snack. He was clearly upset about something, but the day had been too grueling for me to press the issue. I assumed it was because we'd left him to go find Nepasha, but it was too late to quarrel, so I switched topics.

"Hey, have you seen Olivia?" I asked.

He still did not look up. He just raised his arm and pointed out the window towards the barn. I went back to my bedroom, slipped on a pair of shoes, and walked out the door, ignoring him as I left. The placid moon lit the ground as I passed underneath the sign that never failed to evoke haunting memories of Lily.

I unlatched the gate and peeked inside. The barn was pitch black, other than the beams of light that came through the gate and the holes in the wooden walls. All the elephants were oddly quiet in their stalls, considering the events of the day.

"Olivia?" I called in not much more than a whisper. Nothing. I tried a little louder as I passed the first stall. "Olivia? You in here?"

A light flickered on towards the end of the barn in the second-to-last stall: Nepasha's.

"Is that you, Joe?" she whispered back. "I'm over here!"

I followed her innocent voice towards the light, placed both hands on top of the stall door, and there they were, as adorable as ever. Nepasha was deep asleep, lying on her side in a bed of straw, her trunk curled up, her mouth forming a little grin. Olivia, wearing a silky white dress with her hair pulled back into a ponytail, was curled up a few feet away on a dark blue blanket, facing her.

"Hey there, how's she doing?" I asked, trying not to wake Nepasha.

"She was still a little frightened when we got back, but I rubbed her forehead for a bit, and she fell asleep almost instantly. I just wanted to sleep with her tonight, in case she's missing her mother."

"Oh, that's nice. She looks peaceful. I couldn't sleep, and I never heard you come in, so I just wanted to see if you girls were okay. I'll let you get back to sleep."

I took my hands from the top of the gate and turned to leave, when her soft, sweet voice stopped me dead in my tracks.

"You're leaving so soon?" she asked as my heart skipped a beat. "The blanket is big enough for two, you know."

I couldn't believe she'd asked, but I wasn't about to argue. I unlatched the gate and tried not to cause a stir. Nepasha's trunk flopped to the other side as the gate snapped shut behind me. I tiptoed over to her and pulled up a brown blanket that was keeping her hind legs warm. I crouched beside her and placed my hand on her neck, just behind her relaxed ear. I could feel her deep, reverberating breaths as I softly stroked her back near her spine. I did not mean for her to wake, but one long-lashed amber eye cracked open and peeked at my shadowy face, lit by the flashlight next to Olivia. She quickly slipped back into a state of utter content as I removed my hand from her hide.

"Boy, I'm so glad she's okay," I whispered as I stepped around Olivia's feet and lay down beside her. "What a day."

Several seconds went by with nothing but utter silence. A cricket that had found its way into the barn disrupted the growing tension. Olivia was in the fetal position, still facing Nepasha. I could not see her face, but I did pick up the pheromones escaping her body as she inched closer to me, not totally knowing exactly why she wanted me here in the first place. I could sense that she was deep in thought, despite not being able to see her face. I felt an uncontrollable urge to touch her as I scanned the curvature of her hips in the silky dress that hugged her body, partially illuminated by the light. But somehow, I resisted the temptation, as I couldn't seem to pick up her vibe.

And just as I stretched out my right arm to use as a pillow, she cut the light. The moonlight that came through a nearby window outlined her silhouette, but I could see nothing else. My other senses began to take over, picking up sounds of stirring elephants in nearby stalls, accompanied by the incessant cricket. But the scent of a barn filled with pachyderms was somehow completely replaced by the natural scent of her—a smell so sweet that I had to edge closer. As I did, she took me by surprise. Her delicate hand reached back, finding my arm with acute precision, gliding it down until she had the back of my hand in her grasp. She pulled it towards her, wrapping it around her body like a blanket, leaving me no choice but to erase any distance between us. I curled up to her, my bent legs fitting into hers like a puzzle. I could feel the heat escape from her body as her scent became more and more irresistible.

"Are you cold?" I asked her. "I could go grab us another blanket…"

"No, I'm perfect. You just stay right where you are, mister."

A couple minutes went by before she began lightly stroking my forefinger with the tip of hers as I lay torturously still, my body pressed tightly against hers. A sensation trickled over my entire body that rendered sleep impossible.

"I'm so glad you're here, Joe," she said. "And I'm so grateful for what you did today to help save this place."

I wanted to tell her that it was her place that was saving me, but instead, I remained silent as the tingling in my body matured. Her scent became overpowering, and I lost all control of thought. My subconscious took over as I began to react on instinct alone. I lifted my head from my arm and leaned in closer to her exposed neck. Her fragrance hit my nostrils, creating a sensory overload that traveled to my brain and down my spine. I began to breathe softly on her neck, running the tip of my nose ever so gently towards her ear and back down. I could feel her respond as I did it once more. She began to caress my hand with more zeal as any trepidation that I'd previously felt flew out of my body—a body that was increasingly operating on autopilot.

I tenderly kissed her neck, barely touching my lips to her skin as she began to breathe a little harder. My lips opened a touch wider as my tongue started to taste a sugary sweetness that complemented her fragrance. She gripped my hand harder as I kissed the lobe of her ear, causing a ticklish squirm of her body. She tried to hold still, but she couldn't take it any longer. She turned her head towards mine, and our lips interlocked even more vigorously than they had beneath the waterfall. I felt her tongue caress my upper lip as I could feel my arousal reaching its zenith. Without meaning to, I pressed my body against hers even more firmly as she continued to kiss me with vivacity. I did not know where the night was going to lead; we were lying on a blanket in the straw next to an elephant, after all. But Olivia immediately took any guesswork out of the picture. To my sheer astonishment, but undoubted delight, she took her hand off mine, reached behind herself, and started rubbing tantalizingly near my zipper. The excitement was palpable as I began caressing her silky-smooth inner thigh just below the bottom of her dress. But despite my exhilaration, I was not going to force the issue, realizing that it was all happening so fast—perhaps too fast. My conscious mind began to war with my mammalian brain. But before I could even grapple with the notion, she again let me know her intent.

"I want you, Joe," she said convincingly, breathing harder, unbuckling my belt.

I didn't say anything, just kissed her with passion, letting her know that not only did I want what was about to happen, I wanted *her*—all of her. She sensed my sincerity as I began to pull up her dress, but as I did, she grabbed my hand. For a second, I thought I had done something wrong—acted too fast, perhaps. But before I could even speak, she turned and rolled, straddling me like a gymnast, kissing me yet again, seizing control. I didn't know if it was her way of thanking me, but nearly as soon as she was pulling my pants towards my knees, my eyes were rolling back in my head, and a sensation I had not felt in well over a year rendered my brain incapable of thought once again. We moved brilliantly in concert on the hay, savoring every touch, trying not to wake the baby sleeping in the corner.

WEEKS TURNED INTO MONTHS as Olivia and I began to cultivate an effortless love. We simply clicked. The things we cared about and wanted out of life were congruous in all the right ways. Similarly, how we viewed the Earth and our place in the universe was also in alignment. She was impossible not to adore, and for many more reasons than her striking beauty alone. She had a heart of gold, and a soul that could not be qualified by earthly measurements. And being an old soul like me, she helped my soul to not only heal, but to flourish and grow.

I began spending one hundred percent of my time at the sanctuary, and not long after we first made love, Olivia invited me into her quarters permanently—something that Udokwe did not like at first. He subsequently almost quit, perhaps due to jealousy, but eventually let it go.

We took in another orphan, a weary little male, brought to us by another anti-poaching outfit in the region. His leg had been caught in a snare and badly cut. The men who'd found him surmised that the mother, who had been viciously mutilated very nearby, would not leave her bound baby, and she had paid the price with her life—and the baby was almost certainly forced to watch. We healed his physical wounds, but his mind remained shaken as he struggled to fully integrate with the other orphans.

Olivia gave him an abundance of love daily, hoping he'd turn a corner, and named him Jasiri, or "brave" in Swahili.

My work was increasing around the sanctuary, but I loved every second, treating the property as if it were my own. My relationships with all the elephants continued to develop, but my partiality remained with Nepasha. She was my buddy, and we went everywhere together. When I ate, she ate. When I slept, she slept. And she constantly helped me with whatever task I was working on, not realizing that grabbing the shovel from me with her trunk only made the job take longer. But I didn't care. Like a father with his daughter, I never had the heart to scold her. I just loved her company, as I did Olivia's. Every morning when I opened my eyes, I felt so fortunate to be in such a magical place, loved by such special creatures. I had to pinch myself to be reminded that it wasn't all a dream. But as good as it was, one thing kept eating at me constantly, something I could not shake: my abandonment of the team at the reserve, and in particular of my good friend Adam.

I was thinking about him while sitting at the kitchen table on a dreary and unusually cold morning, eating plantains and eggs, my typical breakfast to start the day. Olivia was already tending to Jasiri and the others in the barn. I set down the monthly poaching report and looked out the window at the tips of the eucalyptus trees swaying in the wind. Just as I was about to take my last bite, a cloud of dust preceded by a familiar vehicle caught my eye as it jetted into the courtyard. Aaron emerged in haste, striding towards the house with fervor. A pit emerged in my stomach as the fork I was holding fell from my hands, clanging off the side of the plate and onto the floor. I left it there and rushed out of the house, bypassing socks and shoes. I knew whatever news he had to share was dire.

As I gave him a firm handshake, the look on his face confirmed my suspicions.

"So good to see you, Aaron. It's been a while," I said, waiting for the news. "What brings you to these parts?"

"Well, mate, I wish it was to invite you to a shindig, but quite the contrary. Adam has gone missing. He's been absent for the past couple nights."

I had somehow known it was about Adam. I sensed it so completely that I could have nearly finished the sentence for him. I wasn't shocked, and I wasn't going to pretend to be.

"I knew this day was coming," I said with poise. "The last few times I spoke with him, he was becoming increasingly militant and hostile. I knew he was going to do something brash; it was just a matter of time."

"Any idea where he could've gone?" he asked. "You know him best."

"Actually, I might have one," I said, spotting Olivia poking her head over the barn gate with a look of curious concern, giving an apprehensive wave. "I assume his belongings are still in his barracks?"

"They are."

"His clothing still hanging neatly on the rack?"

"Correct."

"He went after Ahmed, I bet."

"There's no way! He had no method of transportation. It's too far to hike, and besides, he knows that going solo would be a suicide mission."

"You don't know Adam like I do. The man is bold. And he is extremely adept in the wilderness and isn't afraid of death. Ever since you guys acquired those guns, he's become enamored with the idea of hunting down Ahmed. And once you guys found the general coordinates of his hideout, that was all he needed. How far of a hike is it to the nearest main road from the reserve? About nine miles or so?"

"Give or take," he replied, appearing half convinced.

"He left at night when you were all asleep, hiked to the highway, and found a driver to take him the rest of the way. He can be quite persuasive, and he's beyond savvy with direction. I bet if you look a little deeper, his rifle, knife, boots, and flashlight will all be unaccounted for. And probably the map you gave us as well."

"No one is allowed to keep their rifle in their room, but one was missing from the case yesterday morning," Aaron said. "We assumed Adam took it somehow, but he was gone before we noticed."

"So, what now?" I asked him, looking over my shoulder to see if Olivia was still watching us. She was, but pretended to be working on breakfast for the orphans.

"We're discussing a mission to go get him as we speak, which if you are correct, will serve a dual purpose, allowing us to further conduct surveillance on Ahmed's operation as well."

"And let me guess: you want me to be a part of the planning, because I know him so well, correct?"

"Exactly, mate! You brought him here, didn't you?"

I looked at Olivia again, this time for several moments, thinking about my new life that had been carefully crafted at the sanctuary—a life with which I never wanted to part. But the nagging feeling of abandoning my friend that had kept me up nights was pulling from within. And out of nowhere, from somewhere in the deepest caverns of my being, emerged an unanticipated valor. What came from my mouth next shocked even me.

"I'll do you one better: I'll take the lead. He's my friend. I got him into this mess. I brought him here. I'm going to get him out."

The anxiety that was all too familiar returned the second my mouth stopped moving.

"No way. That's suicide."

"I'm not going to be responsible for any of you ending up like Jafari," I said. "You can back me up from a safe distance. But I am sure about this."

"Okay," he conceded after pondering the idea. "But you have to take a rifle with you, even though you aren't a fan."

"Of course," I said, acting as if I knew how to use one. "I'm not *that* insane."

"Alright, come to the reserve tomorrow morning," he said.

I nodded, shook Aaron's hand, and ambled back to the house, a million thoughts racing through my head. He shouted just as my hand made contact with the door handle.

"Hey, mate, I forgot to tell you the good news!"

"More?" I asked with unmistakable sarcasm. "What could be better than the news you just shared?"

"China just put a ban on the buying and selling of ivory. It won't go into effect for a couple years, but make no mistake, Joe, that is a monumental win! A massive development for our cause."

"You're right, that *is* phenomenal news! I'm speechless."

"You get some sleep tonight, Joe. I'll see you in the morning."

I halfheartedly waved goodbye as I opened the front door and sat down at the kitchen table, staring out the window with a blank face, but a cluttered mind. After I had not blinked for what seemed like several minutes, a hummingbird, known as a sunbird in Africa, crashed into the window and fell to the ground. But before I could get up from the table to see if the creature was hurt, the tiny bird shook it off and hovered like a helicopter in front of the window, staring directly at me for at least fifteen seconds. The color on her breast was a brilliant yellow, with fluorescent pink covering her neck. I stared at the little bird in wonderment as I tried to feel the frequency between us. I felt silly for a moment, imagining a connection, but I didn't care; it put my nerves at ease. I took the encounter as a sign—a sign that my decision, again, was the proper one. But I still had to break the news to Olivia.

I gulped down my last ounce of coffee and shuffled down to the barn as if my legs were made of iron that wanted to stay affixed to the earth. Perspiration was forming under my arms as I opened the door. Nepasha broke loose from her bath and came trotting over to wrap her trunk around my arm and say good morning, much to the dismay of Udokwe, who was holding a soapy sponge.

"Hi, sweet girl!" I said, rubbing her trunk. "How's your bath time going? Not too well, I see. You'd better go finish up! I have to talk to your mom."

I led her back to Udokwe, then sauntered into the far stall, where Olivia was fixing a board that Jomo had nearly split in two. She was bent over at the waist, and again, as always, she rendered me speechless, and I nearly forgot what it was that I needed to tell her. She did not look up, nor did she say good morning, but I knew she sensed my presence.

"Whatcha doing?" I asked, but she just ignored me and kept hammering. "Looks like Jomo got a little aggressive in his stall last night, huh?"

Still crickets. I wasn't sure how she could've known anything was amiss, but I had learned long ago that a woman's intuition was a powerful and mysterious thing not to be underestimated.

She stood and turned, looking at me with a steely gaze as the hammer fell to her side. "So, what did Aaron want?" she asked with a rhetorical undertone, as if she somehow knew I had been asked to participate in another mission. I didn't want to lie, but I certainly wasn't about to divulge the whole truth either.

"Well, you remember Adam, my longtime friend whom I came to Africa with? The one you met the day I met you? Well, he's gone rogue. And the team wants me to help locate him."

I didn't even finish my sentence before she turned away and

went back to fixing the board, once again highlighting her curvaceousness, making me further regret my decision to sign up for a possible suicide mission. *Why would I ever want to leave this?* I asked myself, losing my train of thought once again. She stopped hammering, and again she stood, paused, exhaled, and turned to me with moisture welling in her eyes.

"I've gotten close to someone in the past, only to lose them to senseless violence. I don't need that again. But I understand: you have to do what you have to do. We all have a different purpose here on Earth." Again, she took a deep breath. "I was doing just fine by myself. Just me and the elephants."

I picked up some trumpeting from the other side of the barn as once again, I was rendered speechless. Was she telling me not to come back? I didn't want to ask. She dropped the hammer again as a tear rolled down her left cheek. I wanted to tell her how beautiful she was. I wanted to tell her that I wished to never leave her. I wanted to tell her that I loved her. But the words just wouldn't come out. She walked over to me, holding back tears, threw her arms around my neck, and touched her lips to mine for what I prayed was not the last time.

"You be careful out there, Joe," she said, relinquishing her grip and peering into my eyes, wiping an unruly tear from her cheek just before I could. Then with one hand on her hip, she strode out of the barn. And just like that, she was gone. I wanted to run after her and tell her that I would stay—that I would stay forever. But the call of duty was deafening in my mind. Were it not for my friend, perhaps I never would have come to this continent, never would have met Olivia or Nepasha. My soul would have remained lost. I had no choice but to go.

I waved to Udokwe and walked out of the barn, my head drooping as far as my neck would allow, before I crashed down on a knotted wooden bench just under the Lily's Way sign. But for the first time, I didn't think about my haunted past. All I could think about was what was to come, and how I could return with my friend, and to the woman who gave me a reason to get up every morning. I sat there staring at a eucalyptus tree that towered above the rest, swaying in the intermittent breeze that accompanied the morning.

I was just about to go pack my gear when a curious trunk tested the air around the corner. It was Nepasha. She broke away from the others in the yard, who were drying off by hurling fresh dirt at each other. She trotted up as soon as she spotted me, temporarily melting my worries as I stroked her growing ears, whispering into them softly, as if she knew what I was saying.

"I probably shouldn't go, huh? But I must. You remember Adam, don't you, girl? He's my friend, and he might be in serious danger. You understand, don't you?"

She took her trunk and slithered it up my shirt and across my neck before tickling my ear, eventually placing it on my head.

"Hey, that tickles!" I laughed, already feeling better. There was a magic to interacting with a baby elephant, especially when a bond had been created. And just when I thought she was done, she took her gargantuan front foot and draped it over my leg, one and then the other, climbing onto my lap. She then placed her anvil of a head against my breastbone as I could feel the low rumble that she often emitted just before falling asleep. Although the sacs in my lungs were searching for oxygen, I could not tell her to move; it was simply too comforting. I placed my arm around her neck as we just enjoyed the morning sun warming our skin for a moment. An elephant's intuition was an unexplainable thing, and Nepasha's was growing by the day. I was not about to question what she sensed or did not sense; I just knew I was thankful for her presence.

The rest of the day was quiet, with much of the silence coming from Olivia. Whether she was trying to distance herself from me for emotional protection, I could not be sure, but I didn't press; I just let her be. I did as many tasks around the lot as I could to not only keep myself distracted and reduce my anxiety, but also to demonstrate my commitment to her and the elephants.

I didn't eat much the rest of the day, and didn't sleep much more than a wink after switching back to the guest room. The angst was just too overbearing. I forced some nutrition down my scratchy throat as morning arrived all too quick, while guzzling down two cups of coffee to help clear the fog clouding my mind. Like a zombie, I stared blankly out the kitchen window at the sinister clouds that blanketed the terrain for miles. The sky was as dark as my mood. I began to resent Adam for his cowboy ways, threatening my utopian future that was being crafted at the sanctuary. But I knew the decision was ultimately my own, and no one was forcing my hand but me.

I dressed in several layers, not knowing what conditions the day would bring. Before grabbing the keys to the ATV from the dresser, I noticed the arrowhead-shaped black rock that I'd found the day Olivia took me to the waterfall. I tucked it in my inner jacket pocket for luck, crept into her room, and kissed the back of her head. She didn't budge.

As I fired up the ATV, every ounce of me wanted to kill the engine and rush back inside, but my subconscious dread of allowing fear to further dictate my existence kept my legs straddled to the sides as I rode through trees towards the reserve, the morning chill bouncing off my face.

Everything was so familiar as I pulled into the dirt lot, parking in front of the main office. As I opened the door, I thought I would hear the captain on the phone, wailing away at someone, but the halls were silent. No one was stirring in the kitchen, and no aromas permeated the air. It was too late for everyone to still be asleep, and for a second, I fantasized that they had gone on the rescue mission without me. But as I walked down the steps of the main building towards my old barracks, voices began to emerge from the classroom, with the captain's thunderous tone superseding the rest. Class was in session.

I stood on the steps for several seconds, frozen, knowing that if I opened the door, there would be no turning back. I had a vision of hopping on the ATV and riding back to Olivia as fast as the tiny motor would take me. But I just couldn't bring myself to do it. I inched the metal knob clockwise as the door creaked open, hoping no one would notice, but instead, all eyes except Aaron's, the captain's, and Kintu's fixated on me with a punishing glare, as if to say, *"Why did you Americans even come here?"*

The captain stopped talking as soon as he saw me. I prepared for a verbal lashing, but to my surprise, it never came.

"Glad you came, Joe," he said in a calm tone. "Grab a seat. We were just going over the plan."

I sat nervously and studied the aerial reconnaissance photos he was pointing to on the board, doing anything to divert my attention from the stares that I could sense in my peripheral vision.

"Now, if Adam was indeed captured by Ahmed's gang, which is likely, there's a good chance that he will be held here," he said, circling an area in one of the photos, then pinpointing the same location on a neighboring map.

The thought of Adam being captured had never actually crossed my mind. My palms began to clam up.

"There's also a good chance that they would hold him hostage and demand a ransom, but we aren't going to wait to find out. We are, however, going to wait until early morning. Not only does that amplify the surprise factor, but also, as Aaron just alluded to, a rare heavy storm is expected to hit the region overnight and persist into tomorrow. So, we'll go at dawn. I just hope it won't be too late."

After some spirited debate, mostly led by Dota, the meeting was adjourned. I walked out of the building first and stood outside, not really knowing what to do, but I was curious to see if anyone would come speak to me or at least shake my hand. Only one did: Kintu. And for that, I was thankful. Most everyone else just walked on by, except the captain and Aaron, the last two to exit.

"Aaron told me that you wanted to do this alone," the captain began, placing his mighty hand on my shoulder. "But I could never let that happen. Once you come to the reserve, you're like family—part of the team, you see? We take care of all our people, no matter what. It would be highly dangerous for you to go alone. Plus, this will give us the opportunity to get up close and personal with Ahmed's operation, where we believe he keeps his trophies."

"I feel horrible, getting you guys into this," I said.

"Don't," Aaron replied. "It wasn't you who ran off, now was it? Well, at least not to go hunt down Ahmed… Besides, he may not even be there."

"He's there," I said, ignoring his slight jab.

"I think Joe's right," the captain said. "It all adds up the more I think about it. His behavior changed as soon as the guns came in. Part of me regrets ever changing the policy."

Aaron rolled his eyes in clear disagreement.

"Either way, we're going to find out," the captain said. "Train leaves at zero six hundred. Take it easy for the rest of the day. We'll go over the plan again tonight before dinner."

As I walked away, Aaron called out to me. "Meet me in the field an hour before sundown. I'm going to show you how to use the rifles."

I didn't quite know how to spend the rest of the day, so I decided to walk towards the edge of the reserve, like Adam and I used to. I tried not to think about the predicament he was putting everyone in, just tried to clear my head. There was an unusual chill in the air, with the clouds shielding my skin from the sun. I saw no grazing animals off in the distance, and all the wildflowers that had been in bloom when I left were gone.

After several sluggish miles, I headed back the way I came, with a quick nap in my old barrack squarely on my mind. I also wanted to see if there were any clues left behind in the room that would give me more insight into Adam's motives. I thought perhaps I could sneak in with no one noticing, but just before I could open the door, Kintu came up behind me.

"Hey, Joe," he said.

"Oh, hi, Kintu!" I said, acting excited to see him, but really just wanting to be left alone.

"We didn't get a chance to speak this morning in the meeting room, but it's good to see you!"

I had always been fond of Kintu. He was a warm, vibrant soul, so I didn't rush him away.

"It's really nice to see you too. It's been a while, hasn't it? Anything new around here—besides Adam causing everyone problems?"

"We like Adam; he has a good fighting spirit, and he really cares about the work. But yeah, probably shouldn't have gone alone. Not wise."

"You think?"

"We've been learning so much more about the Mambas and Ahmed's operation ever since the day we encountered them in the field. We're getting closer—and they can feel it. And it all started with you and Adam meeting Ahmed in Nairobi."

"That was totally accidental!" I said.

"Yes, but it was critical," he said. "I believe you were meant to meet him that day."

"In a strange way, so do I, Kintu. So do I."

I shook his hand again, and he began to walk away before turning around. "And hey, Joe," he said as I took my hand off the door. "I don't blame you for leaving and going over there. She's beautiful, man. I would've done the same thing." He then flashed his infectious toothy grin and strolled off. I wasn't sure what he knew about Olivia and me, but I just smiled back, appreciating his benevolence.

I opened the door and crept in. The creak of the rickety old floorboards flooded my mind with familiarity. Everything was the same, especially the damp, musty smell of the wood. I scoured the room for anything out of the ordinary that could provide a clue, something that could help me decipher Adam's intentions. His clothes were still neatly aligned on the rack next to the bed. There was nothing on the table besides a book about the Serengeti, and a pen randomly placed with its tip hanging off the edge, as if it had recently been used. I didn't have to meet Aaron for a few hours, and I could feel my eyelids drawing closer and closer together. The stiff old beds that were more akin to cots were screaming my name. Adam's was nearer, so I threw myself down, shoes and all, and tried to free my mind from the prison of anxiety that was growing with each passing minute. I rolled over onto my side, nearly drifting away—until my extended arm felt something sharp, crunchy, and out of place underneath the other pillow.

As I pulled out what I recognized to be a sheet of paper, neatly folded in two places, just enough light came through the cracks in the wood to illuminate the messy scribble on the front in big, bold lettering: *For Joe.* I unfolded it in haste.

*Dear brother,*

*If you're reading this note, I am likely already gone. But take comfort in the fact that although I have lost my life, I lived it to the fullest, in large part because of you. You brought me on this adventure at a time when, like you, I was lost, searching for meaning and truth. Well, brother, I have found it. These past several months have ignited my soul, and I began to feel alive for the first time in years. I know you thought I was happy-go-lucky and indifferent about the world, but I struggled for purpose as well. I kept it bottled up, partly because I knew that I had to discover it for myself. I'm a fighter by nature, and in this world, there is good, and there is evil. We have witnessed the evil up close and personal, and I could not stand by any longer. It was time for me to go cut off the head of the snake. I hope Ahmed meets his fate at the end of my rifle. And although I'm going alone, I am going for you. I am going for the captain. I am going for Jafari. I am going for myself. But most of all, I'm going for the elephants. Please tell the captain thank you for everything. And Joseph, I want you to know, I am not upset with you for leaving. We all have to find our purpose. You*

*found yours. But this one is mine. Godspeed, my brother.*
*I hope to see you again someday, somewhere.*

> *Your friend,*
> *Bach*

The note fell from my hand and hit the floor as tears began to fill my eyes. I was floored and moved simultaneously. I lay there motionless, staring at the ceiling, feeling every beat of my heart. Thoughts spun through my head like a cyclone. There was a good chance that he had already been captured, but a part of me wanted to believe he had been stealthy enough to accomplish the mission and bolt. But I knew that was wishful thinking. He might have already been killed, as his letter suggested, but there was only one way to know. I knew what I had to do.

I looked at the keys to the ATV parked outside. I wanted to leap off the bed and leave, right then and there, but I knew I had to wait. With the cloak of darkness as my cover, when all was quiet, I was going to go get my friend—alone.

I PULLED MYSELF TOGETHER and somehow remembered to meet Aaron out in the field for the tutorial. I did not plan on using the weapon, but I recalled the old adage: it was better to have a gun and not need one, than to need one and not have one. The rifle was so heavy and powerful that it nearly knocked me over upon firing, bruising my dominant shoulder in the process. When we were finished, I took careful note of the combination to the safe where the guns were kept in the main building just outside the captain's office: eight, thirteen, twenty-three. At first, it did not strike a chord, but as I walked down the steps of the building, the synchronicity stunned me. Adam had been born on August thirteenth, and I was born on the twenty-third of October. I did not tell Aaron about the sign, nor did I mention the letter, although I knew I should have. It made no difference. At dawn, the team was heading out to the surveyed area on the rescue mission regardless, and I didn't want to tip my hand in any way as to my plan.

I had Aaron take me back to the classroom one more time before dinner to show me the exact route to and location of the peculiar clearing amidst the trees, which had been gleaned from a few reconnaissance missions over the last couple months. I grabbed a map of the territory that was sitting on one of the desks, telling him that I wanted to study it carefully in my barrack before I fell asleep. Fortunately, he was not on to me. I also pocketed a walkie-talkie from an equipment bag when he wasn't looking, in case my plan went haywire and I needed rescuing myself. Of course, if no one had its mate on hand, it would be totally useless. Still, I felt it was worth a shot.

After dinner, everyone retired early as I sat by the fire, staring into it, envisioning the scene that was about to unfold. All I could see was Adam's passionate, militant face in the flames. I kept waiting for my anxiety level to reach a tipping point and render me incapable of the undertaking, but for once, I had a rare sense of calm. I felt guided by something bigger than myself.

I had the feeling that I was doing the right thing—and because of that, I felt that I would make it back to Olivia safely. Whether it would be with my friend in tow, I could not be sure. What I was certain about was the solo nature of the mission. I was not going to let the team get ambushed because of Adam's dereliction. As my head hit the pillow, I knew my dreams would be faint and sleep would be fleeting, and 4:00 a.m. would come in a blink. I set my watch, just in case.

The wind howled through my old room all night and into the morning, when the alarm sounded. The air was damp, and I knew that the storm that had been brewing the past two days was about to finally show its teeth. I did not mind, however, as the wind and rain would create the cover I needed to escape the reserve before anyone caught on. I just had to make sure to keep my map dry. Time was of the essence, as the captain woke up at 5:00 a.m. sharp, so I slipped on my durable beige camo pants and matching coat, laced up my boots, and grabbed the map, walkie-talkie, and keys from the table. Just before I turned the doorknob, I reached into my pants' cargo pocket to make sure I had Adam's note safely tucked away.

As I snuck across the complex towards the main building, I could feel the moisture in the air sticking to my face, but the hard rain had not yet begun, much to my dismay. The battering of a downpour would have muted my movements, but the gusty, swirling wind had to suffice. My heart began to race and my hands began to tremble as I gently climbed the steps. Fortunately, all the lights were off, and no one was stirring inside.

The door was unlocked, as was customary, so I gave the handle a gentle turn and inched it ajar. I could make out the outline of the gun case down the hall. Tiptoeing to avoid any creaks in the floorboards, I felt like a burglar. I had no story if someone were to catch me red-handed. I would just have to come clean with my motives—motives that I felt were honorable.

I stood in front of the case and used the light on my watch to illuminate the padlock. Eight, turning the dial to the left, thirteen, back to the right, and twenty-three, once again to the left. I gave the handle a yank, but my hand was met with only resistance. I tried the code once again, assuming I had overshot a number, but once again, it would not budge. *The captain must have changed the code last night*, I thought to myself as my mind began to panic. To calm my nerves, I tried telling myself that I did not plan on using a weapon, but the comfort of having one was taking precedence in my subconscious as my hands began to shake even more uncontrollably.

I gave up and got out of there as quickly and covertly as I could, barely latching the door behind me. It would not be long until the team was up, heading out to find Adam. I had to get a head start. It was now or never. Every inch of my body wanted to jump back in bed and forget the whole charade—or better yet, drive as fast as I could and climb back into Olivia's nurturing arms. But as with the day before, something internal kept me going.

I straddled the ATV and fired it up, figuring there was a fifty-fifty chance of the noisy engine waking up the captain. But I had to risk it as I snuck away, trying to avoid revving the motor. I wasn't more than sixty yards past the barracks when an idea hit me: the machete. I ran back as fast as I could to the small red storage shed just beyond the outer barracks. It was unlocked, and again, I used my watch for light, grabbing one of the two-foot blades resting on a wall rack, and scurried off so fast that I couldn't be certain if I'd left the door wide open. I rode off in haste towards the highway, with the machete on the floorboard underneath my feet, just as the downpour began.

According to the map, the clearing was about twenty-eight miles from the reserve—twenty-two miles east along the highway, and six miles into dense bush. Without helicopter surveillance, we might never have uncovered it. But a cleared elliptical gap in the bush, about eight football fields in size, with what appeared from overhead to be huts in the center had aroused the team's suspicions, which were later confirmed by Jemba's squad conducting surveillance on foot.

I was soaked as I approached the twentieth mile, the sideways rain pelting my face. I attempted to stay along the side of the road, cutting through the trees at times, trying to be as undetectable as possible. It was still very early, and few cars were on the highway, but the team was certainly awake and had been alerted to my absence. The old ATV had no odometer, but based on the twenty-miles-per-hour speed I maintained, I knew that I would arrive at the approximate cutover location in just over one hour. There was a small road, Route 11, that I circled on the map, very near where I was to turn north into the bush. Fortunately, my watch had a compass, and as long as I didn't veer from true north, I would run right into the cleared territory.

Very little daylight penetrated the foliage above, which also served as an umbrella, providing some welcome cover from the sheets of water that descended upon the terrain. I knew the team couldn't be far behind, but I also knew they would have to hike a bit more through the bush, as their vehicles wouldn't be able to negotiate all the obstacles. The further I ventured into the forest, the thicker it became. Again, calculating the remaining distance based on my speed, I had about one mile to go, or two as most. The ATV was versatile enough to take me the entire way, but it was too loud, even with the concert of wind and rain swirling about. I knew I had to abandon the vehicle to remain inconspicuous. I parked it by the largest and most prominent tree I could find, grabbed the machete off the floor, and peered in every direction, trying to memorize a landmark or two. But as my boots hit the moist ground, panic again engulfed my body from head to toe. I began to hyperventilate. The only thing that shocked me was that it hadn't come sooner. I had to fight off every urge in my body to get back on the vehicle and turn around. But I had come too far, and Adam was too close.

One cautious foot after another, I hacked my way through the bush and crept towards the target. The rain began to lighten, and the vegetation began to thin, but I had to remain out of sight. I used the widest trunks as my buffer. As I drew near, I no longer needed the map or the compass; the surveillance the team had conducted was deadly precise. The visibility had improved, and the entire area was on display. Still, without binoculars, I couldn't make out many details, but I could see the huts off in the distance. I counted at least ten. I knew I had to investigate, but there was no way to remain covert in such vast openness. I observed from behind a tree for several minutes, scanning for any sign of the Mambas, but the entire area appeared devoid of humans.

Again, I felt the urge to abandon the mission, even if I encountered our team, which was undoubtedly closing in. But something in my gut told me to go on. Something deep within was screaming at me again, overriding any trepidation. Adam was in one of the huts off in the distance; I could feel it. But which one? One of the huts appeared closer to the tree line than the rest, but it was best accessed from the western border, so I kept my cover, stayed low to the ground, and crept my way over to survey the area. I soon realized that I was going to have to make a run for it. It took countless deep breaths for me to calm my body and muster the courage.

I thought I heard a rustling in the trees behind me just before I jetted from the shadows, machete securely in hand. I could feel the wind intensifying, the gusts smacking me square in the face, making the two-hundred-yard dash feel like a mile. Time seemed to tick by in slow motion. I was sure I would be spotted and gunned down in the middle of the field before I could take cover. I closed my eyes and prayed, my legs scampering as fast as my body would allow.

As I drew near, the heinous scene that came into view floored me to the point that I stopped in my tracks in horror before reaching cover. My mind could not believe what my eyes were telling me. The sheer size and scale of it was unimaginable. The huts were not actually huts after all; they were stacks upon stacks of ivory trophies forming the shapes of teepees, just like in my vivid dream the day the captain shot Jafari's killer, with the tips curled toward the dark grey sky and dried blood staining the facades. Some of the smaller ones had clearly been gouged from the faces of hopeful adolescents, but most had been taken from the elders. Many of the tusks were longer than I was tall, making me wonder how massive the victims must have been.

Emotion overtook me as I looked around the sinister site, trying to calculate just how many elephants had been taken from the Earth to produce such a scene. The smell of death saturated the air—or at least, my mind tricked my nostrils into believing it. I nearly fell to my knees and broke down before I remembered that I would become a trophy as well if I were spotted, so I threw myself behind the outermost stack.

Again, I lost focus as I ran my hand down the side of a seven-foot-long tusk six inches from my face. It was dense and cold to the touch. Anger and rage began to replace my sadness as I crawled to the side of the stack and peeked my head around, just enough to get a glimpse of a few of the piles. Still no signs of life. I looked at the forest behind me to see if the team was somewhere watching from the canopy, but I saw no movement. I ducked over to the next pile, like a soldier advancing through a war-torn village. The remaining stacks were all visible from my new vantage point, but that meant I was more detectable too.

The voice in my gut grew louder and louder. I knew Adam was near; I could feel it in every bone in my body. But the question that lingered was, was Ahmed near too?

I darted over to the next trophy stack, and as I did, I noticed something faint wafting through the ivory tips atop the stack in the center. It was the largest heap of them all, stacks upon stacks of tusks reaching over twelve feet. As I snuck closer, checking my flank with every other step, it became clear that something was burning in the heart of the pile, or at least it had been at one point, whispering spirals of smoke into the thick air. For a split second, a vision of Adam's burning corpse in the center penetrated my mind, but I wouldn't allow such a nightmare to take hold. Yet the gnawing in my belly only intensified. I began to feel the earth, the vibration of his presence.

There was a small triangular gap between two of the tusks in the stack that none of the others seemed to exhibit. After several breaths that bordered on hyperventilation, heart racing, I clenched the machete and inched toward the opening. The smoke began to strike my nose, but I smelled no burning flesh. The gap in the pile was clearly meant to be a concealed entrance, as it was not wide enough for a human to squeeze through. I bent down and poked my head through the small gap, but it was too dark to see, and there were no flames to illuminate the center.

"Adam?" I called out softly, but got no reply. "Bach? You in here?"

I knew I had to maneuver some of the ivory aside, but I risked toppling the whole stack over, blowing any sort of cover and crushing anything inside. But I had no choice. I braced my feet on the ground and budged one colossal tusk, then another, just a few inches, opening a seam just big enough for me to wiggle inside without collapsing the pile. I crammed myself through the dark slit and peered inside. My eyes wouldn't adjust to the darkness, so I used the light on my watch to illuminate the center, which was indeed hollow. Images and sounds from my premonition began coursing through my head. Then, behind a wall of smoke, I saw him sitting there in a wooden chair. If he was alive, it was just barely.

"Adam!" I exclaimed, to no reply. "Adam! Are you alive?"

Again, nothing. His chin rested near his clavicle, his head drooping limply off to one side. His hands were roped behind his back to the chair, and the smoldering remnants of a fire sent plumes of smoke towards his face. My watch light was just bright enough for me to see the damage that had been inflicted. He was naked from the waist up, his pants torn, with shallow incisions covering portions of his chest, blood still seeping from several. Clearly, the artwork that was carved into his abdomen was meant to be a deterrent. The slices spelled out the organization's name in all caps: M A M B A S.

Adam was either unconscious, or traumatized and in shock from the torture, or he was dead; I couldn't tell which. I placed my hand underneath his mouth, which drooped open, and detected the faintest of exhalations. He was not dead yet, but he wouldn't last long. I began to panic, unsure of how to revive him. I called to him again and again, lightly tapping his leg, which I could tell had been badly beaten. Still nothing. My heart began to pound harder, and my head began to swirl as fear and rage blended into a cocktail of fury. But I had to stay calm; I knew that.

I grabbed the walkie-talkie from my back pocket, and with the softest of whispers, called out to the team, hoping someone was on the other end. But as with Adam, no reply came. I took my machete and carefully tried cutting through the sturdy rope, but the lack of a serrated edge made it impossible.

"I'm getting you out of here," I said, unsure of my plan, still cutting with little success. I tried ripping the rope apart, but it wouldn't budge. And as I picked up the machete from the dirt, I heard movement from outside the pile of death that nearly stopped my heart. I prayed that it was the captain coming in for the rescue.

"You hear that, Bach?" I asked, as if he were conscious. I gently crawled over to the opening I had created, peeking out. I didn't spot anything, but still heard footsteps in the distance. And then, my worst nightmare was confirmed. Out of the shadows, dressed all in black, Ahmed emerged, with the same black aviator sunglasses, nonchalantly carrying an adolescent elephant's tusk over his shoulder to add to a pile about fifty yards away. He appeared to be alone from my vantage point, which I found incredibly odd, and I couldn't help but wonder why all his valuable trophies were not being heavily guarded.

The fear inside threatened my clarity as I retreated my head from the opening faster than a turtle under siege. I didn't know what to do. I thought about the rifle that I did not have. For a minute, I thought Adam and I were both headed for the same fate. I nearly collapsed to the ground, but as I looked over at him, with his beaten and bloodied body, the fighter in me that burned so brightly in him began to emerge. I decided right then and there, machete in hand, that either Ahmed wasn't leaving alive, or I wasn't.

I knew Ahmed was eventually going to come check on his victim, so I had to get out as quickly but inconspicuously as possible. I placed my hand on Adam's head, said a silent prayer to the universe, and wedged my way out of the seam I had created. When the coast looked clear, I scampered like the wind behind a nearby tusk stack, keeping Ahmed in front of me off in the distance. I peeked around the pile and saw the black truck that was hauling the trophies. He seemed to be alone. I stayed as still and concealed as I could, thinking of my next move—when suddenly, my cover was blown.

*"Joe, come in. Do you copy?"* the walkie-talkie blared, and adrenaline shot through my body like never before. I couldn't believe I'd forgotten to turn down the damn thing's volume.

Ahmed stopped, lowering the trophy from this shoulder, glaring in my direction as I jerked my head back behind a gigantic tusk, unsure if I'd been spotted. Footsteps drew closer and closer, and for a second, I thought about sprinting back to the trees. But I figured he had a gun, even if it wasn't his typical semiautomatic rifle. I stayed put and kept as motionless as I could. Adam was only about twenty feet away in the nearest stack, which began to emanate sounds and words that I could barely decipher.

"Oh. You're still alive, I see," Ahmed said to Adam. "But not for much longer. You'll never escape the Mambas' wrath."

I peeked around the other side of the pile and saw Ahmed exiting into the open. He stood there for a minute, looking around, but decided nothing was amiss. I could only assume he had thought the sudden sounds came from his dying victim.

I could have run. I wanted to run. But a bigger part of me knew what I had to do, or die trying. Time was of the essence. I could not rely on the captain and the team charging in to save us; by then, Adam and I would be dead. Something deep within conjured up the courage to suppress the fear and charge. His back was turned. The time was right. But I knew I couldn't get all the way to him with the machete before he heard the pounding of my feet. I scanned around for other options, but they were limited.

Before he got too far away, I glanced down at the ground—and there was the ticket. Likely a suicidal ticket, but a ticket, nonetheless. A relatively smooth, rust-colored spherical rock, just larger than a baseball, lay near my feet. I picked it up and held it loosely in my hand, feeling the weight, which was heavy enough to inflict serious trauma, but not too heavy to throw accurately. I hadn't thrown a baseball in years, but some things were like riding a bike. I had put faith in my right arm countless times in the past; it was time to do it again.

With my machete in my left hand and the rock in my right, I charged in the name of my friend. I made a beeline straight for Ahmed, knowing he would hear me about halfway there and likely turn and shoot. Thus, like the charging outfielder I had once been, I turned, cocked and loaded my body, reached back, trusted my arm, and let it go just as he spun around. My fate lived in that rock, and somehow, a supernatural force guided it exactly as intended. It was a direct hit, square in the side of his head near his temple, and he collapsed to the ground.

Something paralyzed my muscles as I approached his body, unsure if he was still alive, but I could only assume he was. I cautiously stepped around him as I saw the blood seeping from his head. He appeared unconscious. I kicked his arm that was folded over his body, laying him out flat on his back in the dirt. I felt like taking my blade and filleting him like a fish, but again, something sprung up from within, suppressing any traces of a killer instinct. But that didn't stop me from taking my fist and pummeling his jaw several times until it bled like his cranium. His collared black jacket with silver buttons, covered in dust, was unbuttoned at the top, exposing his upper chest, just as it had the day we met at his restaurant in Nairobi. Again, the top of his tattoo poked through, just under his bristly black beard. Curiosity overwhelmed me; I simply had to finally know what it depicted. I straddled his limp body, ran my blade down the side of his bloodied face to the buttons of his jacket, and ripped it towards me, indifferent to any slices to his chest. My eyes could not believe the image that was revealed, and my heart raced into thumping palpitations. The black tip that ran up his chest towards his neck was the tusk of a dead elephant lying on its side, covering Ahmed's left pectoral.

The rage returned as a fire burned in my stomach. The demon

on my left shoulder was winning the battle against the angel on the other, and I could not repress the anger I felt. The premeditated cruelty and evil that lived within him was being transferred to me. I raised the machete high in the air and glared with squinted eyes at the malicious art covering his heart, and I had a vision of driving the blade straight through it. But something held me back yet again. I was simply not a killer.

Just as I began to lower the blade to my side, I heard a commotion coming from the tree line. I couldn't hear the words, but I knew it was the team, who was watching the scene unfold. I turned to look, knowing help was finally on the way. But as I turned, Ahmed, somehow suddenly awake, swung his arms at me, which sent my blade flying past the pile of tusks several feet to our right. I immediately regretted not ending his life when I had the chance. Fight-or-flight instincts took over as I went to strike him again, but he averted the blow and grabbed me by the shirt. We wrestled and rolled on the ground, crashing into the pile of tusks, which partially collapsed. I thought he would have been weakened by the blows to the head, but I struggled to gain control as adrenaline shot through both of our bodies. With dust filling the air, I managed to work my way back on top of his chest as I felt him release his grip on my left shoulder. I knew he was reaching for his weapon, and once he did, any advantage I had would be gone—and so would I. I had to think faster than I ever had before. My life hung in the balance. I could not wait for the captain.

Fortunately, I spotted an undersized tusk next to my arm that had fallen from the pile amidst the chaos, and without hesitation, just before he was able to raise his gun, I grasped the tusk and clobbered him over the head, splattering his blood on my face. Once more, he lay lifeless. Out of the corner of my eye, I could see the team making their way out of the forest. I didn't know if he was dead, so I kicked his gun away, grabbing a slightly larger tusk from the dilapidated pile that I could fit my palms around. I heard Ahmed moan under his breath for mercy, but I was done with mercy.

I was about to strike a lethal blow to his face, when I recalled a story Kintu had shared with me about what often happened to poachers when they were caught alive. They were offered up to the local native tribes as a gift to be sacrificed—and they were burned alive. I could only hope that Ahmed would share the same fate, and I decided to give him the chance. I took the tusk, raised it over my head, and violently smashed it down on his wrists and ankles, hearing his bones shatter as he wailed in agony.

Finally, the team emerged from the trees, racing across the open field in my direction. A part of me wanted to know what the hell had taken them so long, but there was no time to play the blame game, so I simply waved them over and scurried back to the pile to get Adam out. I separated the tusks, widening the hole even further, and ducked in.

"Adam!" I exclaimed. "Hang on, buddy! I got that son of a bitch! He won't be harming any more elephants, I'll tell you that much!"

His body was as I'd left it, tied to the chair, but his shoulders were more tilted, and his head dangled from his neck as if it weren't even connected.

"We're gonna get you out of here, but you gotta wake up," I urged. "C'mon, wake up, Bach!" I frantically tried to wiggle him free of the rope. But as I touched his depleted body, a chill shot up my spine that was only usurped by the cold that met my hands. I checked for his breath, but I didn't need to. I couldn't even call for help. I was too late.

I fell to the ground and wept as I heard the team surrounding Ahmed. The satisfaction I had felt just seconds prior had swiftly been shattered like a glass egg. And then I recalled what I had always known: there was a yin and a yang to life—sheer beauty, but also utter brutality. One couldn't exist without the other.

I removed the hemp bracelet from Adam's right wrist that he had worn every day since college, and I tucked it safely in my pocket that safeguarded his letter. I put my arms around his neck, kissed his head, and turned to leave as a tear landed in his hair. I didn't even go over to where the team had gathered. I just kept walking, completely drained and delirious, back to where I started, toward a forest of empty nothingness.

I turned my head for just a moment and caught the eyes of the captain, and then Aaron. They were the eyes of ultimate approval. But as I turned back toward the misty woodlands, where the vast openness was met by the living, breathing grove, I felt dead inside.

# TEN

M ore than a year passed before I came to terms with the death of Adam Rorbach. Guilt haunted my being, as I simply could not accept the outcome, feeling responsible for bringing him to the continent. I reread his letter to me hundreds of times, hoping it would provide some comfort and closure, but I just couldn't shed the blame. Moreover, I missed my friend. Not a day went by that I didn't think about him. And what made it even more difficult was that I was just beginning to emotionally accept the death of my daughter.

Adam's body was sent back to his parents in the States, but a traditional African ceremony was held in his honor, despite the absence of an actual burial. I choked through a eulogy, thanking the captain and the team for everything.

If it weren't for the support from the team and the unwavering love from Olivia, I would have succumbed to the destructive thoughts induced by unrelenting depression. At times, suicide seemed like the only way out. But during the darkest moments, I found a way forward through the light that shined in her eyes.

Olivia became my everything. Once I finally found peace

again, we were married on the reserve in a dual celebration, as Abasi and Ashi had added a daughter, Atheni, to the family. We all danced and chanted on a long summer night, drank buckets of *urwarwa*, a Burundian banana wine, and of course, goat's head stew filled our bellies. Fortunately, I managed to keep it down. It was truly a glorious day.

I could never have imagined all that had transpired, but I was beyond grateful. Just Olivia accepting me back into her world was a gift in and of itself—a gift I'd had doubts about the fateful day I left. But she understood why I had to go, just as she also knew why I came back.

However, grief again threatened my world about six months later, when we had to say goodbye to our sweet little Nepasha, who had grown to be not so little. I pleaded with Olivia to keep her, but she convinced me that the mission of the sanctuary was to rehabilitate and release elephants back to their natural habitat, not to domesticate them. Besides, the operation was not equipped to handle full-grown elephants. Nonetheless, I was a wreck watching her cautiously walk over to her new surrogate family, which already had two adolescent girls of its own. I was, however, so pleased that Nepasha was accepted by a new family and would get to live out her days in the wild. But that couldn't fill the hole in my heart, and furthermore, due to her blossoming tusks, I had to fret about her falling victim to the blade, just as her mother most likely had.

But over time, I learned to cope, understanding that acceptance was one of the keys to survival. Living without Lily had taught me that. Each day that went by became a touch more bearable. And it was on one beautiful, bright summer morning three years later that I truly found the peace I had so desperately sought since the day my daughter left the Earth.

I woke to an empty bed as I rolled over, my arm smacking the cold, vacated sheets. The notes streaming from the birds were crisper and more vibrant than on any other morning I could recall. So lively were they that I couldn't fall back asleep, even if I'd tried. The scent of coffee led me to the kitchen, and eventually to the barn in search of my wife. It was a Sunday, a day when we normally slept a little longer.

It wasn't until I walked to the far exterior of the barn and looked around the corner that I spotted her. Along the tree-lined hillside that had finally begun to recover following the fire, there she was, beautiful as ever, her hair glistening in the sun, swaying in a hammock attached to two thriving acacias that had somehow been spared from the blaze. I walked over and kissed her good morning, handing her a cup of coffee.

"I already had some, but thank you, lover," she said, melting me once again with her brilliant smile.

"Just enjoying the morning, huh?" I asked.

"It's such a spectacular day, I thought I'd come bask in the sun for a bit."

"I think I might join you," I said. "But first, I have someone else to say good morning to though. Where is he?"

"He's over there playing with Jasiri."

"I don't see him... Oh, wait, there he is! Behind them all. I'll be back in a minute." I kissed her again and walked toward the group of elephants, some new to the sanctuary, some elder statesmen like Jomo and Jasiri.

"What are you doing hiding over here?" I asked him playfully. He just giggled and initiated a game of hide-and-seek. I scooped him up, kissed his wavy sandy-brown locks, and peered deep into his beaming blue eyes. He had the eyes of his mother. But if I stared long enough, which I often did, another set of baby blues came shining through—eyes from my past, but eyes that could never be pried from my memory. Lily lived not only within me, but somewhere deep within him. I tried not to tear up as I kissed his cheek and put him down.

"Daddy, why do they have these?" he asked, placing his fingertips on Jomo's emerging tusk.

"Your mom and I have told you this before, haven't we, son?"

"Tell me again, please?"

"They're used by these special creatures for a variety of reasons: protection, procreation, survival… They're special and unique, just like you. That's why we named you Tusk. They're also highly coveted in this world for all the wrong reasons, but they belong to no one but an elephant. They should never be anywhere but attached to an elephant. Do you understand?"

"I think so," he said sweetly, though I could tell most of the words I'd presented were out of his range. But I knew he got the gist.

"C'mon, let's go say hi to your mama in the hammock," I said, reaching for his hand.

We said goodbye to the orphans as they stayed in their pod, socializing. As we began walking back to the hammock, a powerful feeling came over me—a feeling I could not quite explain. My gut began to ache with overly stimulated acuity, a sense that I could not simply chalk up to being overly emotional. I could feel the trees. I could taste the wind. I could sense the earth vibrating deep beneath my feet. For a second, I felt like an elephant-like intuition shoot through my heart like a bolt of lightning. I knew something was present, something near, even though it made no sound, with only vibrations permeating the space between us. As I turned, I did not know what would be unveiled, but I was not in fear of whatever it was.

Standing regally in the distant valley, toward the ascending hills that led to the waterfall, was a family of four. The silhouette of their ears flapped in the backdrop of the glowing African sun as they faced us with dignity, all in a staggered line.

"Olivia, look!" I called out, pointing to the spectacle.

She raised her head off the hammock and gazed in awe. "Is that...?"

"I believe it is," I replied.

I didn't even bother wiping the tear from my cheek as our suspicions were confirmed by the distinctive trumpet from Nepasha's trunk raised toward the heavens. I wanted so badly to run to her and rub her forehead once more, but that would have severed the vital bond she now shared with the wild.

"Who's that, Daddy?" our son asked, gazing up at me as Lily's face again blanketed my mind.

I paused for a moment as the group began to retreat, trying to gather my emotions. "An old friend, son. An old special friend. Just like Jasiri is to you."

I watched Nepasha and her new family march back to the distant grove until they disappeared into the haze. I turned toward my wife, who was looking so elegant beneath the trees as I looked down at Tusk and grinned from ear to ear. I panned the valley surrounding the sanctuary, with the orphans rolling in the dirt and basking in the sun, as I flashed back to the journey that had brought me to where I now stood. All the blood. All the tears. All the pain. But also, all the love, all the signs and synchronicities that had led me to exactly where I was meant to be.

And suddenly, it hit me harder than it ever had before. We were all one, all interconnected, all part of the same universe, birthed from the same elemental dust that formed to give life upon a star's death. From the trees to the animals to the rivers that flowed and the air that we breathed, everything in the cosmos had always been and would always be part of the same vibration. And it was within that ethereal, eternal space that humans warped like time and bent like light to strive to become the best versions of themselves, with imperceptible forces guiding the path toward the light. *Humans were never meant to rape and pillage Mother Nature's resources for personal gain*, I thought to myself, glancing at the baby elephants once more, knowing that as they grew, they would one day be leading actors in the never-ending conflict.

As we approached Olivia sitting on the edge of the hammock,

patiently waiting to embrace her pride and joy, Tusk unclasped his fingers from mine, bent down, and picked something from the earth, a beautiful bloom with white petals and a lavender-yellow core. "Here, give this to Mommy," he said, reaching out his tiny hand as a dragonfly hovered above us for a moment before dashing away.

As I handed her the flower and confessed how much I loved her, she touched the tip of her nose to the soft white petals, closed her eyes, filled her lungs, and smiled, letting out a sigh of blissful fulfillment. "It's gorgeous," she said to me, gazing into my eyes, and I could again see my whole life in hers. "Do you know what kind it is?"

I shook my head. "An African lily."

www.ingramcontent.com/pod-product-compliance
Lightning Source LLC
Chambersburg PA
CBHW030155200626
46812CB00017B/2089